MONTANA

MONTANA

GWEN FLORIO

THE PERMANENT PRESS
Sag Harbor, NY 11963

For information, address:
  The Permanent Press
  4170 Noyac Road
  Sag Harbor, NY 11963
  www.thepermanentpress.com

Library of Congress Cataloging-in-Publication Data

Florio, Gwen —
  Montana / Gwen Florio.
    pages. cm
  ISBN 978-1-57962-336-4
    1. Women journalists—Fiction. 2. Murder—Investigation—Fiction.
  3. Drug traffic—Fiction. 4. Whites—Relations with Indians—Fiction.
  5. Blackfeet Tribe of the Blackfeet Indian Reservation of Montana—Fiction.
  6. Montana—Fiction. I. Title.

PS3606.L664M66 2013
813'.6—dc23   2013021081

Printed in the United States of America

For Sean, Kate and Scott

ACKNOWLEDGMENTS

I'm so privileged to work with The Permanent Press publishers Martin and Judith Shepard, agent Barbara Braun, editor Judy Sternlight and copy editor Joslyn Pine; thanks also to Lon Kirschner for his gorgeous cover design and Shaila Abdullah for a striking website.

In each place I've lived over the last several years, I've been mentored by terrific writers:

In Philadelphia—James Rahn and the Rittenhouse Writers Group, especially Joanne McLaughlin; and Peter Kaufman. In Denver—Pat O'Driscoll, Jim Sheeler, Mark Stevens, Alan Gottlieb and Mike Booth. In Missoula, the 406 Writers' Workshop sessions led by David Allan Cates and Brian Buckbee, as well as the group known informally as 406 Gone Rogue—Dana Fitz-Gale, Caroline Simms, Wes Samson, Laura Foster-Wasilewski and Brooke Hewes Carnwath. And Sherry Devlin, for supporting the time necessary to make this book possible.

For shelter and financial backing at crucial times over the years: the New Jersey State Council on the Arts, the Ucross Foundation, the Brush Creek Ranch Arts Foundation, the Cry of the Loon Lodge, and Sally and Andy Lewis.

Missoula police Detective Sgt. Travis Welsh and Lt. Bob Bouchee patiently answered what were clearly "book" questions as opposed to newspaper questions, as did Missoula County Sheriff's Detective Jason Johnson and Sheriff's Lt. Rich Maricelli.

Deep gratitude to my parents, Pat and Tony Florio, for banning television and hauling us weekly to the library; likewise to my children, Sean and Kate Breslin, whose childhood refrain was "Mommy's writing."

Profound appreciation for my partner, Scott Crichton, and his unstinting support. Finally, I'm grateful to Nell for not eating the whole manuscript.

PROLOGUE

A stick snapping beneath a hard-soled boot sounds like nothing else in the woods.

Mary Alice Carr spent much of the night on the slope above her cabin wide-eyed and upright, back braced against a rolled sleeping bag, the minutes an inky ooze of boredom cut by fear, the hours flowing so slow and dreamlike that when the crack reverberated through the darkness she wondered if she'd conjured it from the thin mountain air. Beside her, the young dog raised his head. She'd heard right, then.

The cabin stood against a rocky bluff on one of the rare level shelves where the northern Rockies break their headlong surge toward the sky, out of the path of the unremitting wind whose default force was a full-on gale. The wind's relentless onslaught scoured the land's surface, sculpting strange and brooding shapes out of the local limestone. It toughened the region's animal inhabitants into fierce and predatory opportunists, and caused the human ones, upon occasion, to burst into inexplicable tears. But at dawn the wind lay down, gathering strength for the day's battering siege. Here and there sounds rose up sudden and distinct. Dry needles sifting from lodgepole pines. A coyote's trailing refrain.

Footfalls across the cabin's porch.

The half-grown border collie vibrated low and tense beneath Mary Alice's hand. She closed her fingers around his muzzle and called herself twenty different kinds of stupid. Whoever was down there wasn't even trying to keep quiet.

She felt for her cell phone. Habit, useless. Her cabin sat at the far and unreliable border of the phone's coverage area. Her position up the hill fell well into the dead zone. Her fingers moved past the phone and fastened on the .45 with a *snick* as she thumbed off the safety, another alien noise in the predawn hush.

Mary Alice eased onto her stomach by centimeters. The slick fabric of her puffy down jacket made soft whispery sounds as she set the gun in front of her, resting her wrist on a flat rock. She'd hauled the rock into place the night before, back when she'd attributed the whole elaborate setup to the paranoia resulting from working too long on a story turned too strange.

"It's never as bad as you think," her friend Lola liked to say, of everything from meals to men to the various stories they'd chased as young reporters in Baltimore. "It's worse." Lola's plane would land in just a few hours. They hadn't seen one another in five years, when Lola had gone off to Afghanistan and Mary Alice to Montana, career paths that had run parallel for years suddenly diverging. Lola had promised her some war stories when she arrived. Mary Alice closed her eyes and contemplated the fact that she'd have a war story of her own once this night was over.

Cold pinched her exposed wrists. He'd been in the cabin a long time, probably at her desk, strewn with files baited with misleading labels, flash drives filled with meaningless junk. If she'd called it right, he'd scoop it all up, assume he'd gotten what he came for, and drive away, giving her a precious few seconds to glimpse his face before he got into his car. She wondered how long she should stay up on the hill after he left.

Then realized she'd never actually heard him drive up.

She opened her eyes.

Mist pooled in the clearing below, the darkness cottony around the edges, dawn commencing. He knelt on the porch, solid and dark and real in the vaporous light, sighting Mary

Alice through the scope of an AR-15, its barrel steadied on the porch railing. A hat shielded his face but she had no trouble imagining the crosshairs centered on her own. The sturdy .45, so comforting moments before, felt like a toy in her shaking hand. Fifty yards was pushing the limits of its range. By the time her bullet slowed in a tumbling fall toward the porch, his would have punched through her and beyond, just getting warmed up on its unerring way. The dog began to bark.

Mary Alice dropped the gun and raised her hands high.

CHAPTER ONE

"Miss?" The voice rode the wavering lamplight so softly through the crack in the door that Lola Wicks sank back toward sleep, soothed by the customary noises in the next room.

The endless gurgle of tea into cracked cups. Breathy fricatives of Pashto. The metallic ratchet of magazines locking into place in preparation for the coming day. Lola slid lower in her sleeping bag, inhaling the pleasurable scent of woodsmoke and dung that signaled her most recent foray from Kabul into the highlands, entire centuries falling away the farther she traveled from the city, the only signs of modernity in these mountain villages the terrible weapons hoisted by cloaked men in sandals. The conflict was close here, not like Kabul, where men postured around conference tables with the occasional anonymous grenade tossed through a window to keep things interesting. In the highlands, combatants knew one another's names. It had taken her months to gain the trust of this particular faction, whose stated purpose was to drive the Americans from Afghanistan's borders even more decisively than they'd dealt with the Russians two decades earlier.

Despite the risks of leaving Kabul's questionable safety, any return to the outlying regions always felt like a sort of homecoming to Lola, a welcome respite from filing her stories in the crowded villa whose outlandish expense she shared with a shifting, quarreling cast of other foreign correspondents. Distractions and obligations peeled away as she traveled, until she arrived at a destination where filing the story and staying alive remained the only two things that mattered. Lola pulled the bag tighter around her head. It was mid-June but nights still snapped with cold in these lower reaches of the Hindu Kush.

"Miss."

The door opened wider. Her fixer again, his voice insistent. Lola sat up and reached for her headscarf, the only article of clothing she discarded at night, even keeping her boots on, the laces merely loosened. "*Ho,*" she murmured. Yes.

"A call, miss." He scooted her beeping satellite phone, freed from its generator recharge, across the dirt floor. It came to a stop against the edge of a rug whose rich dyes and labyrinthine swirls mocked the spartan surroundings. Lola cursed quietly, in English. Not even the most publicity-hungry warlord would call her at this hour. It had to be an editor. She flipped open the phone without bothering to look at the number. "Don't you people ever think about time zones?" she asked. Then sat up straighter.

"What?" she said.

"You're not serious," she said.

And cursed again, not bothering to whisper this time.

✧✧✧

A WEEK later found her over the Atlantic, encased within a sleek, gleaming cylinder, its occupants as well-upholstered as the seats, not a Kalashnikov in sight. She'd spent so much time among the casually over-armed that the sudden absence of weaponry unnerved her. Below, the rumpled grey sheet of ocean billowed and flattened. Lola shifted, trying to get comfortable, and apologized for elbowing the person next to her. She wondered when her newspaper had stopped paying for business class on overseas flights. She was too tall for coach. Still, she took a moment to savor the fact that the people around her seemed to take things like flight attendants and readily available alcohol for granted. She calculated drink against dosage, broke a sleeping pill in half, and signaled for a glass of wine. She'd already prowled the cabin's aisles twice, staring hard-eyed at her fellow passengers. But she'd been gone too long. They all looked alike. She'd lost the ability to read her own kind. The pill lay halved and crumbly-edged on her tray table.

She couldn't remember the last time she'd tried to sleep on a plane. She'd spent too many years trying to get to the sorts of places that sane people sought to leave, traveling there on rusting prop planes of questionable pedigree flown by pilots of dodgy backgrounds under conditions that made her wonder why she'd ever fretted over an assignment of window versus aisle; each new trip a gut-liquefying opportunity to wonder when luck would turn on her, demanding payment for past excesses of hubris. She didn't sleep on planes but she would damn well sleep on this one, grab a few hours of oblivion to stave off the reality of that phone call. She scooped up both halves of the sleeping pill and swallowed them dry. She hit the call button again. The attendant was at the front of the plane, the first-class curtain pulled aside, speaking to someone there. She glanced back and kept talking.

Lola balled her napkin within her fist. She leaned into the aisle. Such a short, straight shot, almost too easy, even given the improbable physics of wadded paper and pressurized cabin air. She cocked her arm, then whipped it forward. The napkin streaked the length of the aisle and hit the attendant between the shoulder blades, bouncing into someone's drink with a soggy splash. Lola pressed the call button again. The flight attendant turned, the expression on her face an unmistakable emergency warning.

Lola lifted her plastic cup. "Another, please."

✧✦✧

IN BALTIMORE, an editor, one of the new ones, tilted back in his chair and avoided her eyes. "It's not personal," he said. "We're shuttering all the foreign bureaus. We'll find you something here. Maybe in one of the suburban offices. The layoffs left us pretty thin out there. At least you'll still have a job. Consider yourself lucky."

Lola examined a paperweight of milky swirled glass that sat between a file and a newspaper on his desk. It looked heavy. She picked it up. It was. "The suburbs. Lucky me."

Floor-to-ceiling windows formed one wall of the office, the legacy of a newsroom renovation dating to the days when profits sloshed through the paper, spilling over into heralded new foreign bureaus, yearlong prize-savvy investigative projects, and wink-and-nod expense accounts. That tide had swept out a long time ago, leaving behind pay cuts and layoffs and unpaid furloughs. Packing boxes sat atop several desks in the newsroom. Others looked as though they'd been bare for months. Stubborn cracks left unrepaired veined the tall windows. Grit dulled their surface. The popcorn burst of automatic weapons fire sounded faintly through them, and Lola counted silently, reckoning the distance, before she saw the man hunched at the curb, a jackhammer anchoring his bobbling torso.

"I'd be reporting on school boards," Lola said. "Zoning hearings. Neighbors pointing lawyers at each other over a foot of property line." She tossed the paperweight high. It dropped into her palm with a satisfying sting.

"There'll be some of that. It's what people care about."

"Interns cover that shit."

"We don't have interns anymore. Haven't for three or four years now. You've been overseas a long time. You don't even have a smartphone, do you? We've got plenty of younger reporters in the suburbs who can get you up to speed on the technology. Look, would you mind putting that down? It's expensive." His cheeks were pink and smooth, his shirt starched and palely gleaming against the fine dark weave of his blazer. Lola tried to remember a life that allowed for easy cleanliness. She straightened her legs, taking up too much room in the too-small office, the scuffed toes of her cleated hiking boots nearly touching his pretty polished loafers. Standing, she had six inches on him.

"You can't pull me out now," she said. "The warlords are rearming. Somewhere, somehow, someone's getting money to them—a lot of money. Not to put too fine a point on it, but what's going on there is going to determine the course of history for the next decade at the very least. You know that. And yet you put today's story from Afghanistan on . . ." She exchanged the paperweight for the newspaper. She turned the pages, counting aloud. "Page One—no. Two—no, not there either. Three, four— Here's something about everyone twittering a crotch shot of an actress with no undies. That one's right above a story about a massacre in Congo. Glad to see you've got your priorities in order."

"Tweeting."

"What?"

"Never mind. The wire services can cover Afghanistan."

"Damn it!" She rolled up the paper and slapped it against his desk. The paperweight shuddered. "The wire services aren't getting the job done. They've had layoffs, too, in case you haven't noticed. The only guy the AP's got left in Kabul is too scared to leave the city. He does most of his work by phone. But I'm out there where it's all happening. *Was* there. Until you called."

He reached across the desk and took the newspaper from her. "Our readers care more about how a property tax increase is going to affect them right now than they do about how things in Afghanistan are going to shake out in ten years." He opened the file and slid some forms from it. "You've got some—a lot—of time off coming. You haven't taken a vacation in years. It's really played hell with our accounting. You have to take it. Go get some R and R."

Lola hefted the paperweight again and looked at the ceiling. "I'll take it back in Kabul. Softball amounts to R and R. I play a lot of softball. I'm the pitcher on the Kabul Kabooms. We're on track to take the championship away from the Talibanieri." Her hand flashed. The paperweight shot up and rocketed back down. She snatched it from the air above his head. "Do you really want the Italians to beat us at our own game?"

"Jesus Christ." He righted himself in his chair. "All of you correspondents are a pain in the ass when you come back. It's June. The way I count up all this time, we've got to give you something like ten weeks off with pay. That'll take you until nearly September. You should be housebroken again by then. Take that vacation. Given that we budgeted for flights home that you never took, we'll pay plane fare—within reason. Don't go to Tahiti. And don't run up a big hotel bill. Go someplace where you can sponge off friends. *Put that damn thing down.*"

"I don't know anybody here anymore. You laid them all off. Except for one who beat you to the punch." She realized, too late, that she'd given him an opening.

"Who's that?"

"Mary Alice Carr," she said slowly, wishing she'd thought to offer up another name. "She left a few years ago, back when this place was still giving buyouts. Before your time, I think."

But he nodded. "I remember her. She left right after I got here. Went to some crazy place. Idaho, Wyoming, something like that. She called us a couple of weeks ago."

"Montana. What did she want?"

"She was all excited about something happening out there, trying to sell us the story. Some delusional person sent her my way." He grimaced. "She didn't know we'd gone all local-local in our news coverage. No reason to buy a national story, and no freelance budget for one, anyway, even if we had been interested. Which we weren't."

Lola stood. "I've really got the whole summer off?"

"Legally, we've got to give you the time. Something I'm short on." He looked pointedly at the message light blinking on his phone. "Go to Montana, then. Fly-fish, ride horses, whatever it is they do out there. We still have a travel agent. I'll have her make the arrangements before they cancel that contract, too."

"I don't fish," Lola said. "And I don't like horses. I don't see why it's a problem for me to just go back to Kabul and finish up what I was working on. I'll see you in September." Like hell she would. But first she had to get back. She could figure out how to stay later.

He pushed his chair back. "I don't think you understand," he said. "You *are* finished over there. You can drop off your laptop and satellite phone with the clerk. You won't need them anymore. As of the minute you walked through this door, we no longer have any more foreign bureaus."

"I left the sat phone in Kabul, along with my body armor and all the rest of my stuff. I should go back and get it."

"Nice try," he said. "Just have those French freaks you live with—the ones who think it's so funny to answer your phone and hang up on me when I try to call—ship your stuff. You're not going back. We've already canceled your company credit card and the travel account."

He kept talking but Lola's focus shifted to a panel truck, the perfect size to hold a dozen oil drums packed with a sludgy mix of fertilizer and racing fuel, moving slowly past the building. Lola stared hard at the driver, watching for the quick yank at the wheel that would send the truck into the lobby, the thumb to the detonator that would follow. The concussive force would bend the newsroom windows outward, the panes bubbling like a soapy mass across the face of the building, then suck them back in with such speed and intensity that the glass would burst, shards rocketing across the office, razoring through furniture, paper, flesh. Lola blew out a breath, slammed the door behind her and strode the length of the underpopulated newsroom, the stupid expensive paperweight in her pocket banging against her thigh with each step.

CHAPTER TWO

Baggage Claim stopped Lola dead in her tracks.

She was used to all manner of haphazard Third World arrangements—places where airport workers held Kalashnikovs in one hand and flung the luggage onto a dirt runway with the other, places where bags arrived slit open and regurgitating what remained of their contents, places where would-be porters mobbed her with bags not her own. But she had also forgotten that not every American airport was like JFK or LAX, with acres of briskly revolving carousels forested with identical black roller bags. There was but a single carousel in Helena, Montana, and it emptied fast. Lola walked past with only a small duffel in her hand and her book bag, stuffed with her sleeping bag and her laptop, slung over her shoulder. She cast sidelong glances at her fellow passengers, retrieving an array of towering backpacks and cylindrical cases that looked as though they could contain grenade launchers. Fly rods, she decided after some consideration.

Within minutes it was just Lola and a gum-chewing young woman lounging behind a rental-car counter, idly blowing pink bubbles that she inhaled with audible retorts. An elk head with shiny startled eyes hung on the wall above her, antlers stretching toward a skylight. A grizzly bear stood on its hind legs within a glass case, lips lifted away from incisors that looked capable of punching holes through steel. It was taller than the rental-car clerk, taller even than Lola. Lola walked over to the case and pressed her palm against the cool glass. Claws as long as her fingers curved like scimitars from the bear's raised forepaws.

"Need a car?" the woman called.

"No. I'm waiting for a friend."

Another bubble vanished with a crack. "Your friend's late."

The airport's main door sighed its slow revolutions. Lola headed for it, feeling the woman's gaze at her back, and stutter-stepped through. Beyond the low-slung city, mountains prodded an infinite sky that drew her gaze and held it hard. Lola took a deep breath of crystalline air and scanned a parking lot sardined with pickup trucks. None met the description of the saucy red number that apparently had claimed whatever was left of Mary Alice's buyout money after she'd bought the cabin in Montana. Lola went back into the airport and looked for an electrical outlet. She'd postponed recharging her cell phone, avoiding as long as possible the inevitable outraged calls from her editor when he realized she'd failed to turn in the laptop. Now that there were two thousand miles between them, she plugged it in, settled into a plastic chair and tried to compose an adequate explanation for Mary Alice as to why her summer vacation would amount only to a long weekend.

She'd gone straight from the newsroom in Baltimore to a bank and raided what was left of her dwindling retirement account. Part of it went toward a ticket back to Kabul. She asked for ten thousand dollars in hundreds—old ones, with no telltale crackle to make things even chancier at checkpoints—and took the brick-like packet immediately into a restroom. With quick, experienced movements, she'd lined the cups of her bra, the soles of her boots, the zippered compartment inside her belt and all the pockets of her cargo pants with cash. She reversed the process at the airport, stashing the money in her backpack with the bank receipt rubber-banded around it just before she went through the body scanner, then found another ladies' room and transferred it back to its earlier hiding places.

Over the next few days, the rasp of cash against skin would lessen as warmth and sweat oiled the bills and they molded themselves to the contours of her body, a reassuring shield of plenty in Afghanistan's cash economy. She had enough, she hoped, to pay her share of the rent on the Kabul house and to travel back to the highlands before chaos consumed the region so completely that even inexperienced fixers would refuse the outrageous bribes she was prepared to offer. She'd prepaid the satellite phone's SIM card for the next three months so that it would work when she returned, and acquired a new Internet provider against the inevitability of the paper shutting down her account.

As a last resort, she carried the second passport that she'd obtained some years earlier in the deceptively somnolent riverside town of Gujrat in Pakistan, where forgers—their eyes red and watery and their fingertips brilliant with colored inks—plied their trade. Maria diBianco was an Italian woman with Lola's cropped chestnut curls and a full upper lip at odds with her angular features. Her narrowed grey eyes stared a challenge from the document littered with blurred stamps for exotic-but-plausible destinations such as Thailand and Bali and Mexico. Maria apparently enjoyed beaches. Lola had delayed her trip back to the United States to make a quick visit to Gujrat so that Maria could obtain a new passport stamp showing that she'd gone through customs at Baltimore Washington International Thurgood Marshall Airport on the day of Lola's arrival. The fake passport, for use only in the direst emergency, was as likely to create problems as solve them, but it made Lola feel safer to have it. She was ready.

"Vacation, my ass," she said to herself. She opened her newly juiced phone and, as expected, saw her editor's number stacked repeatedly in her voicemail list. She held her finger to the delete key. Once he saw the stories she'd file when she got back to Kabul, he'd realize it was a mistake to close the bureau. Sandwiched among his messages was a single one from Mary Alice. Lola skipped directly to it.

"Hey, you. I might be late. I've got to take care of something here. I'll call when I'm on my way. You sit tight 'til I get there." A pause. "Love you."

Lola stared at the phone. "Love you?" Theirs had been a spiky friendship based on outward cynicism and the one-upmanship of fast-paced insults. In all the years she'd known Mary Alice, Lola could recall only a single hug, Mary Alice clutching her fiercely before waving goodbye as Lola walked down the jetway to the first in the series of planes that would eventually deposit her in Kabul. A year later, Lola had been on assignment in Jalalabad, unable to return the favor when Mary Alice surprised her with the news of her own unlikely move to Montana. Lola checked the message's time stamp. Mary Alice had sounded rushed, breathless, as though she were hurrying toward the airport, but the message had been left twenty-four hours earlier. Lola punched and repunched Mary Alice's number into the phone, hanging up each time the voicemail began its automated spiel. It was already late afternoon and Lola was nearly a day into her so-called vacation. She tossed the phone high, palmed it on the return, and headed toward the rental-car counter.

"No." Lola told the young woman there what she already knew. "I don't have a reservation." The woman reached for a pair of keys, and shoved a form and a map at her. Lola pulled out her phone to call Mary Alice one last time.

"Is that a flip phone?" The clerk's eyes widened. "I didn't know they made them any more. Can I see it?"

"No." She waited until she was outside the airport before leaving a message for Mary Alice, her voice stiff with annoyance. She glanced at the map and calculated the mileage, irritation flaring anew. There was a closer airport, but Mary Alice had insisted upon meeting her in Helena, saying she needed to do some research there. "I'll see you in about three hours," she told Mary Alice's voicemail.

She bit back an urge to add a sarcastic "love you," and hung up.

✧✧✧

THE CITY was in the rental car's rearview mirror and then it wasn't, vanishing without the softening aspect of suburbs. Ahead, bare foothills bunched like fists, knuckled ridges pressing back against the weight of sky. The road arced around the hills in lazy swooping curves, then without warning hairpinned through cliffs that leaned in above her, slicing the sky to manageable size. Lola stole glances at the scoured rockfaces as the car maneuvered through the narrows, and imagined engineers months into their desolate assignment, laying lines of dynamite, sending up a cheer as an opening blasted through to the valley beyond.

Signs indicated the distance in miles and kilometers to the Canadian border, closer than she'd thought. The occasional billboard rose up, guideposts to this new place. Election season was in full swing. Candidates, some big-hatted and horsed, grinned down at Lola. Others walked through thigh-high golden wheat, stood next to oil rigs, leaned on split-rail fences. One man dangled leather work gloves so yellow and bright and obviously unused as to make Lola smile at the universality of campaign fakery. One candidate's sign had no photo at all, only a puzzling slogan and a name: "Run with the Wolf. Johnny's Chasing Jobs."

Meth apparently was a problem, warnings against it almost outnumbering the candidates' come-ons. One billboard showed a young woman slumped on the floor, cavernous eyes pleading with the camera. Large men, T-shirted and tattooed, leered over her. "Meth—You'll always have a date," was the message. Someone had taken pink spray paint to her face: "Your mom." Lola snorted her appreciation. Her lifeline grasp on the wheel eased. She'd spent the past few days fighting the culture shock of First World re-immersion, bumping up against the hard shiny edges of hygiene and haste; of wide ribbons of highway traveled by smoothly feinting cars unimpeded by pedestrians, donkey carts, or drifting herds of fat-bottomed sheep. She hadn't been allowed to drive herself anywhere for years. Relegated to the back seat, she endlessly negotiated truces between drivers who fought with translators, who in turn sulked and refused to tell her what the hopped-up kids with Kalashnikovs at the checkpoints were saying.

She slouched, steering with two fingers, old attitudes rising from muscle memory. She checked the map again. Mary Alice lived outside a town named Magpie, not far south of the Canadian border. Lola steered the car off the interstate, heading north on a tapering road that picked its way through a rock-strewn valley floor. To the west, a line of mountains higher than any she'd yet seen wedged darkly upward. A pickup appeared in the rearview mirror. Out of habit Lola checked for the telltale glint of sun off rifle barrels, feeling foolish but also relieved when the truck finally whipped past, the driver lifting a forefinger in greeting. She tried the radio, but it hissed and popped like severed electrical wires. She flinched and turned it off. She'd plugged in her laptop at the airport and booted it up while there to scan news sites online, a cumbersome operation that made her envy the people she'd seen simply rubbing their fingers across their phones. The truce between the Islamists and the military—the one that would allow her to slip back into the highlands—was holding, but only just. Counting the time she'd already wasted getting home, she'd been away from the story a week. She'd stay in Montana for three more days. Then, a full day of traveling just to get back to Baltimore. Another couple of days messing with the London-Dubai-Kabul transfers and layovers, not to mention at least a few days on the ground in Kabul once she arrived to dispense the bribes necessary to renew her travel permits and round up a vehicle and find another fixer, her old one barely able to disguise his relief when she'd been summoned home.

"Six children," that sad-eyed man had reminded her. "Would your newspaper have supported them if anything had happened to me?"

"Nothing did," she'd snapped. When she got to Mary Alice's, she'd email him and ask that he line up someone new who'd be waiting when she arrived. He owed her that much, she thought, given that she paid him the equivalent of a year's salary every month or so. Just in case, she'd ask him to find yet another person ready to step in once the new one seriously contemplated the prospect of the car rolling over an innocuous jumble of wires and packed powder, body parts somersaulting high, the white summer sky spattered scarlet.

The car crested a bald ridge. Ahead, the mountains rose like a wall. With some effort, she focused downward, toward a scatter of houses and spindly trees, scraps in the bottom of a vast bowl of valley lipped by those foreboding peaks. A sign pointed: "Magpie."

⟡⟡⟡

LOLA'S CAR coasted along a three-block business district anchored by a square sandstone courthouse with an oversized clock tower. The faded brick storefronts were dark, the sidewalks lonely. The "Closed" signs in some of the windows had a permanent aspect. Lola checked her watch. Nine o'clock. A neon glow beckoned from a convenience store at the far end of the street. Lola drove to it, waiting as a semi hauling a flatbed stacked with rolls of hay maneuvered itself out of the store's lot. She parked and tried Mary Alice's number yet again. "The mailbox is full," the computerized voice repeated with its odd mechanical hesitations. "The mailbox is full." She left the phone on the seat and got out of the car. Something stirred at her feet.

"Got change? Got a dollar? A five? Ten would be better." A man lay beside the store's front door, using a backpack as a pillow. His grin shone pink and toothless. Dirt drew black lines beneath his fingernails and seamed the hand he raised. A few longish hairs straggled from his chin and a filthy red kerchief wrapped his neck. "It's not a handout. I got money comin'. Pay you back."

Lola edged around him into the store. Two teenage boys with gleaming black hair bound into thick braids studied refrigerated shelves of soft drinks. A heavyset woman stood behind the counter, eyes on the boys. "Help you?" she said without turning her head.

"I just need some directions," said Lola.

"Well, now." The woman shuffled her feet until she faced Lola and fixed hooded, unblinking eyes upon her. She leaned against the counter, letting Lola know that she intended to enjoy this new distraction. "That depends on where you want to go." The woman threw a glance at the boys, who hacked up dutiful laughs.

Lola resigned herself to playing her part. How often had this happened to her, in how many places, the stranger in town put through her paces for the enjoyment of the locals? She looked at the woman on the other side of the counter, her green store tunic straining across those hunched shoulders, shapeless feet stuffed into canvas shoes with the laces left untied, and reminded herself that she needed so very little from this woman compared to those whose hazing had been far worse.

The woman lifted her head. "You boys going to buy anything? Because if you're not, you can't loiter here. Sign says so." She pointed to the placard on the front door. The youths conferred, then pooled their change and brushed past Lola with a single can of Mountain Dew. "Hey," the woman called after them. "Take Frank back to the rez with you, why don't you? He's pestering the customers."

One of the boys stooped beside the man and put a hand on his shoulder. The man shook his head. The boys looked back toward the store, then departed without him in a car that was more rust than paint, perched aslant four bald tires.

"Now," the woman said, "where exactly do you want to be?" Broken veins rouged her cheeks. Lola took in her slow, deliberate movements and the way her shoulders mounded up against her neck, and thought of a turtle.

"I want," Lola began, before too much travel and too little sleep caught up with her all at once. She wanted to be at Mary Alice's. Mary Alice would surely be back from whatever had delayed her; would have gotten Lola's messages, would even now be brewing coffee for Lola and smoky-flavored tea for herself in her grandmother's china pot. There'd be two glasses and a bottle of Jameson's within easy reach to supply the "wee drop" traditionally served guests. She'd put on Leonard Cohen or Billie Holliday—"that mournful shit you like"—and then she'd lean her elbows on the scarred antique table that went wherever she did. She'd listen to Lola's stories and laugh and laugh, her breathy girl's voice transformed wholly unexpectedly into the whiskey-and-smokes cackle of a broad. Lola had perfected a tight, economical smile for the times people seemed to expect one, but couldn't remember the last time she'd laughed, really laughed. She was long overdue.

The woman's stomach pressed against the counter, a soft roll of shiny green nylon lapping the dull surface. "You need some sort of help?" Her lids dropped over her eyes, then she opened them wider than before.

"A friend was supposed to meet me at the airport and she never showed. She lives north of here. I just need to know how to get to her place."

"You're Lola."

Lola took a step back. "And you would be?"

"I'm Jolee. Mary Alice told us all about you. Showed us pictures and everything." Her monotone rose a quarter-decibel in what Lola guessed was enthusiasm. "You're a real world traveler."

"I guess right now I'm just a Montana traveler who doesn't know how to get where she's going."

Jolee rooted around under the counter, emerging with notepad and pen. "I'll get you out there. Just give me a minute to write it down so you won't forget. That Mary Alice. She's probably off on one of her stories. She's been working day and night these last few weeks." She made a fist around the pen. When she tore the paper from the pad, Lola saw the letters outlined on the sheet beneath. "Turn west out of town," the instructions began.

"Which way is west?"

Jolee layered her words with superiority. "Look for the mountains. Go that way. The road takes a jog north after about ten miles. That's about halfway. You just stay with it. Mary Alice is up in the foothills, in the old Jepsen cabin. She's fixed it up nice. I'll give you a couple of days to get settled in, but then I'll want you girls to come on over and eat with me. I make quite a pie."

"I don't eat pie," Lola said. But Jolee was out from behind the counter, urging her toward the door.

"You'll want to hurry on up there. You're not used to driving around here, and it gets dark fast back there under the trees where her place is. There's just a little two-track up to the cabin. You don't want to miss it."

Lola studied Jolee's map. "What's the name of the road? Is there a sign?"

Jolee took the map back and added a child's version of a tree, stick-straight trunk and cloud of leaves. "Look for the big cottonwood."

Lola considered the possibility that she might never find Mary Alice's place. She opened the door. "That guy's still out there."

"That's Frank." Jolee came and stood beside Lola. "He's brain-bad. Took one of those IEDs over in Iraq. Goes wandering now. Been weeks since I last saw him. Usually he sticks to the rez but this afternoon he made it all the way down here. I'll call the sheriff to come pick him up."

The man's head had rolled off the backpack. He'd wedged a hand between his bony cheek and the concrete.

"Why?" asked Lola. "He's not hurting anybody."

Jolee's eyes bulged again, importing a significance Lola didn't understand. "It's so nobody hurts him. You go on now.

Mary Alice is probably waiting on you. I'm glad you're here. Maybe you can get her to take a break. I see her outfit go by here at all hours."

The man rolled over onto his back. His hair fell away from his temple and Lola saw the dent in his skull, long and deep enough to have accommodated the heel of her hand. "Mar' Alice," he mumbled. "Poor, poor Mar' Alice." He squinted against the light from the store and flung his arm across his face. His breath caught in something halfway between a sob and snore.

"Yes," said Jolee. "Poor Mary Alice. But she's got a friend coming now. She'll take a rest."

Lola tried to remember whether Mary Alice had told her about Jolee. Or Frank, for that matter. Probably. Mary Alice wrote about her new life in Montana in long emails, dense with detail, that Lola skimmed and then deleted, a calculated choice between maintaining ties to her old life and adapting as quickly as possible to Kabul's bewildering realities. At some point Mary Alice's lengthy missives had tapered off.

"I thought I'd gotten away from all of this when I left Baltimore," a recent one read in its entirety.

Lola held Jolee's directions in front of her eyes, straining to read them in the near-dark. The car swung wide around a curve. A tall shadow skittered bat-like at the periphery of her headlights. Lola dragged at the wheel and the shadow resolved itself into horse and rider, two sets of eyes rolling whitely as she swerved past. Lola straightened out the car, registering the glare shot her way from beneath a wide-brimmed, high-crowned hat. She raised a hand in belated apology as the apparition melded into the twilight. Her first cowboy, she thought, and she'd just about killed him. She stored the thought away, a tidbit to serve up later for Mary Alice's amusement.

She slowed and scanned the west side of the road, looking for the opening Jolee said would appear just past a big tree. Even so, she almost missed it. She stomped at the brake and backed up a few feet, turning onto a track of flattened grass that led through the scrub. Stars emerged, catching and concentrating the fading light. The little rental car labored up a hill, ragged fingernails of brush dragging along its sides. The track took a final turn and opened into a meadow. Lola cut the ignition. The cabin stood at the far side of the clearing, nearly invisible in the shadow of a bluff. To one side, tall pines sheltered a shed and small corral. A spotted horse moved restlessly back and forth, tossing its head.

Lola got out of the car and inhaled the sharp clean scent of evergreen. The trees sighed, their branches rubbing and reaching as the wind wandered through. Lola leaned against the cool stream of air and let it slide across her face, and resisted an inkling that she was glad she'd come. She headed for the cabin, keeping to the edges of the meadow, avoiding exposure out of habit, stepping carefully through the darkness beneath the trees. She didn't see the red pickup until she was nearly upon it. Lola flattened her hand against it. The metal was cold, its surface jeweled with dew. Mary Alice hadn't parked it moments earlier and rushed inside to get her things before racing back out to fetch Lola from the airport, full of apologies for being late. No, she had not.

Lola looked at the truck awhile. Maybe something was wrong with it. Maybe Mary Alice had caught a ride with someone else or borrowed a friend's car. Maybe she'd gotten halfway to the airport and then checked her cell phone and listened to Lola's messages and was speeding back, readying a lecture for Lola on the value of patience.

Maybe.

Probably.

A dog barked.

Lola ducked behind the truck. She raised her head above the hood by degrees, scanning the forested hillside beyond the cabin. A shaggy black and white dog raised itself stiff-legged from the grass and whined. Lola dropped to her knees, knocked off balance by a flood of recall and its accompanying relief. Mary Alice had gotten a dog. She liked to hike with it, she'd written. So that's where she'd been.

"Hey, Mary Alice," Lola called into the woods. "Your dog beat you back."

The words rose on the wind and lost themselves amid the trees. Lola listened for an answering shout, for the sound of footsteps hurrying home. The wind settled. The silence that followed had weight and texture. Lola stood uncertain within it. The dog lay down across something heaped and shiny. It flattened its ears and sent a long, audible growl Lola's way when she took a step, and then another toward it. Lola watched the ground, wary of losing her footing in the darkness. Halfway up the hill, she lifted her gaze. The shiny stuff was a jacket and someone was in it. She forgot about her feet and sprinted, almost falling beside a rolled-up sleeping bag.

Mary Alice's eyes stared upward, a fat fly quivering atop a pupil, despite the evening chill. Lola avoided their unwavering scrutiny and concentrated on the neat hole in Mary Alice's cheek and remembered a time years earlier when, still new on the job, she had held a ballpoint pen to a similar hole in a man's chest, thinking that its very insignificance—so small, so defined—made a good detail for the story she was writing. She hadn't known then, but she knew now, what the hole's counterpart looked like; and so when she put her hands to Mary Alice's head, she was careful just to touch fingertips to temples, and sure enough, when she lifted gently, not even an inch, there was nothing left back there, just a mess of congealed blood and brain and shattered bone, brocaded by long, long strands of bright golden hair.

CHAPTER THREE

The car sidewindered back down the grassy track, the steering wheel spinning in Lola's hands.

Twigs snatched at her through the open window. Lola risked a hand off the wheel to punch 9-1-1 into her phone. "No service," it blinked in response. She flung it to the floor. The car fishtailed onto the main road, slewing around the curve where she'd nearly hit the man on the horse. "Please," she whispered. "Be there." She saw the horse first, riderless, and then the man, crouched beside a ditch, fooling with a wheeled metal contraption. Lola mounted a two-pronged attack on horn and brake. The horse reared, dancing backward, hooves slashing the air. The car spun to a stop. Adrenaline abandoned Lola as quickly as it had rolled in, a tidal wave and its sucking retreat, leaving her fighting for air. She slumped across the steering wheel.

"Miss," a measured voice said, "you have got to learn to drive more carefully."

Lola lifted her head and took in a green-shirted midsection and a tooled belt with a silver buckle of considerable size. The man lifted his hat and she looked up into honed features moving fast beyond middle age, skin shrinking tight across bone, prominence of nose casting shadows across hollows of eye and cheek, an austere landscape made more so in contrast to a lavish sweep of silvering hair.

"Verle Duncan," he introduced himself. "Are you all right?"

The kindness in his voice very nearly undid her fragile control. "Mary Alice." It was all she could say.

"Mary Alice Carr?" He sat the hat back on his head. "You must be her friend who's coming for the summer."

Lola slammed a hand against the wheel. "Stop talking. She's . . ." Her throat closed against the word.

"She's what?"

"She's . . ." Lola tried again.

"Is she sick? Hurt? Did she fall off that horse?"

Lola, mute, shook her head.

He crouched beside the car. "There now. I'm going to get some things and then I'm going to go back up there with you and figure out what's going on. You sit tight." He went to the horse and she heard the creak and flap of leather, something opening and closing. He returned with a flashlight and opened her door and took her arm and escorted her around to the passenger side. "I'll drive," he said, his voice light and even. "The way you handle this car, I think that's better."

"Your horse." It poked a hoof at the ground, head down, reins dragging.

"Don't worry about him. He's a cow horse. He'll stay wherever I leave him."

"A cow horse?" she said. Then, to forestall any explanation: "Never mind. Hurry."

He drove quickly, competently, back to Mary Alice's, pulling up beside the red truck. The darkness was complete. Lola jumped out as he turned off the engine, feeling for the slope of earth with her feet, heading uphill. She couldn't see the horse in its corral but heard its hooves thudding against the dirt. Verle caught up with her and put his hands on her shoulders and turned her toward the cabin.

"No. Up there." She pointed.

"You stay here." He raised the flashlight. His steps receded. It was getting cold. The cabin was a solid black square against the unreliable shadows of trees. She walked to it and sat on the porch steps, near a substantial stack of split wood, and blew one experimental breath after another and tried to think about nothing other than the small, perfect clouds condensing and dissolving before her. The dog yipped, once. There was no other noise. Even the horse ceased its restless perambulation. Some while later, Verle came back down the hill, the dog tucked under one arm, treading the blinding carpet laid down by the flashlight. He paused in front of Lola, and shone the light to one side. She blinked. They were in the aftermath. She knew this part. She started talking in mid-thought.

"The way she looks, it was probably your basic M-16," she said. "Given where he got her—right in the face like that, but from far away—he knew what he was doing. He could have used something smaller. He didn't need all that firepower."

The light bobbed, pale brushstrokes crisscrossing her face. "We don't use those much around here," he said. "Maybe a .30-06 for elk. Shotgun for geese or pheasant."

"Who would do this? Why?"

The light jumped again. "We need to call the sheriff. And we need to get you back to town. But first, we should take care of these animals. A few more minutes isn't going to make any difference now. I'm sorry. But that's how it is. They were precious to your friend." He thrust the dog at Lola. "He'll want food, maybe, water for sure. Take him inside and give him some, but not too much. If he's been up there with her awhile, he'll be dehydrated. I'll deal with the horse."

She grabbed the dog, all hair and eyes and scrabbling toenails, and held him away from her. He torqued, nearly throwing her off balance. She pulled him tight against her chest.

"Go on now," Verle said. "We don't want to be up here any longer than we need to."

Lola walked across the porch and tried the door handle. It was unlocked. She stepped inside. Something hard and sharp went to powder beneath her feet. She ran her hand along the wall until she found a light switch. Wished she hadn't. The kitchen table, the one at which she'd downed entire inky oceans of coffee during more than a decade of friendship and that Mary Alice apparently had hauled with her to Montana, lay on its side in a slurry of what appeared to be the contents of the refrigerator and all the cabinets. Lola lifted her foot and saw the blue-and-white remnants of Mary Alice's grandmother's dishes. She moaned and the dog whined, a quick call and response of sorrow and incomprehension. A folded piece of paper lay amid the mess. Lola saw her own name in Mary Alice's back-slanting handwriting. She stooped and picked it up. Shook it open.

"Lola—Camping on the Two Medicine. Back before you get here. If you beat me home, you know where to find the liquor."

Lola snapped her wrist, as if to free more words from the paper, ones that would make sense. Mary Alice had planned to meet her at the airport. She'd sent an email to confirm the time and flight number. And she'd left the phone message, too. The dog squirmed. Lola slid one foot ahead of the other, skating through the devastation, and found a lone intact bowl in the back of a cupboard. She started to set the dog down upon the floor, but considered the broken glass and instead swept an arm across the counter and listened to things fall. She ran a half-inch of water into the bowl, and set it and the dog onto the cleared counter. The water disappeared in a few frantic gulps. He lifted his head and sought more with a bifurcated stare, one eye brown, the other blue. His tail painted the air in feathery sweeps. Lola reached for the tag on his collar.

"Bub."

Bub.

It was Mary Alice's word.

"You sure that's how you want to phrase that, Bub?" Not Mr. Mayor. Or Congressman. Or whomever she was addressing. "Fine with me, Bub," she'd say to an editor who wanted to soften a story. Letting him know it was anything but. Or, "Sure, Bub, you can have my phone number." When hell freezes over.

The dog looked toward the door. Hackles lifted along his spine. Lola slipped the note into her pocket. Verle kicked his way across the room with a tremendous commotion. The dog took a step away from him, backing into the space between the cabinets and the counter. "This is a sorry business," he said. "Did you find any food for him?"

She shook her head.

"We can pick some up on the way into town. I've called down to Charlie," he said. "The sheriff," he added.

"How? My phone wouldn't work."

He reached for the faucet and held his hands under the water. "It's tough to get service up here unless you've got a local plan. Most of us carry two cell phones, one for local and one for normal. Charlie's on his way up. We can meet him down at the main road. No need to stay here with the . . ." He wiped his hands on his jeans and looked at her face. "We should just go on down."

The sheriff intercepted them halfway back along the two-track, lights flashing red and blue, startling colors in the moonlit landscape of black and grey. Verle pulled over. The sheriff's car came alongside. The siren cut off midway through its rising wail. Verle leaned out the window. "Charlie."

"Verle," the sheriff replied. He'd buttoned up his uniform shirt all cockeyed and his hair stood up in cowlicks. He was about half Verle's age, younger even than Lola, and the disarray shaved off more years still.

"Going all out, aren't you?" Verle asked.

"You said there was somebody shot up here. When was the last time we had somebody shot in this county? On purpose, I mean, not just somebody hunting and tripped? And not just any somebody, but Mary Alice?" Staring through Lola with every word.

"You got a point there," Verle allowed.

The sheriff waited, giving Verle time to make introductions. Verle declined to oblige. Some kind of tussle going on between them, eyes locked, jaws set.

"Who's this?" the sheriff asked finally.

Verle's shoulders relaxed, telegraphing victory. "This is the one found her. She flagged me down. I don't think we were ever properly introduced."

"Lola," she said. "Lola Wicks."

"After I'm done up there, I'll need to take her statement," the sheriff said. "Yours, too."

Lola put her hands flat on the seat and dug her fingernails into the upholstery and jammed her foot against the floorboards as though seeking an accelerator. "Stop talking!"

Both men's heads jerked as though yanked by the same string.

"Mary Alice is lying up there. Do something."

"She's right," Verle said. "You'd better get on about your sheriffing."

The sheriff looked up the track. His car inched forward, then stopped. "The longer we wait to start an investigation, the more time the perpetrators have to get away." Phrases stiff, stumbling, like something he'd memorized out of a book but hadn't had much chance to use.

"From the look of things up there, this happened quite a while ago," Verle said. "Your perpetrators are probably across the border and halfway across Canada by now. You can visit with this one—Miss Wicks?" Lola nodded. "You can visit with her tomorrow. She's not going anywhere. And you know where to find me. I'll take her down into town, put her in the Sleep Inn for you. Unless"—he turned to Lola—"you'd rather not be alone. I'm sure Jolee over at the store would be happy to take you in."

Lola thought back to the woman and imagined a bullying sort of sympathy, one urging avid, moist confidences. "No," she said. "Thank you. I think I'd be better off at the motel." She forced the words, distracted by the reality knocking at the forefront of her consciousness. Mary Alice was gone.

"Fine," the sheriff said. "First thing tomorrow, then. You didn't touch anything, did you?"

Lola looked down at the dog in her lap. "I went into the house," she said. She held the dog up so that the sheriff could see it. "I got him some water. He was thirsty."

"Damn. Verle, why didn't you stop her? There goes my crime scene."

Something nagged at Lola. "I touched Mary Alice, too."

"Oh shit, oh dear." The sheriff lifted his hands from the wheel and moved them helplessly. "Why did you do that?"

"I wanted to see what they used. I always check for that. It's how you tell which side did it. . . ." Then, seeing their faces, added quickly. "It's something you learn to do in Afghanistan. I'm a reporter. I work there. Did."

The sheriff's hands landed back on the wheel. The car lunged forward another six inches.

"Besides," said Lola, "I just lifted up her head and put it back down. I didn't touch her anyplace else." As far as she could tell, her voice sounded normal, if somewhat far away, hard to hear past the words jangling in her head. Mary Alice was gone.

"Look at her, Charlie. Let her get a night's sleep. Talk to her when she's fresh."

"Hell and goddamnation. Fine." Charlie hit the gas. His taillights washed red across the road, bent and disappeared.

"Thank you," Lola whispered.

"That guy," Verle observed, "doesn't know any more about sheriffing than I do about dancing a damn fandango. But don't you worry. This'll all get straightened out, despite Charlie." He eased the car into gear. "Let's get you over to the Sleep Inn. I'll get somebody to give me a ride back to my horse. You'll be fine there. They'll let you keep the dog in the room."

Lola turned. "Me? Why can't he stay with you?"

"You don't seem to know much about animals," he said conversationally, as if Mary Alice were not lying just up the road, blood congealing and limbs stiffening, her body closing itself off against the rude intrusions that would follow the initial indignity of being shot.

Lola wondered how much more she could say before her voice gave out altogether. "No," she managed. "Animals were Mary Alice's specialty."

◇◇◇

WHEN THEY met in college, there was a calico cat named Typo, smuggled into a dorm in violation of all regulations. She sashayed back and forth across Mary Alice's keyboard as she typed stories for the school newspaper, giving her a handy excuse against an editor's red grease pencil. Years later in Baltimore, when Mary Alice began working the neighborhoods where the police felt free to help themselves to the cash and drugs in stash houses after making their sweeps, she acquired Daisy, a Rottweiler whose jowly glare and rumbling bark usually sent anyone who got too close scrambling for cover before he could realize Daisy had only three legs. The dog's handicap came from her habit of chasing cars, a vice that continued in lopsided fashion until she grew too old to muster her former speed and a tricked-out Hummer did her in.

In her room at the Sleep Inn, Lola's lips twitched toward a smile at the memory. She had rearranged the room as she always did, pulling the bed away from the window and safety-pinning the thin drapes closed. She unrolled her sleeping bag atop the bed. After any extended visit to the field, she had a tough time readjusting to a bed's intimidating expanse, its smooth clean sheets and yielding pillows, preferring instead the comfort of the bag's close confines. She forced herself to leave her boots beside the bed and crawled into the bag in hard-soled slippers that would serve well enough for shoes should the need arise. The pup snored softly on the floor, its belly balloon-taut. She'd indulged him with extra food from the bag Verle had bought. He'd stopped at the convenience store on the way to the motel and Lola had waited in the car, sliding low in the seat when Jolee turned toward the blankness beyond the window, face slack as she tried to take in what Verle was telling her.

Lola reached down and scooped the dog onto the bed. He woke with a start, stared around wildly, then burrowed close, snuggling his head into the space under her chin. His hair was long and silky, his body surprisingly warm. Lola shook a sleeping pill into her fist, swallowed it dry, and switched off the light. She wrapped an arm around the pup and closed her eyes. It was always the worst time for her, the moments of half-sleep before the drug did its work. For years, all of the sights and sounds and smells of wherever she'd been that day rushed back in through the pinprick of fast-vanishing consciousness: the banshee wails of mothers at the sight of their own slaughtered children, freshly dead and mummifying quickly in the parched desert air; the dry-eyed grief of the fathers whose ancient Enfield rifles had been no match against errant bombs.

Tonight it was Mary Alice, eyes staring wide, mouth a circle of surprise, the wound like a lipsticked buss upon her cheek, something to be wiped away with a handkerchief. Still scarlet, not yet gone black and crusted, the way Lola usually saw them. But always on strangers. Never on someone who, years earlier when Lola had paid for a transatlantic call to object to Mary Alice's inexplicable career choice, laughingly replied, "It's the smartest thing I've ever done. You're the one going to all the crazy places. Me, I aim to die of boredom."

Lola curved her hand around the dog's head and then the drug did its work, a fast sinking sensation, dark waters parting then closing above her before she stopped thinking altogether.

CHAPTER FOUR

Lola awoke to soft slurping sounds.

A dog sprawled beside her, methodically dragging its tongue between legs splayed wide. Light slivered through an opening in the curtains. Beyond, a slice of jagged skyline. Mountains. The dog detached its face from its nether regions and leapt to its feet, tags jingling. Lola read them again. "Bub." Mary Alice's word. Mary Alice's dog. It was real. Mary Alice was gone.

Lola unzipped the sleeping bag and pushed herself upright, wove a path to the bathroom, swigged water, squirted toothpaste into her mouth and swished. Pain banged away behind her eyes. She tried to remember the last time she'd eaten. The bag of pretzels on the plane so laughably small she'd counted its contents. Nothing since. The dog keened at the door. Lola kicked out of her slippers, stashed her cash and other essentials in their assigned places in her clothing, and pulled on her boots, yanking the laces tight. She cracked the door. The dog shoved past her, the force jerking the knob from her hand. It hiked its leg against the tire of her rental car and pissed an endless stream.

"They'll probably charge you extra for that when you return it."

Lola grabbed for the door.

Verle Duncan stepped out from behind a grey pickup whose side panels flared to accommodate extra tires. "Easy," he said. "Didn't mean to startle you."

"You didn't." She moved back into the room and pulled the door nearly shut, peering at him through the crack.

He stopped where he was, shoulders thrown back in a short man's stance. She looked at the face under the hat and put him at close to sixty, clothing hugging a narrow frame. His boots ended in precise points. "Wasn't sure when you'd wake up," he said. "Been waiting awhile. Figured you'd need something in your stomach."

She remembered the gentle courtesies of the previous night. Let a milliliter or two of tension drain away.

"Coffee," she said.

He gestured toward the truck. "We'll go to the cafe."

She stood still, letting a thought undulate toward the surface of coherence. "The sheriff," she said finally.

"Trust that first instinct. Get that coffee, some food. You'll be more help with a clear head and a full stomach. We'll both need our strength if we're going to talk to By-the-Book Charlie. He'll probably come at us with a checklist straight from the procedures manual. Is that dog coming with us?"

Lola kept forgetting about the dog. She took a step toward the truck and the dog flashed past her, already on the seat before she'd reached the door. She put her foot on the low running board, grabbed the side of the truck and pulled herself up.

"Forgetting something?" asked Verle.

Lola did a quick mental inventory. She'd glanced at her drawn image in the bathroom mirror and reset her face for public display, smoothing her hands over her cheeks until her jaw unlocked, running her thumb between her eyebrows to erase the furrows there, narrowing her staring grey gaze into a semblance of its normal skepticism. She'd run wet hands through her hair and called it good.

"No. I didn't forget anything."

"A purse. Don't you have a purse? Women carry purses."

She felt her hip pocket. She kept a few bills there, folded around her long-unused driver's license with a doubled rubber band. The balls of her feet rubbed against more, layered into the bottom of each boot. She shifted in her seat and felt the rest of her cash sliding against her body, anchored at various points by her clothing. Pens jostled in her shirt pocket. The passports—her own and Maria's—nestled safely in a zippered pocket inside her pants.

"I don't own a purse."

"Huh. I never knew a woman not to." He drove a single block in silence and parked beside about a half-dozen pickups angled in front of a clapboard building set apart from the others by a gravel parking lot. The dog squeezed across Verle's lap as soon as his fingers touched the door handle. Verle elbowed him back. Bub curled his lip and muttered.

"Border collies," Verle said. "They're smart, but I've never trusted them. Look at how they move, slinking around, bellies to the ground like they're half-snake. They need somebody working them every day or they'll turn devil. I don't know what Mary Alice was thinking when she took one on."

Even as he said Mary Alice's name, there was her face, a black-bordered photo smiling from the front page of the local newspaper in the box by the door of Nell's Cafe. Lola stepped wide around it. She'd force herself to read the story later. Inside, she breathed the familiar, forgotten smells of grease and coffee. Formica tables perched upon islands of wan linoleum, the floor between them scuffed to the boards. Men in feed caps sat around a center table, chairs pushed back to accommodate assertive bellies. They nodded toward Verle, eyes on Lola. The newspaper lay open on the table. Verle led Lola toward a spot beneath a window. Beyond the glass, dun prairie rushed toward the ebony blockade of mountains.

Lola hung back. "Let's sit here." She picked out a table just inside the room, but off to the side. "I thought you said we were going to a cafe." She'd envisioned gingham tablecloths, maybe daisies in jelly glasses. "Back home, we'd call this a diner."

"Call it what you want," Verle said. "I call it breakfast." A laminated menu flung choices at her. ScrambledOvereasy-Poached. WhiteWheatSourdough. BaconSausageHam. Conversation rumbled back to life at the center table. Sunlight spilled across the room. Dust gossamered the air. Caution belatedly kicked in.

"Who are you, anyway?" Lola asked. "What do you do—besides squire around crime witnesses? How do you know Mary Alice? What were you doing over by her place last night? Do you live next door?"

Verle tipped his chair back. He wore a denim shirt with the sleeves folded back a triple turn. His throat sagged soft, but hair bristled grey on forearms that meant business. He'd taken off his hat and balanced it on its crown on the chair beside him. That mane was even more impressive in the daylight, shining and senatorial.

"Do you always wake up this cheerful? Must do wonders for your social life."

A teenage boy approached, a hairnet over his braids, coffeepot in hand. Lola recognized one of the youths from the convenience store.

"She'll have the steak and eggs," Verle said to him. "You want a cinnamon bun, too?" he asked Lola. "Nell makes a mean one. Bigger than anything you've ever seen."

"I don't eat breakfast," she told Verle. To the youth, she said, "Just coffee. Black."

"She'll have the steak. How do you like your eggs?"

"I don't."

"Aw, hell. Just bring them over easy. And some oatmeal for me."

The youth poured the coffee in an unsteady stream and left without looking at Lola. "You can drag your jaw up off that floor anytime," Verle said.

"Are you deaf?" Lola snapped. "I don't eat breakfast." She drained her mug. "Where's that kid with the goddamn coffee?"

"Lola, meet Joshua. Joshua, Lola," Verle said, as the boy reappeared and poured with the automatic movements of a somnambulist. Verle put his hand over his own cup. "You may as well leave that pot here. Set it down and back away slowly. She might bite."

Someone chortled. Joshua's expression changed not at all.

"That was a joke," Verle told Joshua's retreating back. Steam curled around Verle's fingers. He lifted his hand from the cup and blew on the palm. "Most people," he said to Lola, "you take them out for a meal, they smile and say thank you."

Lola looked again at the newspaper on the other table. "I don't see myself smiling. Not today."

"No. That's a fact. You do not have a thing to smile about."

Lola inclined her head in gratitude of that simple acknowledgement. "You didn't answer any of my questions."

"I did not."

"What do you do? What were you doing last night when I saw you?"

Fine lines threaded his face. When he smiled, they ran into fissures that bracketed his mouth. "I'd been riding fence all day. Elk got me pretty bad this winter, dragging right through the fences trying to get to the hay. Every time I think I've got it all fixed, I find a new hole. Thought I'd stop on the way home and check the head gate before they start running the water through the irrigation ditch. Good thing I did. Otherwise, you'd have had to go all the way into town to find somebody. Way you were driving, I'm not sure you'd have made it. Then Charlie would have had two bodies on his hands."

Lola fought an urge to pull out a pen and take notes. "I don't think I understood two words you said. Except for that last part. I got that just fine. But riding fence? A headgate? What do you do?"

"I've got a place between Mary Alice's and the reservation. Run some cattle there."

She shaded her eyes against the sun. Through the window, the sky went on and on, lifting effortlessly above the mountains. The cafe felt small. "Does that mean a ranch? And what does little mean? A hundred acres? A thousand? Because nothing out here looks little to me."

The air in the room went dead. Verle leaned toward Lola and delivered an indictment heard by everyone in the room. "You're not from here, so I'll excuse you. You don't ask someone how much land he's got."

Lola's head hurt like a hangover. In Afghanistan, she'd spent years learning how to get along. She never ate with her left hand, never pointed the soles of her feet at anyone, never offered a handshake to a man, let alone looked a man in the eye. She'd draped an extra layer of cloth over her breasts, covered her hair, her face, her whole body in yards of flowing fabric. And now she was up against a new set of rules. "What are those mountains?" she said. Trying for distraction. As if, at this point, a change of subject would help.

"Those mountains?" Verle replied, after he'd given her enough time to wonder if he was still talking to her at all. His eyes signaled amused tolerance. "Those would be the Rockies."

The food arrived in the midst of a collective guffaw, the steak still sizzling around the edges, the eggs goggling yellow-eyed at her. She pushed the plate away. Verle leaned across the table, took her knife and fork, sliced a piece of the steak, jabbed it into the eggs until the yolks broke, and then waved it beneath her nose. "Go on and eat this now."

She turned her head away. The fork followed. She opened her mouth. Bit down, chewed, swallowed. Protein hit her veins like speed. Her mouth fell open again. Verle laughed and handed her the silverware.

"You can take over from here."

Lola sliced at the steak, layering it with some egg onto a piece of toast. She folded the bread and brought it dripping to her mouth. Verle handed her a napkin. "I may have to rethink my bias against breakfast," she allowed.

The youth with the coffee returned and stood beside her, making no move to refill her cup. "Miss."

She strained to hear his voice.

"Wicks," Verle told him.

"Miss Wicks."

"Please," she said. "Lola."

He set the coffeepot on the table. His arms stuck like sticks from a T-shirt that billowed nearly to his knees. "You know—you *knew*—Mary Alice?" he asked the floor.

"Yes." Not a single person in the cafe made a pretense of not listening.

"Mary Alice and my uncle—he works for the tribes—they were good friends."

"They were?" Verle's voice intruded.

Joshua looked up. His eyes, fixed on a point just behind Lola, were rich and brown and liquid, the color of a good strong Arabic brew rather than the watery stuff in her cup. "Do you know what happened to her? All we heard is that she's dead."

"And that's all we know, too," Verle broke in. He lay a ten on the table. "This lady can't be talking to you about it. She's got to talk to the sheriff first." He dug in his pocket and dropped a quarter atop the bill. "You want to find out about it, I'd suggest you read the Daily Distress. Sorry, Miss Wicks. I forgot you were in that line of work. *Daily Express*, I should have said. Looks like they gave it a big write-up."

The boy pinched the money between his fingertips and drifted away. Lola had figured him for seventeen or eighteen, but his hairless cheeks and chin made her wonder if he was even in high school.

"What's his deal?" she whispered to Verle. "He seems so—" She wasn't sure. "Worse than depressed. Almost like he's grieving. Was he close to Mary Alice, too?"

"Naw. His sister's probably back in jail," Verle said. "Best place for her." Then, at Lola's look, added, "Old story. Long story. We should be getting over to the sheriff's office before he sends out a posse."

Lola grabbed the last piece of toast, wiped the egg yolk from the plate, stuffed it into her mouth and followed Verle out of the cafe. At the door, she glanced back. Joshua stood silhouetted against the window, cleaning rag dangling from his hand. Verle had seemed surprised to find out that Mary Alice and Joshua's uncle were friends. Something had slipped across the smooth surface of geniality as he glanced around the room to see if anyone else had registered the remark. Lola ran through the moment in her mind.

They were? Not quite a frown, but close. A couple of quick blinks before his gaze returned to her face. No. She hadn't imagined it. Verle hadn't known. And he hadn't liked finding out.

CHAPTER FIVE

The sheriff sat on one side of a grey metal desk whose heft and dimensions suggested an aircraft carrier.

Lola gauged its immense surface and then the narrow door and wondered if someone had simply winched the desk down onto a piece of flooring and built the office around it. She perched on the edge of a folding chair, fingertips doing a drum roll against her knees, waiting for him to start. The morning newspaper sat to the left of the sheriff's elbow, Mary Alice's black-bordered photo looking up from it, her stare disconcertingly direct. Lola glanced away. A row of pencils lay beside the paper like small spears, freshly sharpened points trained upon her. The smell of graphite and cedar hung in the air. He picked one up and pulled a legal pad toward him.

"I called her parents," he said.

Lola checked her percussive impatience. She'd never given Mary Alice's parents a thought and she could tell that he knew it. In contrast to the previous night's dishevelment, the sheriff was properly buttoned up, cowlicks slicked into damp submission. A couple of fresh cuts crosshatched his chin, as though he hadn't quite gotten the hang of shaving. One of those fake-wood signs on his desk spelled out his full name: Charles Laurendeau. He didn't look French, Lola thought.

"Do they know I'm out here?"

"Figured I'd let you tell them that." Not letting her off the hook, presuming she'd have the belated good grace to call them herself.

"How'd they take it?"

"Quietly."

Lola pictured the home where Mary Alice had grown up, the parlor that resembled every other first-floor room in the claustrophobic rowhouses just far enough away from Baltimore's newly fashionable waterfront to allow the neighborhood to cling to its Irish-Polish roots. Two sway-seated recliners facing the television, antimacassars on the sofa and hand-tatted doilies on the end tables. Pressed glass bowls of candied almonds and Easter-colored mints whose levels never changed. Every object in the room daily wiped free of dust, layers of wax so deep on the furniture that the grain lay wavy and indistinct beneath it. The television's tinned laughter a constant backdrop from morning's rise until late-night's ceremonial thimbleful of Jameson's. "Just a wee drop, girls." Lola had spent an interminable Thanksgiving there with Mary Alice, the two of them occupying opposite ends of the inhospitable sofa, trying to make small talk past the TV. Giving up.

And yet. Mary Alice was their only child. Even after moving to Montana, she paid the punitive fares to fly home for Thanksgiving and back again at Christmas. Telephoned them twice a week, sent chocolates on birthdays and fruit baskets for anniversaries, and postcards and letters for no reason at all. The funeral in Magpie would be in two days, the sheriff had told her when she arrived for her interview. No doubt her parents would schedule a memorial later in Baltimore. Lola made a mental note to call the airlines to push back her flights so that she could stay the extra day. She'd send Mary Alice's parents a bushel-size bouquet. And a card. With a note, a long one.

"What about your parents?" the sheriff asked.

"What about them?"

"Have you spoken with them? You might want someone to talk to under the circumstances, seems like."

"Dead. For years now."

"Friends?"

She thought about that one. She had foxhole friendships with the cadre of foreign correspondents in Kabul, traveling with them in convoys for safety, sleeping with one or another on occasion, and organizing the softball games in courtyards ringed by armed guards. But those ties generally vanished upon departure. The departure in this case being hers.

"No. Mary Alice was it."

He picked up a pencil. "Ready?" He established her full name—"No middle name? Really?"—raised an eyebrow at her exotic address and showed no reaction whatsoever when she told him she was thirty-four. Which, Lola supposed, meant that Afghanistan had taken its toll and she finally looked her age.

"What brings you all the way out here?"

"Vacation."

"You're a long way from home. Couldn't you have found something a little closer?"

She fought an urge to rearrange the pencils, to set something askew on that orderly desk. "Mary Alice and I haven't seen each other for five years. Montana seemed like a better vacation spot than Kabul." No reason for him to know about her job situation.

"For someone on vacation, you sure travel light. They said over at the Sleep Inn you've only got the one bag and the book bag."

Lola thought back to the proprietress at the motel, a tiny alert woman with inquisitive darting eyes, and wondered whether the sheriff had called her, or she'd called him first. "Why are we talking about me? Can we get to Mary Alice?"

His chin crimped in disapproval. Like everything else in his face, it was too big, mouth too wide, eyelids too heavy, nose deserving of its own listing in the U.S. Geological Survey. Lola had known men who managed, through force of personality, to turn their homeliness into an asset. The sheriff was not one of them. "That's what I'm trying to do," he said. "And you were the last one to see her alive."

"*Alive?*" Verle was right. Charlie Laurendeau didn't know squat about sheriffing. "I hope to God you're calling in some help on this one."

The pencil snapped in his fingers, the halves spinning across the desk, wobbling at the metal edge before gravity won out and jerked them floorward. He watched them go, turning his head first one way, then another. "What do you mean?"

"You saw the back of her head."

He picked up a new pencil. His fingertips went pink where he clutched it. "I did. But there was no rigor mortis." She heard the boy in him then, his tone protesting that what he'd seen didn't fit with the way things should have been. "So I asked the medical examiner. Everything is very preliminary. He hasn't completed a full autopsy. But he said as bad as that looked, the bullet missed a lot of important things. It's not impossible that she lived for several hours afterward, probably unconscious, but maybe not. I thought there might have been a chance she was alive when you got to her, that she might have said something. I almost stopped by the Sleep Inn at two in the morning on my way back from the cabin to ask you."

Lola closed her eyes and let it come back to her. But for the staring eyes, the wound like a beauty mark, Mary Alice could have been napping. Lola had put her hands to Mary Alice's face, her head rolling easily as Lola lifted. Fresh blood rippling like satin. A scream—her own. Falling back. Somehow righting herself and stumbling down the hill toward the cabin and her car.

"Her head," she said thickly. "You saw her head." Mary Alice could not possibly have been alive, could not have lain for hours alone but for the dog's mute vigil, the life leaking out of her while Lola dawdled at the airport. "She was dead."

Saying the word aloud for the first time. She took slow, deliberate breaths to steady herself, focusing in turn on each object on the sheriff's desk. Not the newspaper. She couldn't face that photograph yet. But the pencils. The telephone. Files.

Blotter. Calendar. The safety of the mundane. Her inventory ended at a narrow, arched pegboard. She reached for it, fingertips wandering across its polished surface, anchoring herself.

"Cribbage?"

"That's right."

"Ivory?"

"Elk antler."

Lola withdrew one of the pegs, black and gleaming, topped with a blue-green stone. He answered before she could ask. "Buffalo horn, set with turquoise. Wilson Bird over on the reservation made it. The man's an artist."

"Beautiful."

"Yes," he agreed. "Any idea what Mary Alice was doing up on that hill with her sleeping bag? Were you two planning some sort of campout?"

"A campout? Like we were kids?" It was almost enough to make her smile, the idea of the two of them shaking out their respective sleeping bags under the trees, crawling in and whispering secrets, grown women shedding the confusions of adulthood with a return to schoolgirl ritual. It would have been fun. *Fun.* "Not the two of us," Lola said. "Just her. I found this in her kitchen." She pulled out the note she'd retrieved from the cabin and smoothed it onto his desk.

"Don't!" He grabbed her hands and pulled them away. The paper fell back into its trifold creases. Lola extricated her hands.

"I don't suppose it occurred to you not to touch this. The crime lab can lift fingerprints from paper. Could have."

Guilt stabbed at Lola. She rejected it. "Any fingerprints that might have been on this note are probably on every surface in that kitchen."

"Most of which you already touched," he reminded her. "Verle, too."

Lola prodded at the paper, belatedly stopping short of actual contact. "Are we going to talk about something that's too late to fix? Or can we focus on this note?" She'd memorized its abbreviated contents. Mouthed the words as he read them. *Lola—Camping on the Two Medicine. Back before you get here. If you beat me home, you know where to find the liquor.*

She gave him a minute to digest it. A wall clock hung behind his head, second hand twitching audibly in its endless circuit around the face. "The thing is," she said, "Mary Alice was going to pick me up at the airport. She sent me an email a couple of days ago to double-check my flight number and arrival time. So that business about me getting to the cabin before her doesn't make sense. And then there's the voicemail she left me." She pulled out her phone and played it for him. He jotted down the words.

Hey, you. I might be late. I've got to take care of something here. I'll call when I'm on my way. You sit tight 'til I get there. Love you.

The sheriff's hand hesitated over the *love you.* "She didn't say what she had to take care of?"

Lola shook her head. "I've re-checked both my voicemail and my email. She didn't leave me anything after that. But maybe she tried to send me something and it didn't go through. You should look at her computer. I can probably help you unlock it. She's changed her password every two weeks for years, but I know the formula she uses."

"Can't."

The clock ticked and tocked. "Why can't you?"

He dug the heel of his hand against bloodshot eyes. Lola guessed that despite the fresh shirt and hasty shave, he hadn't slept the previous night. He'd knocked away the scab over one of the shaving cuts. A drop of blood swelled and glittered garnet-like in the awful fluorescent light. "You saw that house. We don't know if this was a burglary or what. It was hard to figure out if anything was taken. But one thing we didn't find in all of that was a computer. A television, either. Nor a cellphone, not in the house or on her. The phone's not much of a problem. We'll just get the records from the company. We'd sure like to have her computer, though. Unfortunately, she used the same laptop for work and at home."

"Mary Alice didn't own a TV. But a computer seems like a logical thing to go missing during a burglary. If that's what it was. Besides, even if you find it, it won't help you. Mary Alice was paranoid about security. She bought some pretty expensive software so she could scrub everything, even from her hard drive. She stored all of her files on flash drives."

He leaned forward. "Where'd she keep her flash drives?"

"No idea. But that's what you'll want to look for when you're searching her place. Do you really think this was a burglary?"

"We're considering all the possibilities."

Lola thought she'd probably heard those same words from every cop on every crime story she'd ever worked.

"Speaking of which," he added. "It's really a formality, but I've got to ask: Any reason Mary Alice would want to take her own life?"

"Mary Alice?" Recalling, even as she spoke, a day she'd showed up at Mary Alice's place in Baltimore at dawn, furious and full of self-loathing after her longtime romantic entanglement had retreated yet again to his wife.

"You'll dump him when it's time," Mary Alice had said. Standing in the doorway fully dressed. Warm toast scent from the kitchen. Coffeemaker burbling. Mary Alice held out her hand. "Give."

"What?" said Lola. Her throat raw from the night's shouted recriminations.

"I know how you are," Mary Alice said. "Whatever it is, hand it over." And took Lola down into her basement workroom and handed her a ball-peen hammer so that she could smash the new watch with the engraved anniversary message that Lola had lifted from her lover's bedside table. Then gave her a whisk broom and dustpan. "Clean up your damn evidence." They'd laughed, then.

"Not a chance," Lola told the sheriff now. "Even if she had a reason—and she didn't, not that I know of—she's the least judgmental person I know. I can't imagine her being any harder on herself than she was on anyone else."

"We found a gun at the site. No computer, no phone, but a gun."

"What kind of gun?"

"I can't comment on that."

"It was a .45, wasn't it? She's had that thing forever. If you knew her neighborhood in Baltimore, you'd know why. The drug dealers there had this saying: '.22—Just won't do. .38—Best shoot straight. .45—Stay alive.' Had it been fired? I'll bet it hadn't. Besides, a .45 didn't do that to her. It was a rifle."

"I can't comment on that, either. Did Mary Alice know a lot of drug dealers?"

Lola tried to fashion a shorthand description for the creeping gentrification that led Mary Alice to overcome her parents' objections and bet on a Pigtown rowhouse whose soaring ceilings and marble fireplaces seemed to outweigh the fact that the neighbors on either side had windowless steel doors and curbside parking spaces that no one other than the homes' owners dared use. "Her neighborhood was—in transition, you might say. But Mary Alice managed to make friends with all the folks on the street, not just the ones moving in but the ones who'd been there all along, too. Maybe not friends, exactly. Let's just say they had a working relationship." Meaning that Mary Alice didn't complain about the procession of suburban white boys who cruised the street in their parents' SUVs, barely slowing to a stop for transactions made through windows opened just wide enough to pass cash out and take never-mind-what in. In return, nobody ever vandalized Mary Alice's car—or Lola's either, when she visited—despite the robust level of street crime that served as a sort of welcome wagon for newcomers.

"Any reason why anybody would want to kill her?"

"She'd have told me if there were."

"What about a boyfriend? I never heard about one, but maybe you did. Or, maybe"—he slid his gaze away from hers—"more than one? Sometimes that happens. Two guys, one woman, and for reasons I've never understood, the woman pays."

Mary Alice had occasionally disappeared for long weekends and returned smiling and maddeningly silent, in contrast to Lola, whose liaison with her colleague between and during his various marriages had been open newsroom knowledge for so long that it ceased to be fodder for gossip. Afghanistan had put a stop to that, just as Montana had presumably halted Mary Alice's flings. But maybe not.

"From what I can tell about this place, everybody here would know more about that than I do. She was no nun, but she was the most discreet person I've ever met."

"Girlfriend?"

"I'm straight," Lola snapped. "Short hair just makes my life easier in the field."

The sheriff's pencil added another line to his pad, more words than a simple "no." "I wasn't asking about you." Before the rebuke could settle in, he followed it up with another question. "What about someone mad at her for something she wrote?"

"You'd know more about that, too. Have you talked to the people at the newspaper here?" On surer footing when she was the one asking the questions.

"I called them last night. They were in a tough spot. Trying to deal with what I was telling them, and then needing to write a story about it, too. They're coming in today to talk some more. She'd been spending a lot of time up on the rez—the Blackfeet reservation. There's a guy up there campaigning for governor. Johnny Running Wolf. Maybe you've heard of him."

Lola shook her head. "No. Wait. I think I saw a billboard on the way up here."

"He's gotten himself some national press. Indian candidate in cowboy country, that kind of thing. He's some sort of long-lost cousin of mine."

"Oh."

"What?"

"I'm sorry," she said. "I hadn't realized you were Blackfoot."

"Not Blackfoot. You all named us Black*feet*. Singular or plural, you're sorry that I'm Indian? I didn't know it required an apology." The same challenging tone he'd taken with Verle.

Beneath her own chagrin, Lola again saw Verle and the sheriff facing off from their respective vehicles, the bristling that accompanied their conversation. She wondered what Verle had said during his own interview with the sheriff. She threw a wild pitch. "What about Verle? Is he a suspect?" The clock's second hand clicked its measured progress. Lola wanted to climb up onto her chair so that she could reach high enough to stop it. Then she registered the nod, the words that followed.

"Yes," the sheriff said. "Verle is a suspect."

Her stomach did a slow revolution, an ungainly fish turning in too-deep water. She hadn't given nearly enough consideration to the fact that Verle had been loitering by the road not two miles from where Mary Alice lay freshly dead. Fear and shock had muffled her reason. Lapses like that got people hurt. Killed.

"Are you going to arrest him?" Her voice rose.

"No."

"Because?"

He drew a circle with the pencil and slashed lines across it, dividing it into quarters, eighths. "Sit down."

She hadn't realized she was on her feet. He wrote something in one of the slices of the pie, gave the pad a small turn, and wrote something else. He pushed the pad toward her. "Here's Verle's name. And here's yours."

Disappointment tugged her back into the chair. "Of course," she said. At this stage, everyone was a suspect. She'd have been dismayed by her own lack of judgment if the sheriff considered Verle a strong possibility. Still, it would be a relief to leave Montana with Mary Alice's killer behind bars. The sheriff turned the pad again and wrote another name. "Here's Jolee, over at the store. When I stopped by for coffee this morning, she told me that Mary Alice drove down there a couple of days ago. Said she was stocking up on stuff for your visit. Way it looks now, Jolee was the last person to see her"—those fleshy lips spat the word—"*alive* before she got killed. I'm interviewing her next."

"Speaking of Jolee," Lola said slowly.

"What about her?"

"There was a guy outside her store last night. It's probably nothing."

The sheriff tensed. "Everything counts at this point."

"He said something about Mary Alice. 'Poor Mary Alice,' he called her. It seemed like a strange thing to say. Especially in retrospect."

"Do you know who he was? Would Jolee know?" The weariness had fled his voice.

His enthusiasm, along with the thought that she could be useful, was infectious. "I can't remember his name. But he didn't have any teeth."

The sheriff's pencil jerked, trailing a long jagged line across the pad. "That's Frank. He didn't have anything to do with this." He rubbed at the page with his eraser.

"You just said everything and everyone counted. Why not Frank?"

The sheriff tilted the pad, letting the crumbles of eraser fall into a trash can. "Because he wouldn't have done it, that's why. I know him." Lola started to speak but he cut her off. "Technically, I suppose he's a suspect, just like Verle. But face it. Until I get some more information, half the people in this town are suspects, and I haven't even started talking to folks on the rez. Maybe one of them stopped by her place yesterday. Then I could add another name to my little pie chart."

"What was that guy's name again?" Lola asked. "The one Mary Alice was writing about? Where's his name on this thing?"

"Johnny Running Wolf. He's been down in Denver for a few days, doing some sort of fundraising with rich whitemen. Mary Alice wrote about his trip. He'll be in town for a meet-and-greet at the VFW the day of the funeral. He's probably one of the few people I don't have to worry about." He handed her a business card. "Take some time. If you think of anything, you can call me. Here's how to reach me. We should touch base again after the funeral."

She shook her head. "I'm on a plane out of here as soon as it's over." She reached into her pocket and thumbed one of her own cards, printed in blocky English letters and Arabic curlicues of Pashto and Farsi, from beneath the rubber band and held it out to him. "Call me and let me know the minute you catch whomever did this. Or maybe"—she looked around the office again, at the cheap plastic clock, the government-surplus desk—"you can email me if you can't afford the international call."

The sheriff blinked rapidly. His hands pawed at the keyboard. "I'm afraid not." He angled the computer screen so that she could see it, showed her the standard bulletin that would go to law enforcement departments around the country, as well as to airports, Border Patrol, Homeland Security. She watched him type her name in the blanks. Then he unlocked a steel door behind the desk and walked her down a short hallway and pointed out the cell where he could, if necessary, house her as an uncooperative material witness if she in any way, shape or form attempted to leave Magpie before his investigation was complete. A woman lay on the lower bunk's thin bare mattress, skeletal brown arms clutching her knees to her chest, dark hair waterfalling over the side of the bed. She looked at them with dull eyes.

"Is that Joshua's sister?"

The sheriff's head whipped around. "How do you know about her?"

"Never mind. She looks cold. Why can't she have a blanket? Or at least a sheet?"

"Suicide risk," the sheriff said. "Look. I can talk to the people at the Sleep Inn, try to get you some kind of reduced rate. For that matter, the crime lab folks will be done up at Mary Alice's by the end of the day, tomorrow at the latest. Don't know if you'd feel comfortable staying up there, but it's an option. At least it's free. And likely the safest place you could be right now. Whoever killed her is probably as far away as he could possibly get."

Joshua's sister moaned. She rolled from the bunk and fell onto the floor and pushed herself up onto her hands and knees. She wobbled a moment, then crabwalked toward the lidless metal toilet and wrapped her arms around it and heaved. Lola looked away. "No," she said. "I would not feel comfortable with that. I can't believe you even suggested it."

"Shame to let the place sit empty. You all right, Judith?" he called into the cell. "I know this part's rough. I'm going to call over to the clinic and have Margie come check you out."

Judith's voice surprised Lola with its strength. "She hates me."

"That she does," Charlie said. "Nonetheless."

"How long before you get him?" Lola interrupted.

Charlie led her back down the hallway and into his office and locked the door behind them. "That depends."

"On what?"

"On you—at least in part. Maybe you'll remember something useful. I'll talk to Verle again, too. And Jolee, of course. But please think back. Anything, no matter how insignificant, could help. Maybe there's something you're not telling us."

"Nothing. There's nothing."

Lola slumped against the office wall, limp with a sudden realization. Charlie Laurendeau didn't have the first notion as to who might have killed Mary Alice. She gathered herself for a final effort. "You can't hold me here. That material witness stuff—that's crime show bullshit."

"Try me."

Lola eased her hand into her pocket and closed her fingers around the buffalo horn cribbage peg, pressing the sharp tip into her palm until she felt the skin break, the sudden comforting warmth of blood sealing her inner vow. If Charlie couldn't find the killer, she would. She looked again at the newspaper photo and this time met Mary Alice's eyes. "Love you," she whispered.

CHAPTER SIX

Mary Alice's funeral drew a crowd.

Lola sat in the back of the whitewashed wooden church and watched them file in, the men in starched and creased jeans, big hats dangling from hard hands; the women, even the young ones, trussed up in the sort of dresses Lola's mother might have worn. The flimsy flowered material strained tight across breasts and behinds that had filled out considerably during the years that those good dresses had waited in the back of the closet for the rare occasion demanding their appearance, their wearers stumping uncertainly along on heels no more frequently called into service than the dresses.

Lola had traded her cargo pants for a pair of black jeans and attempted to dress up her usual black pullover by draping her headscarf around her shoulders. She tucked her unwieldy hiking boots as far back under the pew as they would go, and tried not to think about the likely paucity of mourners at her own funeral when that day came, something she'd contemplated several times after close calls. Nothing she'd imagined involved anything like this rapidly filling church standing lonely sentinel over the prairie some miles from town. A plaque inside the vestibule told her it was the old mission church, abandoned a century earlier when the reservation boundaries shrank. Lola had the feeling that most of the time it stood empty and forgotten. She'd grown up in the lush Catholicism of Baltimore, all gilt and garish stained glass and arrow-pierced saints with eyes rolled heavenward. More recently, there had been the centuries-old mosques of Central Asia, gorgeous wrecks with turquoise-tiled minarets and fantastical geometric patterns on the crumbling walls. She'd forgotten about the austere faiths of the heartland, devoid of imagery and comfort, exacting doctrines all of a piece with their unforgiving surroundings.

Still, despite the stark interior, the air in the church was electric, ions of emotion caroming off the tall clear windows, sliding along the severe casket parked up in front. Lola recognized some faces: Jolee, from the convenience store, heavy-lidded and scowling. The toothless vagrant who'd felt so sorry for Mary Alice, face scrubbed, a clean red bandana around his neck, rocking a little in his seat. Fred, Lola thought, trying to fix his name in her mind, eyeing him with heightened interest. No, Frank. She wondered why Charlie had been so insistent that he couldn't have killed Mary Alice. Frank sat between the busboy from the cafe and a small man in thick glasses with heavy black rims, lenses cloudy with scratches.

The sheriff stood alone at the back of the church, raking the mourners with his gaze. Lola wondered how many of these people were Mary Alice's friends and how many were there solely for the entertainment value afforded by the county's first murder in forty years, according to the newspaper story she'd finally forced herself to read. The few funerals for journalists Lola had attended were generally hushed, uncomfortable gatherings in museums or community centers or other secular places, the members of the newsroom generally being an unchurched lot. There'd be some generic music and short speeches by editors fumbling for polite euphemisms for the person's less pleasant qualities. In her own case, Lola imagined words such as "determined," "hard-working," "driven." The subtext ringing through: stubborn, stiff-necked. Nobody's idea of fun. The same sorts of things her editor had implied when he'd sent her off to Montana. What had he said on her way out the door? "Stuck." As in, "You're stuck in those old days. They're gone. Go hang out with that friend of yours, watch some TV, figure out what people really care about. Then come back and write me some stories with pop and sizzle."

Pop and sizzle. Lola silently shaped her lips around the ugly words. They felt like something she shouldn't say in a church. She looked around to see if anyone had noticed her distraction. But everyone was sitting up taller and twisting in their seats, the high-octane event flaming even brighter with a new arrival. Lola saw the suit first, dove-grey, the jacket buttoned over a lustrous black silk shirt and a bolo tie with a big chunk of turquoise. Her gaze slid to his feet and she almost laughed at the idea of anybody picking his way across the sagebrush-dotted churchyard in those paper-soled, butter-soft eyelet oxfords. She belatedly lifted her eyes to his face, to the hair black as oil paint and woven into two short braids gathered into a single ponytail; to the nose that still bore the blow of whatever fist or other blunt object it had encountered years earlier, its high arrogant arch resolving into a shapeless mass. A secondary commotion localized at her pew. Verle Duncan squeezed past people, scattering pardons like confetti in his wake, shoehorning himself into the nonexistent space beside her.

"Johnny Running Wolf sure cleans up good." He nodded toward the man in the suit.

"That's Johnny Running Wolf?" Lola leaned past him for another look at the subject of Mary Alice's recent journalistic focus. Lola had gone online to look up those stories, but the *Daily Express* website had a pay wall that demanded a credit card. Which Lola's newspaper had just canceled. A kilted man cradling a bagpipe stepped to the front of the church.

"Andy Macleod," Verle said. "His family runs sheep." Pronouncing *sheep* the same way she'd heard those words *pop and sizzle* in her mind. "He's always looking for an excuse to put on a skirt and screech away on that thing."

Andy Macleod closed his lips around the reeds, and the opening strains of "Amazing Grace" wailed toward the rafters.

People rose in a deep, rustling sigh. A framed photo of Mary Alice stood atop the casket, the same smiling shot from the newspaper, her eyes coolly surveying the crowd. Lola imagined the elbow in her side, the breathy voice in her ear. "Get a load of this, Bub. Half of them are here to make sure I'm really dead." An elbow nudged her again, real this time. Verle extended a folded linen handkerchief. "Go on. It's clean." She handed it back to him. "I don't cry," she said. Voices lifted around them.

"Through many dangers, toils and snares
I have already come."

The interminable dirge finally ended, the last notes subsumed in a murmur tinged with excitement. Johnny Running Wolf made his way up the aisle, shaking hands along the way. The toothless man waved, trying to catch his eye, but Johnny kept moving, nodding to Verle, his gaze flicking across Lola's face as he headed for the pulpit. The minister, mouth open in preparation to speak, stood frozen as Johnny commandeered the only funeral service for a murder victim the minister was likely to conduct. Johnny paused before him and the minister closed his mouth and stepped aside. Johnny waited until the rustling ceased.

"Mary. Alice. Carr."

He tolled her name, waiting for each word to fall away before intoning the next. Lola shivered. He was going to talk about Mary Alice and it was going to be in the past tense. *Mary Alice was gone.* Johnny paced before the front pews like a lawyer at a jury box, making no noticeable effort to raise his voice, which nonetheless easily reached the rear of a church gone hushed and still as the moment before daybreak. "Mary. Alice. Carr. That name was on top of a lot of stories in the newspaper about me. I didn't always like those stories." He waited as a few quick knowing smiles ran their course through the crowd.

Lola's eyes narrowed at the practiced pause. Mary Alice's voice in her ear again: "What's up with that, Bub?" Verle put a hand on Lola's shoulder, the gesture warm, steadying. Lola shook it off. She didn't want any distractions. The sheriff had said Verle was a suspect and Johnny wasn't. Lola wondered if he'd gotten things backward.

"No, I didn't like many of them at all. But she always told both sides. She made a lot of people mad. They thought she was poking around in places she didn't belong. But she was fearless. She kept on writing those stories and a lot of other ones, besides. We don't know if that's why she was . . ." He left it there, the word worse for being unspoken. Lola sat up straight within the collective held breath.

"We hope not. All we can do, in this time of tragedy, is to hold tight to our memory of Mary Alice Carr, a woman who called it as she saw it." An emphasis on *she,* leaving open the possibility that other people might not see it that way at all. Lola wondered if she'd imagined it. Knew she hadn't. A half-dozen people in the front pew shifted in their seats. Mary Alice's colleagues at the newspaper, Lola decided. She'd need to talk to them after the service. A young woman sitting among them raised a camera and fired a series of shots of Johnny Running Wolf, the shutter's sliding clicks sounding unnaturally loud, intrusive. Johnny faced the camera.

"She went after the truth. And now she's gone. I guess that's what the truth gets you nowadays."

He stood at the front of the church a few moments more, then shook his head and walked back to his seat. Lola pressed her thumb into the wound on her palm from the cribbage peg. She'd heard less subtle warnings, warnings involving gun barrels warming against the flesh of her throat and spittle-flecked shouts mere inches from her face, but this one, she thought, was just as pointed. An organ creaked into another plodding hymn, only slightly more tuneful than the bagpipes, and Lola sank into her seat, wondering what Mary Alice had gotten herself into in Montana.

✧✧✧

"You're her friend, right? The one who came to visit? The one who found her?" The young woman, camera slung over her shoulder, stood at Lola's elbow after the service. She wore a denim jacket over a black dress that wrapped and rewrapped itself around her legs in the wind that swept Lola free of any lingering warmth from the church's interior. Lola stared at the pearly skin nutmegged with freckles and wondered when everyone in her business had gotten so young. "Jan Carpenter," the woman introduced herself. She pulled out a tape recorder barely larger than a cigarette lighter. "I wonder if we could visit for a minute."

Lola scanned the crowd spilling from the church, seeking the dark hair, the braids, finding him at the edge of the throng, talking with Toothless. She turned back to Jan Carpenter. "Tell me you're not trying to interview me at my best friend's funeral." Trying to forget all the times she'd done exactly that, not just at funerals but right at the graveside, for the big stories and the small ones, too, people grieving just as hard after a garden-variety Saturday night shooting in South Baltimore as at a suicide bombing. All the while, Lola standing there among them, offering Kleenex and sympathy, notebook and pen at the ready.

Jan shrugged and the jacket fell open, her collarbones bracketing a neckline far too low for the occasion. She clutched at the jacket, pushing the buttons belatedly through their holes.

"What is that?" Lola asked. "Your old prom dress?"

Jan's fingers stilled at their task. "I just want to ask you a few questions about Mary Alice. About finding her. Charlie—he's the sheriff—won't tell us anything other than that she was shot."

"I know who Charlie is." Lola glanced back toward Johnny. The toothless man, Frank, had taken over the conversation. His body twisted as he spoke. He staggered and nearly fell. The sheriff stood a few feet away, openly watching them. "Forget it," she told Jan.

"It's my only black dress," Jan called after Lola as she pushed her way through the clusters of mourners. Frank showed his gums as she approached.

"Mar' Alice," he said. "She's dead." His cheeks puffed. "Puh-*pow*." He raised his hand and pointed a forefinger and folded the other fingers against his palm. "Mar' Alice got shot. Pow." He dug the finger in his cheekbone. "Right in the *face*. Poor Mar' Alice."

Lola recoiled. The sheriff stepped in, folding his hand around Frank's, lowering the offending finger. "Yes, Frank. That's what happened to Mary Alice."

Johnny used the moment to take his leave. "Frank. Charlie. Good seeing you both again. Shame about the reason."

Lola put her hand on his arm. Firmly. "You're Johnny Running Wolf?" He tried to pull away. She tugged him back, just hard enough to be obvious about it. As soon as one head in the crowd turned, so did all the others, a progressive motion from the core of the throng to the edges. Johnny smiled weakly. "My condolences. Sorry I can't stay. Campaign's got me on a tight schedule."

Lola had always envied people who could cry on command. She couldn't. She put a hand to her eyes anyway, wishing she still had Verle's handkerchief, and injected a pitiful quaver into her voice. "I just want to talk about my friend."

Johnny made a big show of it then, the protective arm around her shoulders, lips pursed in concern. "Sure thing. We'll talk all you want about Mary Alice. She was quite a little gal, that one. Come on over here." Cars and pickups nudged up against the church on three sides. He led her around the back. "What the hell are you up to?" he whispered as they walked.

"I might," Lola said through a clenched smile, "ask the same of you."

❖❖❖

THE WIND caught them as they rounded the corner. Lola stood close to the warped boards of the church, splintery and sun-warmed, and ducked out from under Johnny's arm. "What were you talking about back in there? That so-called eulogy?"

He rolled shock and pain and indignation into a long look that made Lola want to slap him. "Mary Alice was my friend."

"No, she wasn't. She was a reporter. You were a story, not a friend."

Engines stuttered in the parking area. Exhaust swirled around the corner of the church. Johnny coughed. Lola spoke over it. "Why was Mary Alice so interested in writing about you? How come you didn't like what she wrote? And where'd you get shoes like that in a place like this?"

"Hold on," he said. "You know who I am. But you still haven't told me who you are or what you're doing here."

"I'm a friend of Mary Alice's—a real friend. I came out for a visit. It's not going well."

"Guess you'll be heading back now."

"The very minute I can. Just as soon as I find out what happened to Mary Alice." Might as well put him on notice, she thought. She expected defensiveness, maybe a flash of anger. Surprise, at the very least.

Instead, he threw back his head and sent a laugh rolling across the prairie. When he held out his hand, she took it automatically. "You do that. Nice to have made your acquaintance, Miss Wicks."

Lola dropped his hand. He disappeared around the corner of the church. His laughter drifted back to her.

Lola shouted into the wind. "Wait!" She rounded the corner just in time to see him getting into a white Suburban with tinted windows. "Miss Wicks," he'd called her. But she'd never told him her name.

CHAPTER SEVEN

Lola gave it half an hour, long enough for Johnny to be sure that he'd dodged her.

Then she went in search of the Veterans of Foreign Wars hall where the sheriff said Johnny had scheduled a campaign stop. Lola recognized the VFW by the obligatory World War II-era tank slowly rusting in front of the cinderblock building. But for the addition of wives, still in their funeral best, their eyes bright with suspicion, it was as though she'd somehow ended up back at the cafe. Conversation stopped when she walked in. Cutlery cascaded onto plates. Lola walked through the silence and took her place in the line, waiting at the tabletop griddle where Johnny slopped batter out of a plastic bucket with one hand and flipped golden hotcakes with the other. Whispers floated toward the ceiling, mingling with the combined scents of fake maple syrup and real butter and stale beer rubbed into floorboards by generations of booted feet. A man said something about Mary Alice. A woman shushed him. Johnny's voice boomed through the room.

"What'll it be, what'll it be? Short stack or tall? Silver dollar or cover your plate? Just tell me what you want and I'll try to provide, just like I'll do when I'm in the governor's house in Helena. . . . Well, look who's back."

The change in his voice made Lola glad she'd come. "Tall *and* cover the plate," she said. "Please."

He recovered fast. "I've been putting Mickey Mouse ears on 'em for the kiddos. How about you? Want some Mickey

Mouse on your hotcakes?" His broad brown face seemed streaky under oddly spaced ceiling lights that left parts of the room in shadow, others floodlit. It looked hot behind the griddle. He'd changed out of his funeral suit into jeans and cowboy boots.

"Maybe some jackass ears," Lola suggested.

"For me or for you?" He poured three simple circles of batter, no ears of any variety. Bubbles formed on their surface and exploded in slow motion. "What brings you here, Miss Wicks? Business or pleasure?" He turned the pancakes. They browned quickly, edges recoiling from the scalding surface.

"Breakfast brings me here. And the fact that you and I were never properly introduced." She accepted her pancakes with a bland smile and held the plate beneath her nose, letting the steam from the pancakes warm her face, and carried it to an empty table at the far side of the room where she could watch the proceedings without the bother of talking to anyone. Verle Duncan strolled in. Lola bent her head over her pancakes. She wondered if she should go back for another plate and bring it home to Bub. She'd ended up leaving him in the motel, yapping his feelings of betrayal as she drove away. She poured syrup onto her plate. It flowed into the pancakes and disappeared. Lola turned her fork on its side and cut a wedge.

The line at the griddle was down to a few people. Johnny handed his spatula off to a pallid young aide. Lola judged him to be still in college. The line began to move more quickly as the aide dipped and flipped in silence while Johnny worked the room, shaking hands, patting backs, even—Lola wondered if the politician existed who had failed to make this move—picking up each and every one of the few babies there, maintaining the same enthusiasm regardless of whether the brat in question slept or squalled throughout the encounter. He moved within Lola's earshot just as a woman approached him, her voice sugared and warm as the syrup Lola had just poured all over her pancakes.

"Mr. Running Wolf, I am so glad to meet you. There's a question I've been wanting to ask."

Johnny reached for her hand. "Ma'am," he said, "I'll be so glad to answer. Although one of these might tell you what you need to know." He handed her a flier. "This here is put out by a group that very much supports the same goals at the center of my campaign."

The woman dropped his hand. She spindled the flier as she spoke. "If you get elected, Mr. Running Wolf, what are you going to do about your people?"

"Excuse me, ma'am?"

Lola put her fork down.

"What are you going to do"—the woman rolled the flier tighter—"about all of them living off the government tit, sucking my tax dollars dry, being paid not to work while me and my Arlie are going broke trying to hold onto our place? They tax us more and more every year and all of our money goes right out of our pockets and onto your reservation." She might have been talking about orphaned children, so earnest and concerned was her tone.

Lola did a quick survey of the room. People sat pushed back from the tables, lingering over empty plates. A few rose and refilled their coffee mugs from the tall stainless-steel dispensers, while others looked around, waiting to see who would be the first to lead the general exodus. Their gazes swept Johnny and his genteel interrogator and kept moving; and then the woman took a step forward, and rapped Johnny on the chest with the rolled-up flier and said, "You answer me that, mister," and just like that she had everyone's attention.

Verle stood up. His eyes met Lola's.

"Ma'am, I can assure you that my people want jobs," Johnny said, and his words were low and measured and slow. "They want to work hard to earn enough to survive, just like you. But the reason you and I—yes, Indian people pay taxes, too—are getting taxed through the roof is that big corporations aren't making investments in our state because of our tight-assed regulations. There I go with my French, ma'am, and I do beg your pardon." His words pulled people from their chairs, drawing them in close. "Now, don't get me wrong. There's a need for regulation. But there's a place for development, too, responsible development that'll provide jobs—real, living-wage jobs, not just that minimum-wage baloney—for folks like you and your Arlie and for my people, too. I see all of us down at the bottom of the same dark hole looking up at the bright sky, and I'm looking for a way for each and every one of us to climb into the sunshine, with the corporations coming back to Montana, only this time being responsible and paying their fair share of taxes so your road gets plowed every winter, so that you can get to town and buy groceries, and so the school can buy the new books it needs to give your kids that good education they deserve. That way, you can keep working that place of yours in the most efficient way possible so we don't lose yet another family ranch for no good reason at all. Ma'am—what's your name again?"

"Carrie. Carrie Rudbach."

"Mrs. Rudbach, does that answer your question?"

The flier slipped from her hands and seesawed to the floor. "I guess you answered something. By the time you were done talking, I couldn't hardly remember what I asked."

The aide put the spatula down and glided to the woman's side and took her arm. "He has that effect on people."

"Mrs. Rudbach," Johnny said. "This here is Riley. He's going to get your name and address."

Lola knew that whatever Carrie Rudbach might think, Riley's attention meant only that she'd end up with a raft of campaign literature in her mailbox, requests for donations coming every other day. Johnny turned and worked his way around the silent circle that had formed, grabbing dangling hands and moving them energetically up and down, introducing himself over and over again, as though every single person in the room didn't already know his name.

"Johnny Running Wolf. Remember it. Hunting just as hard as a whole pack of wolves, sinking my teeth into every single thing you're owed from your government and bringing it all back to Montana, including the right to be left alone. Pleased to meet you. Here, hand that baby over. I don't think I've met this little princess yet. My, she's a pretty one."

Lola picked up the forgotten flier, looking for the fine print at the bottom. "Paid for by TMResources." Verle waved in her direction. Lola pretended not to see him and put the flier in her pocket and slipped out a side door. She wanted to intercept Johnny before he went to his next event. The steroidal white Suburban she'd seen leaving the funeral was parked down the street, a gleaming iceberg amid a rough sea of pickups crusted in ancient layers of sediment. She ducked behind one as Johnny and Riley emerged from the VFW hall. The wind carried a reedy voice toward her.

"You've got the Chamber of Commerce in Sand Creek at two. Then nothing else until this evening. That would be a good time for phone calls, hit people up for money. The county Dems have their dinner tonight, and if we hustle afterward, we can make it on over to Aster and catch the end of the League of Women Voters' dinner. The state organization wants a sit-down with you, and it wouldn't hurt to meet with some more of the county groups. Tomorrow, there's another breakfast over in Trapp. Then you've got the chili cook-off in Mineral at noon, and the dunk booth for the Children's Fund at the fair in Whiting at three. I still don't think you should do a dunk booth, by the way. It's undignified."

For all Johnny's self-assurance with Carrie Rudbach, Lola knew the very fact of Riley gave away his precarious political status. Before she went overseas, Lola had spent years covering politics—often indistinguishable, she'd joked with Mary Alice, from the police beat—and she remembered the ranks of callow Rileys that trailed the no-chance candidates like runty pups after a lop-eared mongrel, slinking aside when the alpha dogs trotted past, fat and contemptuous. The real candidates, the ones with the party's blessing, got seasoned handlers, not some college-age intern who was in the mix only because his mother had spent the last twenty-five years licking envelopes and baking cookies for the poll workers on Election Day. The fact that Johnny had won the primary but was still stuck with Riley was a sure indication of party unease—which made it likely that, in addition to seasoned staff, the party was withholding serious money, too. Lola wondered how Johnny was paying for his campaign.

He said something to Riley, too quietly for Lola to catch. "What's so funny?" Riley sounded aggrieved. "I had to work hard to get you into this lineup. Except for the dunk booth, you've got to do this stuff, whether you like it or not. It's the only way you've got a prayer."

The hearty good humor that had permeated Johnny's voice during the meet-and-greet at the VFW was entirely gone. "Haven't I done everything you told me? Just look at me. I've jammed my feet into these boots that squeeze my toes and make me feel like I'm tippy-toeing around in high heels. Put one of these ridiculous hats on my head."

"Wait just a minute." Riley's voice climbed a quick octave. "I know you left here when you were just a little boy."

"I didn't leave," Johnny said. "I was taken. Don't forget that. I didn't have a choice in the matter."

"Whatever. Even though you went away, you've still got to look like this place. You're the Indian candidate, not the city slicker from Chicago candidate. And you might be wearing boots, but I can tell you that every single person in the room noticed they were custom ostrich skin. You know I'm right."

"Only because I say you are." The Suburban beeped and blinked its lights. In her brief time in Magpie, Lola had noticed that she was seemingly alone in locking her car. Riley was right. Johnny's background showed in all kinds of ways. Johnny spoke again. "Where'd that reporter go?"

Lola opened her mouth to announce herself, enjoying the thought of his discomfiture. But Johnny kept talking. "We no sooner get rid of one than another one shows up. Poking around, asking questions."

Lola moved back by millimeters, keeping her feet hidden behind the truck's tire. She stooped so that her head was below the window, pressed her ear against the dirt-caked metal as though listening through a wall. A car passed. The hiss of tires on pavement obscured Riley's response. Johnny's voice rose above it.

"If you're so smart, what do we do about her? What if she starts asking the same questions the other one did?"

"You never told me what those were."

Good boy, Lola thought, and waited for the answer.

"Never mind," Johnny said, and Lola slumped against the truck. "I won't make the same mistake of giving this one an interview. No matter what you say to them, they always come back wanting more. The quicker she's gone, the better."

"Maybe you should talk to her anyhow." Riley's voice was thin, as though strained through vocal cords tight with resentment. "You know what they say. Keep your friends close but your enemies closer."

The Suburban groaned as the two men clambered into it. Johnny's voice came from the passenger side. "No," he said, his tone as final as the slam of Riley's door. "We're not going to do that. Here's some city advice for you, something you need to know if you mean to stay in this line of work. A reporter is never a friend. And the closer they get, the more they find out."

✧✧✧

"You all right?"

Lola lifted her head, thinking Johnny had returned. She folded her fists against the impulse to strike him. Verle Duncan stood before her. Dust billowed in the wake of the departing

~ 79 ~

Suburban. Lola blinked grit from her eyes. Her frustration escaped before she could stop herself.

"Do I look all right? My friend's dead. Not just dead, but murdered, and nobody can tell me who did it."

"Take a little ride with me." Verle held his hat in his hand and he slapped it lightly against his thigh, once, then again, the motion soundless beneath the wind's raucous gusts.

Lola drew back. "Where? Why?"

"My place. Come on out and have some lunch there. As to why, you've had a rough time of it ever since you got here. You look like you could use a break." His eyes were bright, only a little pouchy, but Lola thought that it wouldn't take many more years to turn Verle into an old man, the eyes frankly leaking, the body's wiry frame bent in on itself. Yet he stood in the sun on a summer day, issuing an invitation to a woman nearly half his age as though he had every expectation of success. Lola wondered when men quit being so sure of themselves. Or if they ever did. She aimed a hard stare at him, hoping her demeanor masked her inner uncertainty. Her radar was all out of whack here. The sheriff hadn't ruled Verle out as a suspect. But he hadn't called him back in for more questioning, either. Verle's smile told her to trust him. Conventional wisdom told her to trust no one. But conventional wisdom also had told her that a Kabul posting meant job security for the duration of the war. She settled for playing it safe, but keeping her options open.

"I just ate," she said. "Maybe later."

He looked neither surprised nor disappointed. "Just stop by. No need to call."

Lola turned to go.

"Wait," he said. "Let me tell you how to get there."

"I don't have anything to write with," she lied.

He reached for her hand and eased her sleeve up her arm. "Now," he said and pressed his forefinger into her palm at the base of her pinky. "This is where we are right now. Main Street, Magpie." He drew his finger across her palm to the middle of her hand and stopped. "This here is Jolee's store. Take the road out of town." His finger trailed over her wrist, warm, persuasive. Her pulse throbbed against it. "Right about here, you'll see the tree that's the turnoff to Mary Alice's. Keep going." His finger stopped a little past her wrist. He traced a small circle on the delicate skin of her inner arm. "You'll see a break in a grove of aspens to the left. There's a bridge over the irrigation ditch. Take it."

Lola's forearm burned. She jerked it away. "What if you're not there?"

The wind lofted his hair. Lola resisted an urge to comb it back into place with her fingers.

"If you're coming," he said. "I'll be there."

CHAPTER EIGHT

Lola sped toward the sheriff's office, trying to shake her arm free of the lingering sensation of Verle's touch.

She repeated Johnny's words to herself. "We no sooner get rid of one reporter than another shows up." She passed the convenience store. The courthouse loomed.

Get rid of.

Suspicious, yes. But not conclusive enough to take to the sheriff. She needed more. Lola's car slowed. Behind her, someone honked. She waved the car around her and did a U-turn in the middle of the main street and mulled her next move. She wished she hadn't been so rude to Jan after the funeral. She'd need to go to the newspaper at some point and look through Mary Alice's files. Now she'd have to wait a day or two, and hope that in the meantime Jan would write her behavior off to the shock of finding Mary Alice's body. She passed the cafe. The busboy stepped from a side door. He swung his arms. Dirty water leapt from the basin in his hands. He'd told her she should talk to his uncle. Lola pointed the car toward the reservation. She could ask the uncle about Johnny, maybe find out something useful.

Hers was the only car on the reservation road, a black seam stitched across the rippling fabric of prairie. Parched sagebrush hills gave way to gold-tinged grasslands, a billowing sea parted by a fleet of glossy black cattle. Heads lifted as she passed. Puzzled protuberant eyes followed the movement of her car. A cottonwood towered by the side of the road and receded in the rearview mirror. Lola recognized the turnoff to Mary Alice's house, almost insultingly unremarkable in the sunlight. A line of slender aspens shivered beside an irrigation ditch that traced the main road. Wind swept across the water, fragmenting the mirrored surface into clear sparkling shards. She saw the grove marking the turnoff Verle had described and resisted an impulse to pull in. Later, she told herself. Maybe. Another one of those meth billboards appeared, everyone in it, men and women alike, with waist-length black hair, probably meant to be Indians although the sign was so defaced with graffiti Lola couldn't tell. She hoped some Indian kids had done the extraneous artwork. She thought the billboard offensive. In fact, the meth billboards were high on the growing list of things she disliked about Montana. She swerved to avoid one pothole and drove into another. The impact lifted her from the seat. She wrangled the steering wheel until the car was back in its own lane. Two white crosses marked a curve. Three more were spaced out along the straightaway, too far apart to attribute to a single crash. Bullet holes ventilated the speed-limit signs.

The empty road wrapped itself around a rise and without warning she was in a town. Concrete-block buildings painted once and never again housed a video store, a pizza shop and a laundry, all of which seemed closed, whether for the day or for good, Lola couldn't tell. The houses were boxy prefabs that had started falling down the minute they went up. The wind blew hard. Plastic bags pirouetted above the street like kites. Young men standing at a corner turned impassive faces her way. A round brick citadel anchored the far end of the street. Its blinking dollar signs advertised a casino. A near-deserted parking lot negated the neon come-on. Lola turned around in the lot and headed back down the main street. She turned one corner and then another, finally encountering a long brick building whose paired American and tribal flags signaled an official capacity. The flags popped and cracked above her head, folding back on themselves, then standing out straight against the sky. Lola hesitated at the building's door until a blast of wind propelled her into the vestibule. Papers levitated from a desk. Lola scooped them from the floor and handed them to a woman who took them without looking up from a fat textbook. She dropped the papers to one side without reshuffling them and wet her finger to turn a page. Lola saw the hieroglyphics of mathematical equations. She cleared her throat. The woman turned another page.

"I'm looking for Joshua's uncle. Joshua who works at the cafe in Magpie. He sent me here."

The woman picked up a pencil and filled in some numbers on the page. Then she folded down a corner and closed the book. "Joshua has a lot of uncles."

Lola wondered if she'd made the drive for nothing. She'd have to go back to Magpie, talk to Joshua again and get his uncle's name, something she could have done on her way out of town if she hadn't been so distracted by the encounter with Verle.

"But you probably want to talk to Wilson. Right?"

"Right." Lola had no earthly idea.

The woman lifted a receiver and pushed a couple of buttons on the phone. "Somebody here to see you. Don't know. Whitelady." She put the phone down and opened her textbook again.

The vestibule lacked chairs. Lola leaned against the wall, closed her eyes and tried to make her mind go blank. In Afghanistan, she'd spent hours that felt like entire weeks, waiting for interviews, permits, necessary papers. Pockets crackling with bribe money, American dollars only, please. At first she'd fidgeted mightily. Hoarded crossword puzzles from yellowing English-language newspapers, brought books, anything to pass the time. Her French housemates swore by a strategy that involved smoking copious quantities of hashish before heading off to the ministries, where they passed the time smiling vacantly, humming a little.

"You know, we were worried that wall might fall down. But with you here to hold it up, looks like we've got nothing to fear." A man in a plaid snap-front shirt stood before Lola. Glasses thick to the point of opaque. She'd seen him at the funeral, sitting with Joshua and Frank.

"I'm Wilson Bird. I believe you've met my nephew. And now you've come to meet me."

She extended a hand. He touched his fingertips to hers.

"Come on back." He led her into a conference room of sorts, a couple of plastic tables placed end to end, islanded with a half-dozen cribbage sets made of wood, horn, stone, their polished surfaces reflecting her own wavering image.

Lola touched one, letting her fingers linger. "You're *that* Wilson Bird. I remember now. The sheriff has one of these."

"Pretty much everyone in the county has one of these." Words dismissive, tone pleased.

"They're beautiful. And I don't even play cribbage." The game, from what little she knew about it, involved cards. And patience. She was no good at one and entirely lacking in the other.

"If you're going to spend any amount of time here, you might want to learn."

"That's why I came to see you. Because I don't want to spend a minute more here than I need to. And because your nephew said I should talk with you about Mary Alice."

He pulled out a chair for her. Waited until she had settled herself and then sat across from her. "That's the thing about whitepeople. They're always in a hurry."

Lola bit back a response. He wanted her to wait, she'd wait. She sat back and let her gaze drift across walls of madhouse green. The single window might well have framed a painting, so devoid of activity was the street outside. A display case against a wall held a beaded dress. A map showed a ragged-edged territory checkerboarded in green with a single straight line cutting across its upper quadrant. The wind groaned outside.

"You know," he said. "Mary Alice wasn't."

"Wasn't what?"

"In a hurry."

"It sounds like you spent a fair amount of time with her," Lola parried. "There has to be a reason Joshua wanted me to talk to you."

He shrugged one shoulder.

"Maybe because of Johnny," she pushed again. "Or Frank."

He jerked in his chair. "Frank? Frank had nothing to do with what happened to Mary Alice."

Johnny had earned no such denial, Lola noticed. But since Wilson had mentioned Frank first, she decided to go with it. "Funny thing. That's what the sheriff said, too. Why not? Because he's brain-damaged? Or because he drinks?"

Wilson took off his glasses, pulled out his shirttail and polished the lenses. There was no discernible improvement. His eyes were a blur behind them, but his square unlined face hardened as he replied. "He doesn't drink."

"But I thought . . ." Lola stopped. She remembered Frank reclining on the sidewalk outside Jolee's store, hitting her up for booze money. Or maybe she'd just assumed that's what he wanted. She heard a voice in her ear, that of every editor for whom she'd ever worked: "Assume makes an ass out of u and me."

"A lot of people think that." Wilson's sigh was deep and lasting. "The staggering, the slurring. That's the brain damage. You should have known him before. He could shoot a bird out of the air before anybody else even realized it was up there. Came back from the war with so many medals he looked like a pincushion. Yeah, they handed out those medals like candy. Shame they couldn't hand him a new brain. Then he could have gotten a real job when he came back instead of the trouble he got caught up in."

Lola wondered what kind of trouble people got into around Magpie. She thought of the billboards, of Joshua's sister retching into the jail's lidless steel toilet. "Meth?"

"Booze."

"But you just said he didn't drink."

Somewhere in the building, a phone rang and rang. A child's high voice floated along the corridor outside the conference room. "He doesn't drink the stuff," Wilson said. "He smuggles it. At least, that's what I think is going on. He's been wandering more than usual. And he's been flashing money around."

Lola thought he'd finally said something she understood. The Canadian border was so close. No matter the country, no matter which side of the border you were on, she thought, there was always something that sold for more money on the other side, and somebody was always scrambling to cash in on that fact. Entire tribes in Afghanistan supported themselves by hauling everything from opium to ammo to melons across the border. Booze was a prized commodity in all of those places, being theoretically off limits in Muslim countries. But here? She said as much to Wilson.

"Only the worst drinkers go to the package store. Alcohol's such a problem on the reservation that there's a stigma to buying it in public."

"Why not just go to Magpie and drink there?"

"Think about it. You can go to town with a lot of white-people in your face remarking about drunk Indians. Even though they're sitting on a barstool right next to you, you nursing one drink for an hour while they have four or five, somehow you're the one who's the drunk. Or you can sit at home. What would you rather?"

Lola didn't know how to politely phrase her next question. "How'd he do it? I mean, if he couldn't hold a job—"

Wilson seemed to know what she was getting at. "How's a dummy run a smuggling operation? Easy. He doesn't. Somebody else does. Frank's just a courier. The people who set him up know what they're doing. They need an Indian, and who better than Frank? One who can't think his way to why he shouldn't do it, and won't question why they're only paying him half the money they'd pay somebody with a working brain."

"Why do they need an Indian?"

The phone rang again in the other room. It stopped, and then a phone at Wilson's elbow buzzed. "Just now?" he said into it. "Okay. Thanks." He put it down and rested his hands on the table. They were stiff and twisted as old rope. Lola tried to imagine the diminutive bits of obsidian turning within them as he crafted the cribbage pegs. "Smuggling's easier for us," he said. "Stuff comes in from Canada. The reservation goes right to the border. And don't forget, we're a sovereign nation. Homeland Security might not like it, but we don't need passports to cross the border as long as we've got our tribal ID cards. Frank's contacts could hand over the stuff in Canada and he could bring it down here and sell it for twice what somebody'd pay in town. Tribal police have been watching him, trying to figure out who's supplying it. But they've got to patrol the whole reservation, three thousand square miles. And they mostly deal with misdemeanors. The serious stuff goes to the FBI. And it gets even more compli- cated if a crime involves both a tribal person and a nontribal one, which is likely in this case. Then the county gets in on the action. When something crosses the border, you can add Customs and the Border Patrol to the mix. The confusing stuff falls through the cracks. And up here, everything is con- fusing. As you can see."

"Except for murder," Lola said, trying to bring him back to the matter at hand. The last thing she wanted was a disser- tation on reservation crime. "That's pretty straightforward. What if Mary Alice found out who was behind the operation and they killed her? Or, better yet, got Frank to do it for them? Did the brain damage affect his aim?"

Wilson rearranged the cribbage boards. "Doesn't matter whether it did or didn't. Frank didn't do it."

"But he knew Mary Alice had been shot." She told him about the first time she'd seen Frank, in front of the store, crooning "Poor Mary Alice." And then again at the funeral.

Wilson got up and walked across the room and rummaged through a stack of newspapers. He returned with a copy of the *Express* from the day after Mary Alice's shooting. "Everyone in town knows how she died."

Lola took the paper from him and skimmed through the story. "Here," she said. She ran her finger under the sentence. "'Carr was shot in the head,' said Sheriff Charlie Laurendeau."

"The head," she told Wilson. "It said the head. Not the face." And she drilled her forefinger into her cheek, mimicking Frank's motions after the funeral. "The only people who knew where Mary Alice was shot were the ones who saw her. That's me, Verle, Charlie, and the coroner. And then, the person who shot her."

She knew her irritation showed. Didn't care. The day was slipping away with nothing to show for it. Lola wanted to go back to her motel and check out the name of the group that had paid for the campaign flier she'd picked up at Johnny Running Wolf's meet-and-greet. But first, she needed to ask Wilson about Johnny. Not when he was pissed, though. Which he appeared to be, in about equal measure to her own frustration.

"So Joshua's your nephew," she said, hoping to lessen the tension. "That's such a Biblical name."

Wilson went to work on his glasses again. Lola heard the building's outer door open and close. The woman from the front desk crossed before the window. The wind shook out her hair in a dark shining sheet and laid it back down over her shoulders. She walked a few steps away from the building and bent the upper part of her body. She straightened, her lips pinched around a cigarette.

"Joshua's mother was one of those Jesus Indians got dragged off to boarding school," Wilson said. "Some of those people listened to the missionaries. Some not. She was one who did. She named her daughter Judith because she liked the story about how Judith saved her people by deceiving Holofernes and cutting off his head. Same thing with Joshua—the way he blew his trumpet, the walls coming down. Said those old-time Indians could have used a Joshua when they attacked the whiteman forts. I don't think that's quite what the missionaries had in mind when they taught her about Joshua and Judith."

Lola wrested her attention from the window. She imagined Joshua's mother, a young girl torn from her family, force-fed Bible stories along with strange unpalatable foods and customs. Taking the stories and turning them to fit her own world. "I like that," she said. "Is their mother still alive?"

Wilson shook his head. "No. She died. Long time ago. Their gran'mother raised them. But at least we got to keep them. Not like Johnny."

He'd circled back to Johnny without any urging from her. The conference room door swung open and the woman from the front desk stuck her head in, delivering warring scents of fresh air and cigarette smoke. Lola directed murderous thoughts her way. "I've got to go to class," the woman told Wilson. "I've ordered a pizza for the council meeting later. If the phone rings, can you grab it?"

Lola looked at the telephone at the other end of the table and wondered if she could disable it by the sheer intensity of her stare. She needed Wilson to keep talking. The woman left without closing the door. "You were telling me about Johnny. About how you didn't get to keep him," Lola said. She added a nugget from the overheard conversation between Johnny and Riley. "I know they took him away when he was a little boy. That must have been hard." And just like that, with Lola nodding as though she'd heard it all before, he told her.

How Johnny's mother ran off with a whiteman from Chicago, taking her son with her, cutting off all connection with her people so that nobody heard from them again, not even when her mother died. Wilson's voice eased into singsong recitation. "That old lady went to church twice every day, praying for their return, mourned in the old way, too, just for good measure, singing songs all day and night, but couldn't do it right because no one knew whether they were alive or dead. Wore herself out. Couldn't sleep, wouldn't eat. Some say she just blew away, like the fluff from a cottonwood tree, floating up into the sky. That she's a cloud now, up there still, flying over the land, seeking her child and gran'child." His big hands sketched a wispy flight and Lola followed their motion.

"But he came back," prompted Lola. Afraid to say even that much. Which, apparently, was too much.

Wilson got up and walked away from the story. He made a slow circuit of the room, stopping before the map. A dog the color of dust sneaked past the window and lay down in the middle of the road. A car approached. The dog stirred and settled itself more comfortably on the sun-warmed pavement. The car swerved around it and continued down the road in the wrong lane. If Wilson needed a break, Lola was willing to give him one. She was not, however, going to leave. She joined him at the map. "What's this?"

"That's the reservation."

"All these squares, I mean."

"That's the land that the whitepeople gave us that wasn't theirs to give. After they put that land in one of their forever treaties, they turned around and opened it up to homesteaders. So, whitepeople own a good chunk of this so-called Indian reservation. We're trying to buy it back, bit by bit. You can see." He put a round-knuckled finger to the map and she could indeed see how some of the squares were darker than the others, more recently colored in. But there were still plenty of blank spaces among them. He rubbed his thumb over one of the bigger blanks. It took a misshapen bite from the reservation's southern border, a tongue of land probing abruptly north in an otherwise unbroken east-west line. "This one here along Two Medicine River—we thought we had it. But the deal fell through."

She drew her finger along the Canadian border. "What's this?" A few miles to the north of the border, another area was colored in.

"That's the Blood Reserve in Canada. We're all the same people, but the whiteman governments saw fit to split us up. Used to be their reserve came down to the border, but then Canada pushed the reserve boundary north. Don't know why. Did they think a few thousand Indians were too dangerous to have us all together?"

Lola wondered when he would get back to Johnny. He turned to the display case with the beaded dress. The glass was dusty and he pulled his sleeve down over his wrist and ran his forearm across the surface. The dress within was pale and sueded, its yoke and sleeves covered in beadwork zigzags of blue and orange, sky and sunset. "That must have taken forever," Lola said.

"Winters are long here. Especially back in the old days."

She thought that maybe Wilson was trying to teach her a lesson about forbearance. She gave a tense nod, trying to imagine a woman, hands red and stiff with cold, sitting within a wind-buffeted tipi whose fire threw off uneven bursts of heat and light, forcing a needle through the thickness of hide to form those lightning designs with beads no larger than sesame seeds. Maybe the women sat together as they worked. Gossiped, laughed. Friendship an insubstantial barrier against hunger, cold, too-early death. The beaded patterns shimmered on the dress. How had her thoughts wandered so far from Mary Alice?

"Johnny Running Wolf, he'd been gone a long time when he came home," Wilson said.

Lola held her breath and kept her face to the glass.

"Long, long time. Frank was the one first recognized him. They're cousins. It was Frank's wild pony smashed Johnny's nose when they were kids. Johnny tried to ride him. Pony threw back his head. Blood everywhere. His mother drove him to the whiteman doctor in Magpie, thinking he'd be better than the reservation hospital. But that doctor just wiped up the blood and left the nose the way it was. Wasn't for that nose, nobody would have known him when he came back. All that time gone, and living amongst whitepeople. He didn't know anything when he returned. Not our prayers, our traditions, our ways. Not even something as simple as turning left going into a house or a lodge. Take this business of running for governor."

Lola turned to him but nothing in his face had changed, and he was standing there with his hands in his pockets like he was still talking about the dress. "He never even asked the elders. Just up and drove to Helena one day and filed the papers. We found out about it in the newspaper."

Lola floated a theory. "Is there any chance Johnny could be involved in the smuggling? To get money for his campaign, maybe?"

Wilson's "no" was quick, decisive. "Sure, people can support themselves on it. But as I understand it, campaigns need big money. Just look at how Johnny's running around all over the state. Driving that outfit, taking private planes for the longer trips. Where's he getting the money for that? We got him a job when he came back, a good lawyering job, going down to Helena and lobbying for the tribe. Paid for a new suit and gave him a per diem and everything. But we didn't pay him enough for that big white outfit, and it's for damn sure he's got more than one suit these days."

Lola thought of the oxfords she'd seen on Johnny's feet at the funeral, the ostrich-skin boots he'd worn to the breakfast. She guessed Johnny's footgear alone was probably worth nearly a month's pay for most people on the reservation. She remembered the campaign pamphlet. "What's TMResources?"

"No idea."

"It's got to be some sort of political issues group. By law, they're not allowed to coordinate with candidates. But at least candidates have to list their donors. The groups don't. They can throw all kinds of money around."

"I know how they work." Wilson's words came on a fading breath, as though he'd run out of steam. He gathered himself for a last effort. "Maybe Mary Alice was wondering about some of those same things."

No shit, Lola very nearly said aloud. Even if Mary Alice hadn't fixated upon them on her own—and she almost certainly had—then someone like Wilson had probably put those very same questions into her head, talking to her then just the way he was talking to Lola now. Needing to raise the questions but hoping someone else would do the dirty, disrespectful work of digging up the answers.

"Those are good questions," she said. "Thank you for talking with me."

"You think those are good questions?"

Her hand was on the door. She stopped. "Sure."

"Then maybe you want to ask Johnny yourself. He's home today, first time in a long while. That's what that phone call was. Renata said that outfit of his went by a little while ago, heading north. He stays out to his gran'mother's house sometimes. If you're not in too big a hurry, I can tell you how to get out there."

CHAPTER NINE

Wilson's instructions were simple. "Go north. Look for that white outfit. You'll see it before you see the house."

The road ran fast toward Canada. From a distance, the surrounding grasslands looked deceptively smooth, all sweep and roll, but the gravel road quickly devolved into a two-track, rocky and carved with ruts, challenging the rental car. Lola tried to imagine traversing it in the rain. The landscape swelled for mile after empty mile. Even the cattle disappeared, leaving nothing but sky and clouds and tall grass endlessly bowing and kneeling before the invincible wind. Lola felt lost in it, lightheaded. She wondered how Johnny Running Wolf had made the adjustment from Chicago to a world where the horizon was the only delineation. Then she saw the Suburban, looking more consequential than the house itself, which was the standard swaybacked reservation model, siding peeling in lazy curls away from the plywood frame. Lola pulled up beside it and cut the engine. Johnny Running Wolf's bulk filled the narrow doorway. He shaded his eyes against the sun and waited. "Should've guessed. You've been following me around all day."

"I've got a dead friend and a sheriff who won't let me leave town until he figures out how she got that way," Lola snapped. "I was hoping you could help me."

He stepped aside to let her in. The kitchen's thin cotton curtains with their cabbage rose pattern were drawn against the harsh prairie sun. The wind caught the door and whapped it hard against the frame. Lola jumped.

"I was going to offer you coffee," he said, "but it looks like you're already pretty wired."

"Coffee would be great." Her voice clanged in the claustrophobic kitchen, its half-sized appliances crouching beneath a ceiling so low it nearly brushed her head. She took a seat at the small wooden table.

Johnny filled a saucepan with water and set it on one of the stove's two burners. The smell of gas filled the air, then the burner caught. "Hope you don't take cream. All I've got out here is powdered. But there's sugar." He joined her at the table and lifted the lid from a china bowl whose fading lavender splotches might originally have been flowers.

"Black is fine."

He got up again and dumped instant coffee into two mugs. He splashed in some of the water from the saucepan, stirred the contents with a knife, sat one mug in front of Lola and held the other in his large hands. He picked up a sugar spoon, the souvenir kind sold at highway filling stations, and measured two heaps into his mug.

Lola looked across the kitchen into the living room, all doilies and Jesus pictures and sweet-grass braids on the windowsills, the walls giving off the faint smell of grease and kerosene that she associated with poor people's homes the world over. Her gaze flicked to his face, the spreading mass of nose. She looked away. "When did your grandmother die?"

"Long time ago," he said. "Before I came back." Johnny gave his coffee another stir. An enamel shield topped the sugar spoon. It showed a green mountain and brown bison. Lola was pretty sure bison stuck to the prairie. "She was a great lady," Johnny said automatically, the way Lola imagined him saying it to people he'd meet on the campaign trail: "I knew your mother. Your sister. Your aunt. She was a great lady."

Lola sipped at her coffee, predictably awful and tepid besides.

Johnny rested his arms on the table. The backs of his hands bore the telltale pointillist pattern of a recent shave. Vain, Lola thought.

"You didn't come out to talk about my grandmother," he said. "You came out here to see me." He stretched his legs and spread them wide, a classic invitation. His teeth flashed.

"I came out here to talk to you," Lola corrected. "Because I've heard that Mary Alice was writing a lot of stories about you."

"Nothing unusual about that. I'm running for governor. A 'historic campaign,' I believe she called it."

"Speaking of your campaign," Lola said, "what's TM-Resources?"

He did an approximation of a drum roll with the sugar spoon. "From the sound of it, I'd guess that it's a resource company." He winked.

"Cute. But what's TM stand for? Two Medicine? Who runs it?"

He took the brochure she held out and scanned it. "Is that who's paying for this? Nice to know I've got fans. Listen, these groups put out all sorts of campaign literature. You know I can't coordinate with them. I'm just lucky this one likes me. Not all of them do."

Lola snatched it back.

"When did you get so interested in the campaign?" he asked.

"I'm not. But Mary Alice was and I'm interested in Mary Alice." She thought back to her conversation with Wilson. "And Frank."

Johnny didn't so much as blink. "Here I was hoping you'd come in search of me. Knowing we'd be alone together. All the way out here. You don't even have that dog with you today, do you?"

It was the funeral all over again, Lola thought, the silky threat in the guise of normal conversation. Nothing but bluff now, both of them knowing that he had the upper hand if things went beyond bravado. Lola hefted the heavy ceramic mug. She took a long, leisurely swig, the Nescafe grainy on her tongue, and wondered how much damage she could do if she bounced the mug off his head. She calculated distances, to the door, to the car, the unlikely possibility that she could get through one and into the other before he caught up with her. He shifted, the chair creaking beneath him, and she gripped her mug tighter. Her pitching arm wouldn't do her much good in such a cramped space. She'd just have to smash the mug against him, going for the weak spot on the temple. Or maybe the ruined nose. Throw the coffee into his face first to get him off balance. Wondered if he'd made it lukewarm on purpose. Outside, a dog barked. Another one joined it.

"Rez dogs," Johnny said. "I don't know where they come from or how they know, but whenever I show up, they come around, looking for food."

Shut up about the damn dogs, Lola thought. "It seems strange," she said, "that all those years in Chicago, you never even heard from your grandmother."

"When I came back here," he said easily, "I heard that she'd tried to get in touch with me, over and over again. But my stepdad didn't want my mom to have any contact with her family. Sent all those cards and letters right back to my grandmother, hung up on her when she called long-distance. Didn't want anything to lure my mother back here, I suppose. Those whitemen may love their Indian princesses, but they don't want 'em too Indian, you know what I mean?"

Lola didn't know and didn't much care.

"Mind if I use the bathroom?" she asked.

-◆◆◆-

LOLA CLOSED the door behind her. She stood at the sink and turned both the hot and cold water handles as far as they would go. She opened the medicine cabinet, hoping it would yield more information than the conversation. It contained only minimal signs of occupancy. A toothbrush, the bristles still stiff and straight. Deodorant. Some disposable razors. A box of condoms. She opened it. It was only about half full. She wrapped her hand in toilet paper and ran it through the contents of the trash can. A small, colorful cardboard box lay mashed beneath some stained paper towels. She retrieved it. It was a box of hair dye. She looked at the fanciful label. "Dark of Night," and recollected the shaved knuckles. She wondered at what age men turned to such foolishness. She dropped the box and reached for the little plastic squeeze bottles in the trash. Some of the color leaked and stained her fingertips. She let the bottles fall back into the trash, and held her hands under the water and dried them on the paper towels in the trash can. She'd forgotten to pee. But she'd already taken too much time. She flushed the toilet and turned off the water, and went back into the room with her hands in her pockets so he wouldn't see her discolored fingers.

—◇◇◇—

HE WAS at the door when she returned, holding it open. The extra light did the room no favors.

"I guess that's my cue," Lola said. She stepped outside and nearly trod on a couple of dogs of indeterminate parentage. They sat hard by the door, disturbing the dirt with ratlike tails.

Johnny kicked at them and they sidled just out of reach, then turned and stared, tongues a startling pink in the dusty landscape. "I wish I could help you with this Mary Alice business," he said. "If I think of anything, I'll be sure and call Charlie."

"Thanks," Lola said. *For nothing*, she thought.

Some of his hair came loose and blew across his face, kinked from the braid, curly as a girl's. He reached and pulled it away from his eyes, his nose.

"That must have hurt," Lola said.

"What?"

"Your nose."

"You know what they say. You should see the other guy."
He dropped his hand and the wind lashed his hair across his
face again. He turned away. The wind carried his words back
to her. "Taught him not to mess with an Indian."

More posturing, Lola thought. Not wanting her to know
it was just a stupid childhood accident. "You sure showed
him," she said, playing along.

A cloud scooted over the sun, dropping the temperature
a good ten degrees. Lola got into the car and turned on the
heater. Another gale-force gust swept through, shaking the car
on its axles. Johnny slapped the hood. "Sure you won't stay?
Saw you with Verle at the funeral. I'd be quite the change of
pace." He threw back his head and laughed. The sun flashed
through the clouds. His throat was pale in the sudden light.

Lola threw the car into reverse, wishing she could run
over Johnny Running Wolf. She hit the dog instead.

⟡⟡⟡

THERE WAS a thud and a yelp and the ugly lift and drop of
the tires. Lola stopped the car and stepped out into a fading
howl. One of the dogs lay partially beneath the car, hindquarters collapsed and indefinite, front legs stretching for some
sort of purchase. Its mouth opened and closed, making that
sound. Blood flowed darkly, clumping in the dirt. The other
dog circled, eyes avid.

"I'm sorry," gasped Lola. "I'm so sorry. Get a blanket or
a sheet or something, so we can lift it into the car. I'll bring
it to a vet. Think there's one on the reservation? Or should I
just go straight to Magpie?"

Johnny bent over the dog. It rolled its eyes and lifted its
head and snapped at him. Johnny stepped back to avoid the
spray of blood. He moved around behind it and put his stocking foot on its shoulder, pressing the dog deeper into the dirt.

He grabbed the dog by the back of its head, lifting and twisting hard. At the crack, the other dog stumbled backward. Then it lunged forward, stopping just out of Johnny's reach. Another dog raced from around the corner of the house, then a third. Johnny dropped the dog's head and wiped his hands on his jeans. "Go on," he said to Lola. "Get out of here. You don't want to see this."

"I'll chase them away," said Lola. She picked up a stone.

"Forget it. They smell blood now. They'll all be on him in a minute." Still another dog slunk out of nowhere.

"Hurry up." His tone had lost its gloss. "I'd hate to see your delicate sensibilities offended."

Lola got in the car and waited until she'd put three ridges between herself and the house before she stopped in the middle of the road. She pressed her hands to her eyes. They came away damp. The dust, she thought. She wiped them on her pants and tried to focus on her conversation with Johnny. He'd never answered her question about TMR. And he'd ignored the subject of Frank altogether. She reached into the front of her shirt and extracted the narrow bundle anchored stiffly in her bra and unwound the toilet paper from the sugar spoon.

CHAPTER TEN

Lola passed the aspen grove before she registered the break in the trees, the bridge over the irrigation ditch, and remembered Verle's invitation.

Her pulse throbbed anew against the skin of her wrist. The car slowed. She thought of Bub, locked for long hours in the motel room, the way he leapt joyously against her whenever she returned, no matter how brief the absence. She felt again the sickening thump beneath the wheels, signaling a dog that would never leap again. "Damn," she said. "Damn. Damn. Damn." She looked skyward. The sun was still high. She pressed a reluctant toe to the accelerator. Twenty minutes later, she was on the Sleep Inn's floor, knocked to her knees by Bub's welcoming assault, turning her face away from his apparent determination to coat every inch of it with his tongue. He left off briefly to dash outdoors to do his business, but was back before she'd finished filling his bowl with kibble.

"You shouldn't eat all of that now," she said as he nudged her hand out of the way and attacked the bowl. "I might be late getting home. Be good while I'm gone and you'll get an extra treat when I get back." He raised his head and gave her a doggish grin, his tail on fast-forward. The food was already gone. "Listen to me," Lola said. "I'm trying to reason with a dog." His outraged howl followed her as she left. "That's not what I meant by being good," she called through the closed door. And spent most of the drive to Verle's trying to tamp down a sense of guilt, dislodged only by the rattle of planks beneath the wheels as she turned onto the bridge over the irrigation ditch. The car slid through the stippled shade of the aspens. The trees ended and the view began. Lola stopped the car and rolled down the window. Verle appeared from someplace, walking toward her. Saying something.

"Shut up," she said. "I'm looking."

✧✧✧

THEY WERE at one end of a crooked valley. A low log house stretched before her, deep eaves shading a porch where rocking chairs invited lingering occupancy. The house was sizeable but the mountains framing the valley turned it toylike. Lola had to readjust her gaze downward to fend off the sense that she'd somehow shrunk. When she looked straight ahead, things regained their normal proportions. But to glance upward even for a moment at those ice-wrapped peaks was to be sucked back into a world of miniatures.

"What is this place?"

"Mine," Verle said, and everything about him changed when he spoke, the pride and pleasure encompassed in that single word tinged with defiance, his intensity almost unseemly.

Lola looked away. At the far end of the valley, smoke crawled up into the sky. "What's that?"

"A fire. They start up about this time every year. Lightning and such gets them going. Don't you want to get out of the car?"

Lola stayed put. "Shouldn't you call somebody?"

"Naw. It's up in the national forest. They'll let it burn unless it gets too close to houses. Though, dry as it's been this year, that's a distinct possibility."

Lola rolled the window back up and got out of the car. It beeped behind her as she clicked the keychain's automatic lock.

Verle raised his eyebrows. "I'm not going to try to steal your car."

~ 103 ~

"Habit." She turned a slow circle, trying to orient herself. "I thought you said you were Mary Alice's neighbor," she said. "Shouldn't we be able to see her cabin from here?"

"The property line's somewhere over that way"—he pointed vaguely back the way she'd come—"just a few miles south as the crow flies. It's a lot farther by the road. To the north, this place goes all the way up into the reservation. Glad you like it. I figured you could use a change of scenery before you head back."

"Didn't you hear? I'm not going anywhere." She told him about the sheriff and his edict. The mention of Charlie Laurendeau acted like a ragged cloud across the sun, stealing warmth from the day.

"Well, now," Verle said. "That seems extreme. Walk with me. Let's put this ugliness aside for a while."

Lola had to hurry to keep up with him. He was shorter than she was, but he had a deceptive loping stride. He led her toward a high-fenced enclosure, where a man leafed segments from a bale of hay as a trio of horses stood at quivering attention before him. Lola noted their elegant faces, the flowing excess of mane and tail, and figured they were a step up from the stolid, serviceable mount she'd glimpsed in Mary Alice's corral. The man threw what was left of the bale onto the ground and backed through the barn door when Lola and Verle turned his way.

"It is a sad fact that Charlie couldn't find his ass—sorry, ma'am—with both hands, let alone find out who killed Mary Alice. I hate to see you caught up in his incompetence. But the whole point of inviting you out here was to get your mind off things. This should help. They're Arabians."

"Excuse me?"

"The horses. They're purebred Arabians. One of the world's oldest breeds." He lifted a latch and held a barred metal gate aside as she reluctantly followed him into the enclosure. The horses wheeled and trotted toward them. Verle dug in his pocket and brought out a handful of white sugar packets from the cafe. He tore one open with his teeth and poured the contents into his palm and held it out. Imperious arched necks stretched and straightened. Fleshy wet tongues wrapped his hand.

"Here," he said, tossing one of the envelopes her way. She caught it before she could think about it. "You do it."

The horses were small, but with powerful deep chests, smoothly muscled hindquarters and absurdly delicate legs, hooves dainty enough to perch atop teacups. They blew hot breath through flared pink nostrils and turned wise dark eyes upon her, making low, considering sounds in their throats. Lola took a step back, the sugar clutched within her fist.

"Not a horse person?" Verle asked.

She shook her head and backed into a fencepost. The horses surged forward. Verle distributed the last of the sugar and slapped their rumps. He opened the gate to free her right about the time she was seriously considering climbing the fence. "What do you do with them?" Lola asked, once the gate had safely closed behind her. "I assume you don't chase around after cows on horses like that."

"Breed them. Show them. They go all over the place. Colorado, California, Idaho. There's a roomful of ribbons in the house. Come on. I'll show you."

Sunlight gilded the valley. Lola and Verle trod their own angled shadows as they drew near the rambling house, its logs almost black, an emphatic brushstroke at the base of the sky's enameled blankness. Verle pointed beyond the house, to a shed wedged against a bluff overhanging a creek, its boards gone gappy beneath a caved-in roof. "See that? My grandfather, his wife, and eight kids homesteaded there and called themselves lucky, given the dugout where they spent their first winter. My mother wanted to tear that shack down once they built a real house, but my father wouldn't let her. Said it was her heritage. She told him she kissed her heritage goodbye the day she got indoor plumbing."

"What happened to that house?" Lola looked around for a logical step up from the homestead cabin. The home before her, she realized as they approached, was considerably larger than its unassuming profile suggested.

"It's the center part of this place." His hand sketched the outline in the air, the faint seams where old logs joined older ones. "I sent people all over the state buying up wrecked homesteads so the additions would match. Couldn't tell, could you?"

Wide warped planks echoed their footsteps back at them as they crossed a porch where generations of boots had worn a path of hollows toward the front door. A rifle leaned against the doorjamb. "What's that?" Lola asked. The worker had reappeared, holding a wooden-backed brush in his hand. He approached one of the horses. She wondered what he'd do if he heard a shot's innocuous *pop*. Whether he'd run to her aid, or continue stroking the brush along the horse's commodious back, his own back obligingly turned. Then she saw the bulky sidearm on his hip. She hadn't noticed it before.

"What's it look like?" Verle picked up the rifle and held it out to her. She took it and checked to see that the safety was on. She jacked the lever, the action liquid, the steel almost warm against fingers gone icy. She'd half-expected a spent shell to fly out. None did. She checked the chamber, clicked it shut and rolled the gun back over in her hands, giving herself time to let relief wash away the spike of fear. A load from a gun like that would have taken off Mary Alice's entire head.

"Why all the firepower?" she asked, once she was sure her voice would sound normal. "This rifle. That man's gun." She pointed toward the corral.

"Grizzlies."

"Here?" Lola whirled and studied the valley.

Verle laughed, easy and full-throated. "You won't see them this time of day. Dawn and dusk, they come down out of the foothills—where your friend has her cabin. A big griz has been hanging around, scaring the hell out of the horses. Eduardo's had to put them in the barn at night. If I catch him down here again—the bear, not Eduardo—he's a goner."

"Isn't that illegal? Aren't they endangered, or something?"

The laughter left Verle's eyes. "Way I look at it, he's endangering me. He's already taken a couple of my calves. This is my land. His home is up there. As long as he stays there, he and I will get along just fine. But if he comes down here, I could drop him at a hundred yards with that." He nodded toward the rifle.

Lola hefted it anew, appraising its easy balance. The stock's tight-whorled walnut gleamed like good furniture. She ran her fingers over the trigger guard, where a tiny, hand-engraved elk lifted its head in a long bugle.

"It's custom. From Germany. Come on in." He held the door for her.

She replaced the rifle by the door, stepped inside and waited for her eyes to adjust. High-backed leather sofas rose up within the cool dimness, anchoring either end of the room. Patterned woolen rugs sectioned the vast space between them. Verle clicked a switch and light splashed onto recessed shelves, where pots nestled in their nooks like plump hens. Lola crossed the room and examined one, narrow of neck and wide of base, its surface a high jet gloss cut by matte lines.

"You've got a good eye. That's out of San Ildefonso Pueblo. If I'd started collecting before the woman who made it died, I probably could've gotten this for a quarter the price I paid. Even so, it just keeps going up in value. Not that it much matters. I'd never sell it."

He turned her attention to another shelf bright with small, carved animals of polished stone, turquoise, serpentine, carnelian. He selected a bighorn sheep the size of a chestnut, its horns painstakingly ridged, swirls on its rump suggesting its thick woolen coat.

"Zuni fetishes," he announced. "Look at the workman-ship. You're supposed to feed them."

"The Zuni?"

"The fetishes," he said. "Give them cornmeal, or some such, to help them keep their power. I don't hold with all of that superstition." He led her around the room, reciting the provenance of rough-surfaced sand paintings and scowling Hopi kachinas.

"All of these things," Lola said. "They're from the South-west, aren't they? What about the tribe here? Don't you have anything of theirs?"

Verle waved a dismissive hand. "You want to create art, you need leisure time. People like the Zuni built high-rises, cultivated crops, created thousand-mile trade routes. Nothing against the Blackfeet, but they were nomads, dragging their tipis all over the Plains, chasing buffalo, one step ahead of starvation."

Lola thought of the beaded dress she'd seen in Wilson's office. She sank onto one of the couches and ran her hand across the supple leather. She entertained a moment's notion of stretching out across the sofa, closing her eyes, letting undrugged sleep carry her away. The silence within the house as Verle's words died away was absolute. She'd forgotten the restfulness of a real home. Verle took her hand and pulled her to her feet. He dropped her hand the instant she resisted. Which, she knew, was a little too late. He'd caught the split second when she'd tightened her fingers around his.

"Carlos has been busy in the kitchen," he said. "You want art? Wait until you taste his cooking. I think you'll agree it's an improvement on the cafe."

✦✦✦

LOLA PICKED up her glass and rocked it in her hand, watching the complicated dark wine slide along the sides. Lamb bones curved like quotation marks on either side of her plate. Lola hadn't spoken since her first bite of the chops, edges charcoaled and crisp, centers pink and tender as rose petals. Verle tilted the decanter. She put her hand over her glass. She had things to ask him, questions to be formed while she was still able to think clearly.

"What did you mean about the sheriff?" she said. "About him being a problem." As soon as she lifted her hand, Verle refilled her glass.

"He's young. Inexperienced. Inclined to be overly conscientious rather than rely on common sense—which should tell him that you would be of absolutely no use to him in figuring out who killed Mary Alice."

"If he's so inexperienced, what's he doing in the job?"

"It's the Indian thing," said Verle. "He's got a grandmother who was full-blood. He didn't grow up on the rez, but he campaigned hard there, yammering about protecting their civil rights even though he'd never had a problem with such in his natural life; and all those Indians who'd never voted in a sheriff's race in their lives turned out for the last election."

Lola played with the lamb bones, puzzling over what he'd said. "Indians have been here a long time. Why the difference in this election? Surely you've seen Indian candidates before?"

"Not really. It wasn't worth their while. Indians didn't vote much until a few years ago, when the ACLU sued over voting districts. Forced the state to redraw its districts so as not to divide up the reservations and dilute their vote. A whole bunch of Indians got elected to the legislature after that. Once the tribes realized they had some power, people started voting like mad."

"Is that why Johnny Running Wolf is doing so well? At least, I presume he's doing well, if Mary Alice was writing so much about him." Lola still hadn't been able to read those stories, but based on her conversation with Wiilson, she hazarded a guess as to their contents. "About how he was managing to fund his campaign, given that he's considered to be such a long shot."

"I wouldn't know about that. I don't much pay attention to politics. Long as a candidate supports policies that help ranchers, he gets my vote. And in Montana, that's every candidate. I could pull any old lever come election day and I'd come out all right." He leaned back and rapped on the kitchen door. Carlos appeared with another bottle of wine. Verle took it from him and spent a lot of time with the corkscrew.

"Where were we?" he said. "Right. Charlie. You should brace yourself for the long haul in terms of this investigation. It'll make things harder on him, investigating his own people."

Lola tried again. "You mean, like Frank?"

"That old drunk? Why would he shoot anybody? Even more than why, how? He couldn't hit the broadside of a barn if somebody gave him a baseball bat." He pushed back from the table. "Excuse me." Murmurs rose and fell behind the kitchen door. He returned. "You know what I think?"

"What?"

"Mary Alice was always a big one for camping," Verle said. "To the west of her place, on the other side of the river, it's all national forest. She was forever going off with that dog, sometimes on the horse, a few days here and there, exploring. She knew that backcountry better than some people who grew up here. Here's what I think happened. Because nine times out of ten—hell, ninety-nine times out of a hundred—the simplest explanation turns out to be the solution."

"Which is?"

"She'd been off on one of her trips. Came back and caught somebody breaking into her cabin. It happens all the time. Local kids get into those places, rip 'em off, sell or swap the stuff for drugs. We've got a little meth problem here. You've seen the billboards."

Lola nodded.

"Somebody catches them in the act, they'll usually just run off. But your friend came across the wrong guy. Probably a drifter. We get them here. People who want to play mountain man, live in the woods. They're crazy when they go in and the longer they stay, the crazier they get. Bad luck, nothing more."

Lola picked up the wineglass and knocked the rest back, looking for something to blame for her sudden dizziness. The idea of a random killing—the thought that a few minutes' delay, a different route taken, could have changed everything— seemed almost too cruel.

"She had a gun with her," she objected. "Was she afraid of guys like that? Or maybe someone else?"

"Sure she was afraid," said Verle, and Lola sat her wineglass down so abruptly it tilted and fell.

Verle righted it. "Remember those grizzlies? Everybody around here carries a gun when they go into the backcountry. The environmental types will tell you to carry pepper spray, but that's a crock. Your friend was smart that way, although for griz she should've been carrying a rifle. She did everything right and then one day something went wrong. Sorry you had to be the one to find her."

"It just doesn't make sense," Lola insisted. "She was wearing a jacket on a summer day." Lola thought of the phone message, the note. Verle had rejected her other theories so thoroughly that she was embarrassed to mention them.

"The jacket's like the gun. You want one with you just in case something goes wrong and you end up stuck out there overnight. It's pretty basic. You seem determined to turn this into more than what it might be. You ever think about just letting it go?"

"I don't let things go."

The corners of his eyes crinkled. "Another don't."

"What do you mean?"

"You don't carry a purse. Don't eat breakfast. Don't ride horses. Don't cry. Jolee says you don't even eat pie. What kind of person doesn't eat pie? What *do* you do, Lola Wicks?"

She heard her editor yet again, essentially suggesting that it was time for her to be more like other people. Ignoring the fact that the thing that made her different was the reason she'd presumably been hired in the first place.

"I get the story," she said. "That's what I do."

"But what if there's no story?" he asked. Before she could speak, he followed with another question. "This is your day off, remember? And it's almost gone. We don't need to figure it out today."

The kitchen door swung open. Carlos padded into the room and took their plates away, and came back with crystal glasses of dessert wine whose color recalled the day's golden sunshine. Three bluish dots triangled the web between his thumb and forefinger. A dark teardrop dangled at the corner of one eye. Prison ink, Lola thought as he disappeared again into the kitchen, returning a moment later with two little crocks of amber-glazed crème brûlée. Lola tapped through the craquelured surface with her spoon, and let the custard's rich creaminess and the caramelized sugar crystals mingle in her mouth as she watched the pinpoint bubbles ascend in the glass. The sun had set. The room grew dark. Verle's features were indistinct, whether from the wine or the sombrous gloom, she couldn't tell. Lola heard water running in the kitchen, the splash of pots and pans sliding into a full sink, homey sounds long forgotten.

"Where's your wife?" In her experience, they all had wives.

"Long gone."

Lola paid particular attention to her dessert.

"She never liked it here," Verle added. "Seattle or Denver is more her style. She liked to shop. Always"—he shot her a glance—"carried a purse."

Old rascal, she thought. Then she thought maybe she didn't care. He was a handsome man yet. That hair. She inclined her head toward the wall. The framed sketches, he'd told her, were Charlie Russell originals. "So do you, apparently. Like to shop, I mean."

"I collect. It's different." Then he asked: "Husband?"

She shook her head. "Not now, not ever." Could hear Mary Alice's voice in her ear: "None of your own, anyway." Her spoon sought a final scrape of custard. "What do you do for company out here?" Aware as she asked the question that she'd made a decision. Had done a quick calculation of the months of drought and decided that they easily outweighed a twenty-year—she sneaked a quick glance and added a decade—age difference.

"For company?" he said. He lifted his glass toward her in a toast. "I'm doing it right now." So he'd made a decision, too.

Lola stood. Any more chitchat a waste of time.

"I take it," Verle said, "you want to see the rest of the house."

CHAPTER ELEVEN

Lola dreamt in red.

Fields of poppies bending low in the backwash of a military helicopter. Trios of rocks splashed with scarlet paint in the international warning for land mines. Archipelagos of blood and dust beneath her feet in a just-bombed bazaar. A hole punched through a chalk-white cheek.

Beside her, a heavy turning. "You all right?"

She woke with a gasp. "Fine," she murmured automatically, before she knew where she was, or to whom she spoke. The response a rustle and a snore. She slid a hand along her throat, down her sides. No tight, reassuring wrap of sleeping bag. Just sheets against skin. Bare skin. She was in a bed. Not alone. The rest just a dream. Mary Alice, though. That was real. As was the person beside her. Lola edged a tentative toe across the bed until it bumped a sinewy calf. Verle. She lay a few moments longer, remembering a slow savoring that had unfolded as deliciously as the dinner, one welcome surprise after the next. Verle had not been past the stage of some basic acrobatics; knew how to use his tongue, too, not something you could always count on with an older guy. She'd been happy to overlook the blue pill he'd slipped into his mouth as they left the table. Lola stretched and registered the easeful fluidity of the movement, muscles too long tensed for danger gone languid, knots worked free.

Moonlight slatted across the bed, shadows shifting within it, resolving into recognizable human shapes. Verle's ranch hands, doing whatever they did at—she checked a nightstand clock radio—three-thirty in the morning. A horse nickered. Lola slid from the bed and knelt by the windowsill. A long trailer was backed up to the corral, a horse's rump disappearing into the blackness within. On their way to a show, she thought. A man led another horse into the trailer, hooves thudding against the ramp.

Verle turned over and exhaled in a ragged snore. Lola wondered when he normally got up. Wondered how he'd react when he did. Would he try to clasp her hand across a basket of muffins still warm from the oven, Carlos remaining tactfully in the kitchen squeezing oranges for juice? Or would there be lingering glances toward the clock, the little throat-clearings that prefaced the old excuses? She'd experienced enough of the latter to last a lifetime. It wasn't worth chancing. She scooped up her clothes, feeling for the brick-like packet of money she'd condensed from its various hiding places when she'd undressed in the bathroom after dinner. She crept from the room, slipped into her pants and pulled on her shirt, stuffing the money along with her bra and panties into a pocket, moving fast toward the front door with boots in hand, detouring only to grab one of the Zuni fetishes from the herd on the living room shelf.

◆◆◆

A MOLTEN filament of sunlight outlined the prairie. The town still slept. Lola drove to the Sleep Inn and unlocked the door to her room. The dog, in full frantic flight, hit her a split second before the smell. At least, she thought as she tackled the entirely foreseeable mess with a hand towel and the miniature bar of soap, Bub had confined himself to a corner of the bathroom. She sat back on her heels and thought of the hours of inertia until she could talk to Mary Alice's colleagues at the *Express*, her only diversion making coffee that tasted of the room's sulfurous tap water. There was Nell's, a delaying tactic, but that meant facing the tables of men whose desultory conversation ceased altogether whenever she opened the door, curious faces turned in unison her way. Wondering what she knew that they didn't. Which, she thought, was not much of anything at all.

The motel had its own newspaper box. Lola stepped outside and fed it two quarters and extracted the day's flimsy offering. Mary Alice was still front page news, although the *Express* had gone with a different photo for its most recent story. In it, Mary Alice was in working mode at what the caption told Lola was a powwow, her head bent over a notebook, interviewing Wilson. He wore a warbonnet, its feathers standing up straight around his head like a crown, at odds with his clunky glasses, their frames thick and black as the headline above the photo: "Questions Remain in Reporter's Death."

"Here we are sitting on our butts with no answers," Lola said to Bub, who deigned to return to the room only when she shook a generous amount of kibble onto a page of the newspaper. "Mary Alice would not be happy with us. Not one bit." The dog crunched at his breakfast with one anxious eye on the door. Lola used up the rest of the soap on her hands. She wrote an apologetic note to the housekeeping staff, laid a ten dollar bill atop the television, rolled up her sleeping bag and stuffed it, along with her toiletries and sleeping pills, into her duffel and bundled Bub into the car. They headed through the softening darkness to the convenience store where a neon sign blinked its red and yellow greeting. "Open. Open. Open." Jolee stood motionless behind the register. Lola wondered when the woman slept.

"Figured you'd show up here again eventually," Jolee said by way of greeting. "Saw you at the funeral with Verle, but couldn't get through the crowd in time to pay my respects."

"I wasn't *with* Verle at the funeral. Is this coffee fresh?" She selected the largest cup and poured without waiting for an answer, then paced the store, gulping coffee with each step, returning occasionally with an armful of dimly remembered implements that she deposited on the counter before attacking the next aisle. Floor cleaner. Sponges. Bleach. Rubber gloves. Trash bags. Detergent. Soap. She ran a hand through her hair, and grabbed a bottle of shampoo, then looked for scissors. The store had only the kind for school kids, too small for her hands, with blunt, rounded edges. She took them anyway.

She turned to the food section. What did people put in their refrigerators? She hadn't had a refrigerator in years, hadn't cooked for herself in longer than that. Milk seemed like a start. Bread. Peanut butter. Jelly. Cereal. Ramen noodles. Student food, the kind requiring as little thought as possible. She got the biggest can of coffee the store offered and started to walk away, and returned for a second can. Through the window, she saw Bub in frantic motion inside the car, leaping from back seat to front and then back again. She went back into the aisles. Dog food. A box of bone-shaped biscuits. On the way to the register, she passed a small selection of wine. The stuff in the bottles looked pink and poisonous, nothing like the elixir with which Verle had plied her. But alcohol might make her food choices more palatable. She tucked a bottle under each arm, then picked up the dog food and treats and sat it all beside the heap at the cash register. Jolee's hand hovered over the keys.

"That gonna hold you?"

Lola ignored the sarcasm. She pointed to a display of what appeared to be small fire extinguishers next to the cash register. A cub-size cardboard grizzly bear loomed above them. "What are those?" she asked.

"Bear spray. A grizzly bear tries to eat you, you squirt this stuff in the air. Wind blows the wrong way, well, the bear has himself a nice spicy meal."

Lola moved a can from the top of the display to the top of her pile. "Now I'm done," she said.

Jolee's hand remained suspended in air. "You know you could get this stuff for half what you're paying if you went to the grocery. They open at six."

"I want it now."

"Suits me. Seeing as you're my biggest sale all month, I won't charge you for the refills." The register began a series of steady beeps.

"What refills?"

"The coffee. You drank the whole pot." Jolee detached a filmy plastic bag from the metal hooks by the register and began filling it. "Looks like you're planning on staying awhile. You must of got one of those rooms with a little fridge. That's handy."

Lola hadn't known that some of the rooms at the motel came with refrigerators. "Yes," she said. "It's handy." She reached into her pocket for cash and came out with her panties.

"You'll want to wash those in Woolite," said Jolee, her eyebrows in frantic motion. "Want me to add it on?"

"Never mind," Lola muttered, and located her cash. She strung the bags along each arm, bumped the store door open with her hip, and loaded everything into the car's back seat. She retrieved the box of dog treats and pried open the lid, Bub's tail a blur. She turned the car onto the main drag, and gunned it out of town, the sky pinking prettily to the east, mountains still a black curtain to the west as she barreled straight at them, ignoring the speed limit signs, heading toward Mary Alice's.

✧✧✧

THE SUN was reduced to alpenglow by the time Lola peeled the rubber gloves from her hands. They smelled of bleach and spoiled milk. She'd stacked a dozen trash bags out on the porch, full of the sharp puzzle pieces of broken china, fruit going malleable and foul, and the bruised and shredded remains of what Lola guessed had been a welcoming bouquet of late-blooming lilacs. She righted a living room chair. A softball, its surface blindingly bright, thudded to the floor and rolled away. Lola thought about Mary Alice buying the ball, waiting to surprise her by suggesting they toss it around, persisting despite Lola's longstanding derision for her friend's inability to catch. Or throw, or hit. Lola held the ball in her hand and pressed her fingertips against the stitches and reminded herself that she didn't cry. Not given the fact that she'd just allowed herself to enjoy a night with Verle while Mary Alice's killer mocked her with another day of freedom.

The damage to the cabin wasn't as bad as she'd feared. The sofa cushions were upended, but not gutted; likewise with the mattress. And despite the mess on the floor, the contents of several cabinets remained undisturbed. Lola explored everything as she cleaned, hoping to find Mary Alice's flash drives. She went through each and every one of the files that had been dumped from the cabinet beside Mary Alice's desk; probed the inner pockets in long-unworn blazers, slid her fingers into the toes of balled-together socks and between the lining and the leather skin of handbags. She picked up the books from the floor and flipped through them one by one, then ran her hands across the tops of the bookcases. She poked around behind the fridge and along the bottoms of drawers for the telltale slickness of duct tape, walked the floors in search of a loose board. She emptied a bag of rice and another of cornmeal into bowls and sifted the contents through her fingers. She shook out the folded sheets and towels in the linen closet, even removed Bub's collar and turned it in her hands, wondering if maybe a hiding place had been stitched into it. Nothing.

She went back into the bathroom with the schoolroom scissors she'd bought and sat the trash can in the sink. Standing in front of the mirror, she pulled hanks of hair straight and snipped off anything past three fingers laid against her scalp. Longer, and her hair corkscrewed into unmanageable curls, utterly impractical. She put the trash can back on the floor and wiped stray clippings from the sink with toilet paper. She unhooked a waterproof radio from its spot on the shower head and brought it into the kitchen, seeking distraction to still her buzzing thoughts. But nothing happened when she twisted the knobs. She made a mental note to buy batteries the next time she went to town.

What if Mary Alice's killer hadn't been looking for anything all, she thought as she dragged a mop across the floor, leaving inexpert streaks. Verle's theory of vagrants or kids, the sorts of people who might have trashed the cabin just for the hell of it, seemed more and more likely. Except for the note, she reminded herself. And the phone call. Impossible to shake the sense that the mess in the cabin was just a diversion. The mop's movements slowed. Bub rushed in from somewhere and marked up the floor with paw prints and ran out again. Lola shook the mop after him. "Don't you ever get tired?" she called. The dog that had seemed so friendly initially now challenged her at every turn, dancing away when she tried to pet him, stealing the sponges and towels as she cleaned. She heard a thump from the living room and turned just in time to see the dog disappearing into the bedroom with the softball in his mouth.

"Put that down!" She brandished the mop at him as he emerged from the bedroom at a full run, whipping past her in palpable triumph. Lola looked around the kitchen for something that wouldn't do too much damage and grabbed a packet of ramen noodles and hurled them his way on his next victory lap. The cellophane-wrapped square caught him in the face, startling him into dropping the ball. He pivoted and dove for it, but Lola already had it safely in her hand, holding it high as he flung himself against her, barking his frustration. She pulled a chair up to the refrigerator and climbed onto it, kicking at the dog to keep him from joining her there.

"You're persistent," she told him as she opened the cabinet above the refrigerator. "Which is the nicest way possible of saying you're a royal pain." Apparently the killer had overlooked the cabinet—she'd found a bottle of Jameson's in there, no doubt awaiting the traditional wee drop upon her arrival—and it seemed a safe enough place to stash the softball. She slid her hands around the cabinet's interior as she had done before, hoping maybe she'd missed the flash drives on her first foray. But she felt nothing more than the bottle and the same stack of papers that had been there before. She'd glanced through them quickly. Bills, all with Mary Alice's handwritten notations as to the dates she paid them. She put the ball on top of them and started to climb down. Then she stopped. She'd been working all day. Maybe a wee drop was in order. She grabbed the bottle and, for good measure, the papers, and sat them on the table as she poured a spoonful of whiskey into a china teacup, the sole surviving piece of Mary Alice's grandmother's collection. The dog fell at her feet with a dramatic groan. A ploy for a treat, Lola thought.

"Not a chance," she told him. "You've done nothing today but get in my way." She settled herself at the table, took a sip from the cup and gave the papers a more thorough examination. Maybe Mary Alice had debts she didn't know about. The whiskey warmed her in an entirely different way from the previous night's wine, no low seductive embers but an instant flare. A single card about the size of a paperback cover slipped from the stack of envelopes in her hand. Lola whooped and jumped to her feet. The chair fell over. The dog scrambled to safety.

She called him back. "Look at this," she commanded, waving the card in his face. "Just look. I don't know what it means yet, but it's something." The dog hovered warily in the doorway. "This calls for a celebration." She held the bottle above the teacup, heedless of the lengthy gurgle. She drank and coughed and drank again. She screwed the cap back on the bottle and replaced it in the high cupboard. She braced her back against the cabinets and slid down onto a tile floor still warm from the day's sunshine and studied the campaign postcard.

"Changing the color of politics in Montana," it proclaimed. "Working in harmony with farmers and ranchers and developers, too. . . . Responsible development means more jobs for Montanans." It never mentioned a candidate by name. It didn't have to. Lola had just heard Johnny Running Wolf utter some of those same words at the pancake breakfast.

She turned it over. There was a phone number on the back, written in Mary Alice's large, looping hand. She didn't recognize the 403 area code, but so many strange new codes had proliferated in her years overseas that she no longer could match the numbers with their locations. Earlier in the day, she had thrilled to the miracle of a dial tone after she'd reassembled Mary Alice's landline. She looked at the clock—nearly ten—and tried to fashion an excuse for calling Johnny Running Wolf so late at night. But the phone went to voicemail on the fourth ring. She'd expected Johnny's hearty delivery but instead heard a wholly unfamiliar voice, at once drawling and curt.

"Gallagher. Leave a message."

Lola couldn't remember being introduced to anyone with that name in Magpie. She answered the message in kind. "Lola Wicks. Call me." She read the number from Mary Alice's phone into the receiver and hung up.

She called Bub and opened the door to let him out one last time before he went to sleep. The horse whickered, a comforting sound in the near-dark. Lola looked around the kitchen, searching for an apple she knew wasn't there. She hadn't bought a single piece of fruit at the convenience store. Verle had fed his horses sugar packets. She opened and closed the cupboard doors until she found a cookie sheet, then poured onto it what little of the sugar remained in Mary Alice's canister. She carried the tray across the yard to the corral. The horse's pale rump caught the moonlight. Lola put the cookie sheet on the ground and pushed it beneath the fence with her foot and moved quickly back. The horse shied away from the unfamiliar object, then approached it in tentative steps and pauses. His nostrils flared. He bent his head to the tray, rolling his eyes once toward Lola before giving himself fully to the task at hand. Lola found it oddly reassuring that he appeared as wary of her as she was of him. "Tomorrow," she promised him, "we'll start to get to know each other."

The kitchen light felt needlessly harsh after the night's cloaking comfort. Her open laptop mocked her from the table. She needed to look up TMResources, the name of the group that had paid for the campaign literature. A yawn caught her, then another. That particular task, she decided, could wait until morning. She closed the laptop and dumped food into the dog dish and stumbled toward the bedroom. She reached to draw the curtains. There weren't any. The bed itself—an outsize log affair that must have been Mary Alice's idea of an over-the-top Montana-style joke—took up most of the space, frustrating Lola's routine of dragging it away from the window. She kicked off her boots and removed the packets of money from them, pulling the rest from her clothing. She slid the bills between the mattress and box springs, and fell onto the bed and dragged a quilt atop her. She realized she'd forgotten to lock the door and remembered Verle's comments about locking her car. Maybe it was time to let go of some of her precautions, along with her sleeping pills, she decided, reaching for the bottle before replacing it unopened in the nightstand's drawer. She took a last look out the window and realized why Mary Alice had chosen to forego curtains. Stars confettied the sky in a great glittering display, flawless diamonds on a jeweler's black velvet swatch. A flash of heat lightning merged the stars' light into a single crackling vein across the sky. "Oh," Lola whispered to Bub, who had crept on the bed and was nosing about, seeking maximum warmth. "It's so beautiful."

She floated into blessedly dreamless sleep, not waking until a chunk of limestone exploded the bedroom window and landed an inch from her head.

CHAPTER TWELVE

Lola, half-sunk in sleep and waking fast, rolled away from the window and off the bed, crawling backward on knees and elbows.

She lunged for the kitchen, sweeping her hand along the counter, wrapping her fingers with relief around the bear spray. She slid back to the floor in a far corner of the kitchen, clutching the canister in both hands. Tried to still her breathing to listen for footsteps—as if she'd be able to hear anything over Bub's crazed barking. She hissed and he quieted immediately. It was not an improvement.

The sounds of the night flowed in. The wind swept past with its usual fanfare. Branches scraped irritably against one another. Lola's heart walloped her ribcage. Things took shape. The bedroom doorway, with its glimpse of the bed, serenely adrift in the starlit darkness, trailing shards of glass like phosphorescence. The window's jagged hole, larger than Lola would have thought, indicated considerable velocity. Whoever had flung the rock had been close. She tightened her hands around the bear spray and wished she'd read the instructions more closely. It was meant for grizzly bears, five hundred pound behemoths whose teeth could pierce her skull with the ease of a toothpick sliding into an olive. Anything that might discourage a grizzly could certainly knock a man on his ass. Then she thought of Mary Alice. She'd had a gun. It hadn't stopped a goddamn thing.

She whimpered. Bub's head whipped around. Then he resumed his singular, quivering stance. The phone mocked her from its spot across the room. In the time it would take her to whisper a plea to a 9-1-1 operator, someone could come through the door and dispatch her. Besides, she'd interviewed too many snipers. "Movement and sound, they're our best friends," one had said. He spoke approvingly of deer and rabbits, the way they froze. Lola had never liked the analogy. Deer and rabbits were prey, she'd pointed out, meek, trembling creatures.

"But they're prey that have figured out ways to survive," came the laconic response. "Ever notice how many deer and rabbits there are in the world?"

So she sat frozen with her back pressed into the corner, barely daring to breathe, reasoning that her only chance was to hear her assailant before he heard her. The microwave's green glowing numbers showed three A.M. Two hours before the sky would brighten. Of course, Lola thought, daylight meant only that she'd be able to see his face as he came for her.

She wondered what Mary Alice had seen.

She drew her knees against her chest and rested the bear spray atop them, and pressed her lips tight against the moan trying to escape.

✧✧✧

SOMEHOW, AT some point, she dozed. She awoke to grey light leaking through the windows and Bub's low, humming growl. She caught her breath and squinted toward the bedroom. As far as she could tell, Bub had not moved from his place all night. His growl lowered and deepened. A moment later, she heard a car. "God," she said aloud. Her stalker must have left at some point. She could have dialed for help. But now he was coming back and it was too late. "*God.*"

She leapt to her feet, possibilities racing through her mind as the sound of the approaching car grew louder. If she fled through the front door, she'd run right into him. She reached for the phone, but realized she could be dead several times over before the sheriff could get to the cabin from town. She heard the car make the final turn that would bring it into the yard. Bub began to bark. Lola cast a last, frantic look around the kitchen. The two bottles of fruity wine from the convenience store sat on the counter. She jammed the bear spray into the waistband of her pants, grabbed one of the bottles and flattened herself against the wall by the front door.

Slam of car door. Scrape of Bub's nails skidding into the kitchen, his barking hitting a crescendo. Footsteps on the porch. The doorknob turned.

Lola raised the bottle and swung it like a bat at a rising fastball. The glass exploded in a pink, sweet-smelling froth against a man's head. She yanked the bear spray from her waistband, slid the safety away with her thumb and depressed the spray tab and held it down, following the man as he crumpled. He let out a gargling scream. Bub fled. The man hit the floor and rolled onto his back, hands over his face. Lola dropped the spray and reached for the shattered bottle and fell onto his chest, her knees digging into his ribs, holding her breath against the burning cloud of bear spray. She grabbed at his hair, but it was too short for purchase. She put a hand to his forehead and shoved it back, pulling his neck taut. With the other, she pressed the razored edge of the broken bottle against his throat, drawing it across the skin to a wildly throbbing spot. "Feel that?" she gasped through the spray. "It's your carotid artery."

He groaned. His throat convulsed. A thin scarlet thread arose beneath the glass. The floor beneath his head was a mess of blood and bits of glass and pink wine. Smell of fruit cut by blood's coppery tinge, the bear spray overwhelming it all, searing Lola's eyes and throat. She turned her head to one side and spat. Her hand twitched. She wanted, badly, to slide the glass deep. But she needed something else first. "Move your hands," she commanded. "I want to see the bastard who killed my friend."

His Adam's apple jerked again and a different sort of noise came from him. He let his hands fall away, and despite the blood and the wine and the eyes already puffing shut from the bear spray, there was no mistaking Sheriff Charlie Laurendeau.

❖❖❖

HE SAT at the table, pressing ice wrapped in a tea towel to the back of his head. Lola counted the towel ruined. He'd already stained a bath towel and the entire kitchen sink, trying to clean himself up. "You'd better hope I can get this bleeding stopped," he told her. "Then I won't need stitches. I don't know how I'd explain this to Margie at the clinic." He'd moved the bear spray and the second wine bottle to a spot behind him, and then he'd gone through the kitchen drawers and removed the sharp knives and put them in the same spot, positioning himself solidly between Lola and anything she might conceivably use as yet another weapon against him. His gun lay in his lap, his hand resting atop it. "You're lucky I haven't cuffed you."

"You're lucky I didn't kill you."

All the windows in the house stood open, welcoming the wind, which obligingly rushed in, lifting the cloud of pepper spray and carrying it away. Lola and the sheriff glowered at one another. Bub crept to Charlie's side and lay his head on his thigh, rolling a fishy eye toward Lola when she turned her glare his way. Charlie dug a finger behind the dog's ears.

"What are you doing here?" she asked. An explanation occurred to her before he answered. "You came to make sure I haven't left town. Well, I haven't. Not even for a minute."

He adjusted the ice pack. "Not unless you count that little side trip out to old Verle's last night. Which I don't. Lucky for you." *Old* Verle's. "Nice setup he's got out there," he continued. "You should have seen it a few years ago. You wouldn't know it's the same place."

"What do you mean?" Not liking the conversation, not one bit, but grateful for a shift in focus. Sleeping with Verle was one thing. People knowing about it was quite another.

"He about lost it. He was on his way to bankruptcy, along with a lot of other folks around here. You could get yourself a Montana ranch for peanuts. Problem is, nobody even had peanuts. A lot of folks went under. Verle, though, he came back from the edge. Hooked up with some oilmen down in Denver and did well for himself. Real well, by the look of things."

As the sheriff spoke, Bub oozed by degrees into his lap, curling like a cat beneath the big caressing hand. "I'm pretty sure he's not supposed to do that," Lola said. Anything to get Charlie off the topic of Verle. "Bub. Get down." The dog opened his eyes just long enough to shoot Lola a heavy-lidded stare before falling back into some sort of canine fakery of contented sleep.

"He doesn't respect you." The sheriff pointed out the obvious. "You've got to fix that. He's a working dog. He needs jobs. And you've got to take care of that horse. I've fed and watered it a couple of times already. That's what brought me up here this morning. I saw your car and then the window when I drove up. Hustled on in here to make sure you were all right. Sure glad I made the effort." He took away the towel and touched his fingers to the back of his head. They came away scarlet. He replaced the towel and pressed until his knuckles whitened.

"I checked on the horse yesterday," Lola said. Meaning she'd stood a good distance from the corral as the horse bobbed its blocky head at her and stamped its feet on the other side of the fence. She'd gotten just close enough to ascertain that there was water in its bucket and hay in some sort of a manger affixed to the side of the shed. Other than the sugar offering before she'd gone to sleep, she'd ceased to give the horse another thought. She didn't want to think about it now, either, given the matter at hand. Charlie would be well within his rights to charge her with assaulting an officer of the law.

He pushed himself to his feet, leaving a wet red handprint on the table. "Let's get this over with."

Lola sat rooted. "Are you taking me to jail?"

"No. I'm going to go take a look at the bedroom. Have you touched anything?"

She shook her head, speechless with relief.

"That's a nice change," he said. "Do you remember what time it happened?"

"A little before three," she said. "I looked at the clock right afterward."

"Okay. That's good information. I'm going to look in the bedroom and then I'm going to look out on the porch and around the yard to see if I can find anything. You sit right here. I mean it. Don't move." He grabbed Bub and dragged him over to Lola. "Hold onto him. I don't want him running around through my crime scene. Do you have some baggies?"

She started to get up, but he held up his hand. "Do. Not. Move," he said. "Just tell me where." She pointed toward a drawer.

He pulled plastic gloves from his pocket and snapped them onto his hands, then retrieved the baggies from the drawer. He was in the bedroom a long time. He emerged holding a jagged rock, encased in one of the bigger baggies. "Here. Look how sharp it is. You're lucky it didn't hit you in the head. You'd look like me right now."

Lola tried a smile. He didn't return it. He left the rock on the table and went outside, and came back after a few minutes with a red bandana flapping between his gloved fingers. "This yours? If it is, I won't bag it."

Lola's breath came quick. "Bag it. It's not mine. But I think I know whose it is. And I think he killed Mary Alice."

⟡⟡⟡

Fifteen minutes later, the sheriff and Lola remained at an impasse. The sheriff tried again. "Do you know how many people here have red bandanas either riding in their back pockets or tied around their necks?"

"That may be. But I've only ever seen one. And each time, Frank was wearing it. Wilson Bird thinks he was smuggling booze. What if Mary Alice had figured that out and was going to write a story about it?"

"I don't know how many different ways to tell you that Frank didn't do it. You're going to have to take my word for it. Besides, booze smuggling is no story at all. People have been doing it for generations. Different gangs come and go but nothing ever shuts off the spigot. Any other bright ideas you want to lay on me?"

"As a matter of fact, there is. And it's not about Frank, either." She showed him the campaign postcard. "I'm sure this is about Johnny."

Charlie handed it back to her. "I told you. He was in Denver."

"What about this?" She turned it over and held it up so that he could see the telephone number scrawled there. "I thought it was Johnny's, but somebody else answered. Does the name Gallagher mean anything to you?"

Charlie's disinterest was clear. "No. Probably somebody else who couldn't have done it. When you find out who, let me know."

"I found the card with the liquor. Up there." She pointed. "Don't you see?"

The sheriff opened the cupboard and retrieved the bottle and held it up to the light, assessing the level. "You did this in one day? Is this par for the course for you? It's not a good idea, you know. Drinking alone, especially when you're upset."

"I'm not upset!" She lowered her voice and tried again. "I'm not upset."

The dog and the sheriff stood side by side, heads tilted at identical angles, eyes accusatory.

"Mary Alice's note. The one she left me. It said, 'You know where the liquor is.' But I didn't. I had no idea. The only other thing in that cabinet besides the Jameson's was a stack of bills. Who keeps bills over the refrigerator? She's got a whole file cabinet next to her desk for stuff like that. And this card was tucked in the bills in the cabinet. You can't tell me that was just happenstance. There's something else, too."

Charlie sloshed the Jameson's around in its bottle again and sat it down. "What?" he said. "Convince me that none of this is the booze talking."

"Campaign literature has to say who paid for it. Something named TMResources funded this." Her finger skittered across the microscopic type at the bottom of the card.

"Never heard of it."

"Me, neither. But—*TM*. Couldn't that stand for Two Medicine? The note said, 'Camping on the Two Medicine.' Maybe she meant that as some sort of signal."

"Half the things around here are named Two Medicine. It's because of the river."

"What river?"

"The Two Medicine River. It doesn't look like much but if it weren't for that water feeding all the irrigation ditches, nobody could ranch here. It runs along the edge of this place and drops down into a canyon not far from here. You should check it out. There's a trail that cuts right behind the cabin. It's a great hike."

"I don't hike."

Charlie put the Jameson's back in the cupboard and picked up the bags with the rock and the bandana, the dog moving shadowlike beside him. "You'll want to get that window fixed. Call down to the hardware store and give Hank the measurements. He'll help you out. He was supposed to come up here anyway, take out a couple of these trees. There's too many, too close to the cabin to be firewise. You're probably best off going back to the motel, but you need to cover up the window, keep the place protected after you leave."

"I'm not going back to the motel," Lola said.

Charlie stopped at the door. "What do you mean?"

"I'm not going anywhere. I'm staying right here."

CHAPTER THIRTEEN

Lola sat back in surprise at her own words.

Charlie dropped the bagged rock onto the counter with a thump. "Ma'am—Lola. I'd have to advise against that."

"So?"

"I'm ordering you not to."

Lola tried to sound more sure than she felt. "Sheriff. I do not understand a single thing about what's going on here, but I do understand my rights. You may have the legal authority to order me to stay here as a witness, although I'm pretty sure if I pushed it, it wouldn't stand. You have the authority to jail me if I don't cooperate, and God knows, you have the authority to arrest me and charge me for bashing you over the head. Although I appreciate that you apparently aren't going to. I appreciate that greatly."

"I'm considering changing my mind."

"But you do not have the authority to tell me where I'm going to stay while I'm here. And I'm going to stay right here in this cabin."

Bub's head whipped back and forth, regular as a metronome, following the conversation.

"You're crazy."

"So I've been told."

Charlie sat down again. He slid his hand around to the back of his head and then studied his fingers anew. The blood was darker, finally coagulating. "Miss Wicks. I need you to listen to me. Which I don't think you've done, not to a single word I've said, since you showed up here."

The sun announced itself above the ridgetop, turning the kitchen into a sudden hullaballoo of light. "I'm listening."

"You're up here a good twenty miles out of town, all by yourself, right where Mary Alice turned up dead and where somebody seems to want to do the same thing to you."

"It was just a rock," Lola said with considerably more hubris than she felt. "If somebody had been trying to kill me, he could have. I think he was just trying to scare me."

"And I'm saying that I think you should be scared."

She forced a laugh.

"Stop it. It's no laughing matter. You're really going to do this?"

"Yes," she said, nearly as surprised as the first time she said it. "I really am." She stood up. "I'm really going to make some coffee, too. Am I allowed to do that?"

He slumped and rested his head in his hands. "Just tell me why."

"Because I need caffeine." She switched on the coffeemaker that she'd set up the night before. She held a mug beneath it and waited until the cup was nearly full, then slid another beneath the stream of coffee and handed the first to the sheriff. When she'd filled the second cup, she put the pot back onto the coffeemaker and sat down. She spoke slowly, not convinced she'd truly made the decision until she heard her own words.

"I've been moving for a long time. Forever, it feels like. But it seems like wherever I go, somebody's always trying to chase me away. Either it's the Taliban trying to keep me from working the border, or it's an editor in Baltimore trying to keep me from working overseas, and now some creep doesn't want me here, and apparently you don't, either—even though you won't let me leave. Well, to hell with all of you. I'm not going anywhere. Not this time. Not until I'm ready." She drained her coffee, and stood. "Refill?"

He shook his head more adamantly than necessary for a simple refusal of coffee.

"I've got to get going. If the last few days have been any indication, today is going to be a continuation of hell." He looked at the rock on the counter as though he'd never seen it before. He picked up the baggie. It swung heavy in his hand. "Do you have a gun?"

"No. Don't want one. I'd probably shoot myself."

"Go buy yourself some more of that bear spray, then. You seem to have emptied the whole can on me. I'm glad you've got the dog. He's not big enough to stop anybody, but he'll let you know if something's coming. If you hear anything, call 9-1-1 right away. Better yet, call this." He took a business card from his wallet and wrote a number on the back of it. "That's my cell. Don't waste time by calling 9-1-1 and waiting for dispatch to track me down." He stood on one foot, then the other. Lola wondered if he was waiting for her to change her mind. When she'd first met him, his uniform shirt strained to contain his stomach, but already, after only a few days of strain, it bagged loose. "About that horse. Don't forget to exercise him."

"You told me. And give the dog some jobs."

"You'll always want to latch that corral gate," he said, still going on about the horse, "even if you're just stepping in with him for a minute. Spot's an escape artist. One day he let himself out and ran all the way into town. Ended up in front of Jolee's store. She fed him a slushee and got a rope on him, tied him to the newspaper box and kept him there until Mary Alice could come get him. Speaking of trips to town, you might as well unload that rental car."

"Then how am I supposed to make those trips to town?" Staying at the cabin alone was one thing; being trapped there another entirely.

"You could ride the horse," he said. Then, at the look on her face, "I was joking."

"Not funny."

"Use Mary Alice's truck. You can drop off the rental car at the gas station in town. Mel's got a contract with the rental company. I'll talk to him, tell him it's special circumstances, so he won't charge you the one-way fee. I'll give you a ride back up here. The dog should be okay here while we're gone. Maybe along the way, I can change your mind about staying in the cabin. In the meantime, come on. I'll show you how to take care of the horse. Then we'll get out of here."

~⟡~

DESPITE HIS vow to harangue her about her decision, Charlie drove in near silence after they'd dropped off the rental car, humming or occasionally singing under his breath, bits drifting her way. "Prairie lullaby . . . sweet Montana home."

"What's with the tunes?"

He flashed a not-quite smile, the closest she'd seen him come to one yet. "It's genetic. My dad used to dance my mom around the kitchen every night, singing this song to her. It's really about Wyoming, but he changed the words. They'd make me join them while our food just sat there. I ate a lot of cold dinners, but I know how to dance."

Lola tried to imagine him shambling bear-like around a dance floor and fought the amusement rising within her. "Sweet Montana home. I guess that's how Mary Alice thought of this place. She said coming here was like"—Lola hesitated, the words so sentimental as to embarrass her— "falling in love. I don't get it. It's just so empty." She turned her head toward the window, the desolation emphasizing her point, and caught a flash of movement across the road. The sheriff stomped the brake. The seat belt yanked tight between her breasts and a moment later, she felt Charlie's arm across them, bracing her from hitting the dashboard. A tailless brown dog darted off into the brush. Lola looked down at the arm across her chest.

Charlie jerked it away. "Sorry." His face was red. "That's Old Man Frazier's dog. It's always out along here. Some-day it's going to be nothing but a grease spot right in the middle of the road. For my money, that day can't come soon enough."

The dog's rear end protruded from a bush, its nub of a tail helicoptering excitement. Its haunches bunched and relaxed, bunched again as it tugged hard at something on the ground. Charlie lifted his foot from the brake and put the car in gear.

Lola looked back. "Is that . . . ?" she cried. "Stop the car!" She unlatched the belt and flung open the door. She took the irrigation ditch in a bound and sprinted toward the dog, which raised a low, warning rumble, its jaws clamped tight around a dead man's ankle.

✧✧✧

LOLA JUMPED back from the dog and the dead man and crashed into Charlie Laurendeau. They fell together, his weight a sudden surprise atop her. The dog dropped his prize long enough for a wrathful bark, then sank his teeth more deeply into the leg with a rolling, elemental growl. Charlie pushed himself off Lola, eyes on the dog. He pulled his pistol from its holster.

"Are you going to shoot it?" Lola got up, brushing her hands along her torso from shoulder to hips, all the places his body had touched hers.

"Not unless I have to. I just want to get close enough to see who this poor soul is." He pulled the whippy red willow branches aside. "Oh, dear lord."

Lola peered around him. The man lay next to an empty nylon backpack, arms flung out, chest caved in, a couple of ribs splintering white through all the red. Blood slimed his hair. His jaw skewed to one side, pink gums gone grey. Lola thought of the outstretched hand, the toothless, ingratiating smile that had greeted her that first evening in Magpie. His hand, now clenched in a useless fist, forming a gun at the funeral. The slurred voice. "Poor Mar' Alice." She took a step.

Charlie flung up a hand. "Don't move," he said. "I won't have you messing up another crime scene."

Lola's legs wobbled beneath her. She sat down before they gave out altogether.

"What's wrong with you?" Charlie asked.

She pointed to Frank, to the ring of clean skin around his neck, presumably protected from dirt by his ever-present bandana. Which was not present upon his corpse. "You take that bandana you just bagged to the Crime Lab, Sheriff. You and I both know that Frank's DNA will be on it. Now we'll never know whether he killed Mary Alice."

"Goddammit!" The sheriff's vehemence chased away the shakes. "Leave it alone. How often do I have to tell you that Frank had nothing to do with that?"

Lola lobbed a quick, defusing softball. "What happened? Hit and run?"

Charlie twisted in place without moving his feet and surveyed the road. A tumbleweed cartwheeled across it, riding a skiff of grit shoved along by the wind. The road crested the prairie swells, rising and falling, disappearing over each ridge and reappearing at the top of the next.

"What are you looking at?"

"Not at. For. Skid marks. But I don't see any. Not that I expected to." He squatted and trained his eyes on the ground at their feet. Lola followed his gaze as it swept quadrants from Frank's body to the road. "Look, there. In the mud by the ditch." He pointed to a muddle of wide footprints with the pointed toes common to the boots everyone seemed to wear. "Look at all those different sizes. I'm seeing three, four people, minimum. Kids, likely."

"How do you figure kids did this?"

"I forget you're not from here. Come on. I've got to call this in. Try to step in your own footprints back to the car. I'll wait here for the ambulance—and until Old Man Frazier comes and gets his damn dog. Maybe he can get you back to Mary Alice's."

"Ambulance? Sheriff, I think he's past help."

"Standard procedure."

She followed him back toward the car, concentrating on placing her feet in the flattened places in the grass. She stopped in front of the ditch, not sure she could jump it without adrenaline. "What does my not being from here have to do with anything?"

Charlie tucked his gun back in its holster and cleared the ditch without visible effort, his ungainly body suddenly graceful. He turned and held out his hand. Lola bent her knees and jumped, grabbing for his hand in midair. "This road," he said, "it goes to the rez. The boundary's just over that hill." He opened his fingers and her hand fell from his.

Lola flexed her fingers. "So?"

A magpie swooped into the willows, its gaudy black-and-white plumage an affront to the dusty leaves. Another landed nearby. The birds turned their heads this way and that, assessing Frank's body. They chattered across the distance, their bold enthusiasm rebuking Charlie's bitter monotone.

"They probably saw him walking." There was something wrong with the sheriff's voice. Lola thought back to her conversation with Wilson, how Wilson had said Johnny and Frank were cousins. And then Charlie, when he'd interviewed her after Mary Alice's death, called Johnny "some long-lost cousin." So somehow Frank and Charlie were related.

Charlie opened the car door and reached for the radio.

"Wait," said Lola. "I still don't get it."

He slid into the car and she walked around and got in beside him. The car was hot from the sun and he turned on the ignition and lowered the windows. "People see an Indian headed into town, no matter how he's getting there, they'll figure he's going there to drink—and that he's got some money on him. Kids roll them for money, or sometimes just for fun. It happens. Frank's had more than his share of it. That's how he lost his teeth. Bum-stomping, they call it. Brave-stomping,

~ 138 ~

when it's an Indian guy. Some fun, huh? But these kids went overboard. They must have been pretty hopped up."

"Jesus." Lola tried to ignore the tiny, shameful wriggle of relief at the knowledge that Frank's death at least had a reason, however unpalatable. Not like Mary Alice's. "At least you have an idea who did it."

"Oh, I'll figure out quick enough who beat him up. But I already know who got him killed."

"Who?"

He curled his fingers and drove his hand into the dashboard.

"Me."

✧✧✧

SHE HAD to ask three times before she pulled an explanation from him.

"Everybody thinks that homemade bomb his Humvee hit left Frank retarded. He was brain-damaged all right, but it didn't mess with his intelligence. Just his speech, and some coordination. He understands things just fine. But everybody looked past him. That made him perfect."

"For what?" Even as she spoke, Lola thought of her own reaction to Frank, the way she looked quickly away. Charlie was right. People didn't want to see him.

"Somebody's running quite the smuggling operation on the rez."

"I know. Wilson told me."

"He thinks it's just booze, maybe a little meth. Same-old, same-old. But things are changing, getting bigger fast. Not sure the FBI's let Wilson in on just how fast. God forbid they should tell people on the rez about the shit rolling down-hill toward them. You saw Judith in that cell the other day. Multiply that scenario exponentially. Usually people die of other things before overdoses get them. Car crashes, mostly. Sometimes they fall asleep smoking, or cooking the stuff, and the house burns down around them. But they die. More and more of them, misery upon misery. And it's not just on the rez anymore. It's leaking down into the county. That level of traffic needs foot soldiers. I asked Frank to let it be known that he was looking for money. That's all it took. He figured out fast who the middlemen were. We could have taken them out months ago. But I asked him to keep after it, find out who the big guns were. And now he's dead."

"Do you think Mary Alice was onto the same thing?"

The tight curved muscles at the corners of his mouth bulged. "I think it's possible. A couple of days ago I let Frank go ahead and make one more run. He told me it was something big. I thought I'd kill two birds with one stone, excuse the expression—figure out who's running this stuff, and get whoever shot Mary Alice, too. Instead, I got Frank killed."

"And I got Mary Alice killed by hanging around the airport instead of heading straight for Magpie when she didn't show up," Lola said.

"That's ridiculous."

"No more than what you just said about Frank. We're a pair, aren't we?"

The hard set of his mouth softened. "That we are."

"Thank you, Sheriff," she said. "Charlie."

"What for?"

"For telling me about Frank. I think it's the first straightforward thing anyone has told me about what's going on since I've gotten here."

His lips curved. "You took me down with bear spray and a wine bottle. Figure I'm better off with you on my side."

They sat for a moment that was almost companionable. Charlie sighed and lifted the radio mouthpiece and pushed a button. The radio buzzed static. "No matter whose fault this all is, we've got to deal with it." He tried the radio again, with the same result. "Huh," he said. He pulled out his cell phone and hit a couple of keys and spoke after a brief pause. "Hey, Tiffany. What's wrong with the radio? Well, put it down and talk to me. We need the ambulance out on the reservation road by Old Man Frazier's place and . . . what? *What?* Where?"

Strangled sounds from the phone.

"Tiffany, calm down. And call somebody, Highway Patrol maybe, or the next county. I don't care where you get them from, just find somebody. Oh, and get another somebody up here to guard my damn crime scene before Old Man Frazier's dog pisses all over it. Make sure they know not to let Frazier go wandering around in here on his own, either. I'm on my way." He dropped the phone and whacked at something on the dash and the siren screamed as the car surged forward, wheels grabbing the pavement in a yawning U-turn back toward town. The hills blurred past, the speedometer needle quivered past ninety, a hundred, Lola's hands braced against the dash, wind rushing through the window, catching her breath and tearing it from her. She fought an urge to shout with the relief of it all, the exhilaration of activity, the familiarity of rushing toward something happening, even if she had absolutely no idea what it was.

✦✦✦

CHARLIE TAPPED the brakes as they came into town, rocketing around the lone pickup moving along the street, the quick dodge throwing Lola hard against the door before her seat belt caught. The car turned off the main street and shot past small faded houses that leaned away from decades of wind. It hit the railroad tracks with no evidence that shock absorbers were part of its assembly. Lola came up off the seat and her head knocked against the ceiling. Shrieking brakes competed with the siren as the car careened into a trailer park and stopped in a head-high backwash of dust. Kids spilled like feral cats out of one of the trailers, stumbling away from the cruiser. Charlie held a mic to his mouth.

"Get back here!" he shouted, his magnified voice booming through the park. "You are material witnesses and you could face charges . . ."

They were gone. He dropped the mic. "Hell and goddamnation," he said. "You stay here," he said to Lola.

She got out of the car.

The trailer had once been white. Tires sat on its roof. A lunk-headed dog leapt and slobbered at the end of a dragging rusted chain. The wind caught the open trailer door and slammed it shut and yanked it open again. Charlie sidled toward it, gun held high. "Stay here," he said again to Lola, and disappeared inside. She ran up the steps behind him as he kicked his way through an ankle-deep layer of beer cans on the floor. The yeasty smell of hops and dope and old sweat thickened the darkness. Charlie headed down a hall, Lola crowding close behind. They moved into the bedroom. Stopped.

A boy and girl lay on a bare mattress. The boy fat, shirtless, skin the color of irises in full bloom, a slug trail of saliva across his cheek. Eyes open and unmoving.

"Oh shit, oh dear." Charlie whispered it like a prayer.

The girl, skinny, hair dark and brittle as Spanish moss across her face. Jeans riding low on bony hips, T-shirt of thin, cheap stuff over braless buds of breasts. A flutter between them. Lola fell to her knees and shoved the girl onto her side, forcing her finger through stiff lips, prizing apart clenched teeth.

"What the hell are you doing? Stop touching things."

"Help me, you idiot," Lola hissed. "Can't you see she's alive?"

Charlie crouched beside her. "Tiffany said the ambulance is over in the next town. Guy had a heart attack. It won't get here in time."

"Shut up," said Lola. "Listen."

Gurgling.

"If that noise stops," Lola whispered, "we'll have to give her mouth-to-mouth. Let's just keep her on her side, keep her airway clear, until the ambulance shows up." She slid a hand beneath the girl's shirt and ran it up her spine, spreading her fingers wide to better feel the breaths. Ribs like twigs beneath her fingers. Skin chilled and clammy as supermarket meat. Lola eased her other hand from the girl's mouth and pulled her hair away from her face.

"Oh shit, oh dear." More of a sob this time.

"Stop staying that." Then Lola saw why. "Oh, no," she said. "Is that . . . ?"

"Judith. Joshua's sister."

Lola studied her. Slash of green shadow across each eyelid, garish against the purpling flesh. Dirty hand curled against her face, bits of green polish flaking from bitten fingernails. A star the size of a spiky thumbprint, tattooed on the tender brown skin of her neck, just below her earlobe.

Gurgle.

"Take it easy," Lola murmured. She stroked Judith's forehead. Tiny pimples like Braille beneath her fingertips. It was very quiet in the trailer. Lola looked at the dead boy. Wished somebody had pulled down his eyelids. Impossible not to think about Mary Alice.

Gurgle.

"Fucking heroin," Lola said.

"What are you talking about?"

She'd seen addicts in the narrow streets of Kabul, the by-product of the brisk opium trade; even a dead man once, needle still in his arm, probing the bruised flesh there like an outsize mosquito. Face the color of the eggplants piled like prizes in the market stalls. "The only overdose I ever saw was heroin. In Afghanistan."

"You're in Montana. They're tweakers."

"Tweakers?"

"Meth."

Gurgle.

"Shhh," Lola said. "Shhhh. Let's just listen to her breathe."

CHAPTER FOURTEEN

By the time the ambulance drove away, the circus was in full swing, people three deep outside the trailer.

Charlie retrieved a roll of yellow tape from the glove box and handed it to Lola. "Make yourself useful," he said. "Mark off a perimeter."

"I'm a reporter. I can't be part of a story."

"You're not writing a story," he reminded her. "You're just along for the ride."

Lola stalked away. She wound an end of the tape around a propane tank at the front of the trailer and began spooling a wide outline, the tape dancing behind her in the wind. She turned and considered, then laid the tape on the ground and anchored it with rocks. "Step back, please," she said to the clusters of feet in front of her. "Please step back."

She heard the accelerated clicks of a camera shutter and glanced up to see the woman from the newspaper, the same one who'd been at the funeral, taking aim at the trailer. Lola turned her face away and stooped to pick up another rock. A viscous, coffee-colored splatter landed next to her hand. A woman whose wide hips contrasted oddly with her narrow, hunched shoulders looked down at her. "It was only a matter of time," she said. Her lower lip pooched out. A droplet of brown liquid wobbled upon it before gravity grabbed it away. "They're in there every week, partying. Boys and girls both. Half the babies born in town this year were made in that trailer."

Lola looked at the woman's face and put her in her parents' generation, then factored in wind and dry air and a lifelong lack of access to expensive moisturizers and thought she was probably closer to her own. "What happened?"

"Just what everybody thought would happen." Pause. Spit. "They were in there like always, blasting that damn rap music, and then one of 'em comes out screeching, 'They're dead, they're dead.' So I called 9-1-1. Finally drank themselves to death." Spit.

"Hey. Hey, there." Charlie crossed to where they stood. "Don't talk to the witnesses," he said to Lola. "That's my job. Trudy, I'll need to get your statement." He raised his voice. "Anybody else who saw anything—who was here, who left, what these kids took—I'm going to need to talk to you."

A man began to back away from the crowd. "Hey!" Charlie called. He started after the man and three other people moved swiftly away in the other direction, disappearing among the trailers. Engines turned over. Exhaust fouled the air. A fast-approaching car wove its way among the general retreat.

Backup, Lola thought. About time.

A brown Chevy pulled up beside Charlie's cruiser. A round-faced woman in an apron shiny with grease flung open the door. "Billy?" she called. "Billy?"

The sheriff stepped forward and caught her wrist when she tried to dodge around him. "You can't go in there, April."

She ducked to one side, then the other. "My son. They said he went to a party here. They said . . . Billy!" Her voice floated above a crowd gone silent, attentive. She looked from one face to the next. "Did anyone see him? Billy Worden? Do you know him?"

Charlie wrapped her other wrist in his free hand and swung her to face him. "I don't know your boy, April. He hasn't gotten into the kind of trouble that would bring him to my attention. That's a good sign. The kids all went home. You should, too. He's probably there. Or maybe at a friend's house, hiding out, hoping not to make my acquaintance."

April had the sort of face that people meant when they said apple-cheeked, and Lola imagined that on a normal day it was open and pleasant, its expression inviting a chat if you found yourself waiting behind her in a checkout line. But now its curves were drawn tight with the fear that narrowed her eyes and sharpened her voice.

"What do you mean, went home? I just passed the ambulance. Was it coming from here? He's not answering his phone. And he's not with his so-called friends. I already called them, the ones I could find, anyway. I'm not stupid. Billy? Billy?"

Wind kicked through the park, lifting a corner of the trailer's roof, letting it down with a slap. Lola realized why the tires were up there. She caught Charlie's eye, held her hand to her ear, miming a phone, and tilted her head toward the trailer. He could call the hospital from inside without anyone hearing him, get the name of the boy lying so still in the ambulance next to Joshua's gurgling sister. Charlie dipped his chin in understanding. He pulled the woman closer.

"Pay attention," he said. "I'm going to go in there, check to see if . . . if anybody left anything. Maybe your son was in a hurry to get out, dropped his cell phone or an ID or something. Lola here, she's going to wait with you. Okay?"

"Okay," the woman whispered. "Thank you." Beneath her apron, she wore jeans and a "Go Scavengers" T-shirt with an absurdly fierce magpie pecking at the words. Lola pegged her as a school cafeteria worker. The door shut behind Charlie. Lola heard him latch it against the wind.

The young woman with the camera eased toward Lola. She wore the same denim jacket from the funeral, this time with jeans and scuffed cowboy boots. She pulled her little tape recorder from her jacket pocket. "I'm Jan Carpenter. We met at the funeral. What happened in there?"

Billy Worden's mother tensed.

"How the hell should I know?" said Lola.

Jan persisted. "Tough scene, huh?" She lifted the recorder. "What's it like?"

"No."

"But you just said . . ."

"I didn't say anything. You said, 'Tough scene.' Nice move. You didn't ask me a direct question. You just said something sympathetic. The idea is that I'm supposed to start talking, and then you'll have a story."

Jan dropped her hands to her sides. "Worth a try."

At least she didn't fluster, Lola thought. That was something. Lola lowered her voice. "I'd like to come by the paper, talk to people about Mary Alice. When's a good time?"

Jan put the recorder away and reached into the jacket's top pocket and retrieved a pack of cigarettes. She shook one out, lit up, and took a drag, spitting smoke in Lola's face. "How the hell should I know?"

Billy Worden's mother flinched. Lola stepped away. Jan followed. "I just want to talk to someone about what Mary Alice had been working on," Lola said beneath her breath.

Jan nodded. "Sure you do. And I just want to talk to you about what's going on here."

"Fair enough," Lola said. "But quid pro quo. I want everything you've got on Mary Alice."

"Watch this," said Jan. "I can blow smoke rings." Wispy ovals slid from her lips and writhed away on the wind. "That's all you've got. Smoke. If you don't tell me what's going on here, I'll find out anyway. I live here. Sooner or later, people will talk to me. But without our stuff, you're up the creek. You want to find out what happened to Mary Alice? Read it in the *Express*."

Lola wondered what was keeping Charlie. She checked to make sure April hadn't moved from her designated spot. "The *Express*," she said. "How many people are going to read that? Five thousand, maybe?"

"You forget about the Web," Jan said. She straightened and Lola heard the same sort of pride in Jan's voice that she'd detected in Verle's when he talked about his ranch. "We might be a little local paper, but people from all over read us. We double our circulation online."

"My paper hits a half-million people every day. And that's the dead-tree version." She tried to remember what her editor had said about the most popular stories. "When it comes to the Web, we're in the double-digit millions."

Jan rounded her mouth. A few more smoke rings floated away. "So?"

"So, all those millions are going to read my story about Mary Alice," said Lola. No reason, no reason at all for Jan to know that story was nonexistent. "Help me out with it, and I'll cut you in. I'll double-byline it." No reason, either, for Jan to know that even if she could talk her editor into a story about Mary Alice, he'd never go for a freelancer's name atop a story. At best, Jan would get a notation in tiny italic type at the end of a story that she'd contributed some information. "Think about it," Lola urged. "Your name on the lead story on one of the leading news sites in the country. And everybody will want to read it, whether they knew Mary Alice or not. City girl chases her dream West and ends up dead. Something like that can jump-start a career. I know the paper is looking for younger reporters." A statement that had only a distant relationship to the truth. Lola was pretty sure that despite the paper's fervor for jettisoning its older, overpaid, non-blogging-tweeting-Skyping staffers, not a one of them was being replaced.

Jan choked on a smoke ring. She dropped the cigarette and stepped on it and licked her lips. Lola watched the idea take hold. "You being from here," Lola nudged, "you could help me see angles I might miss. Give it authenticity. Keep me from making any stupid mistakes."

"I heard down at the cafe you asked Verle how much land he's got. Bad form. Very bad form."

Lola knew then that she had her.

"What do you need to get started?" Jan asked.

"Access to your archives. I want to read every single story Mary Alice wrote for the *Express*. And I don't want to pay."

"I'll give you my password. Your turn." She and Lola moved in unison still farther from April Worden.

"One dead, a boy. A girl—Joshua's sister—still alive, but barely. The rest of them ran."

"Shit," said Jan through unmoving lips. "I heard Judith had been dating a town boy. That's always trouble. We're going to have to remake the paper." She pulled a cell phone from her pocket.

"Wait," said Lola. "There's more. Frank, that guy with no teeth? He's dead, too— Hey. Be cool."

Jan bent her head and let the wind comb her hair across her face, hiding her expression. "What was Frank doing here with those kids?" she said to the ground.

"He wasn't. He's up the road a ways. It's near a house. I can't remember whose. Some guy with a crazy dog."

Jan blew a strand of hair from her mouth. "Old Man Frazier."

"That's it. Anyhow, Frank's all smashed up. Looks like he got hit by a semi. Your sheriff doesn't think that's what happened. He thinks some kids beat him up. That maybe they were—tweaking? Is that how you say it? Don't tell him I told you. Just be sure to ask over at the hospital how many bodies they've got and whether they're all from the trailer. That'll get you started."

Jan nodded. "Thanks." Voice small and stunned.

"You really need to work on your poker face," Lola said.

"I hadn't much needed one until this week."

"We'd better get back." The conversation had already gone on too long. They returned to April Worden's side, standing with everyone else, waiting. The wind sliced past with a steely edge. Clouds the color of soot clumped above. People moved restlessly, talking to break the tension.

"Weather coming."

"About time. We need the moisture."

"Maybe it'll knock down that fire over on the Two Medicine."

"More likely not. When was the last time anything wrung moisture out of one of these clouds? Wind'll stir the fire up worse, more like."

Something stung Lola's face. Then again. She touched her hand to it, wiped away a bit of cold. The air blurred. "Is it . . . ?" She turned and looked at Jan. "Is that *snow*?"

Jan turned up her collar. "Just a squall."

"But it's June."

"Wait 'til July," Jan said. "And August. It snows then, too."

The trailer door opened. The crowd inhaled. Charlie stopped on the step and Lola knew. But April Worden didn't, not yet; she searched Charlie's face, then his hands, looking for her son's cell phone, a wallet, a piece of paper.

Something. Anything.

Pinpoints of snow struck Charlie's uniform, melting in small, spreading starbursts. He brushed at them. "What did you say your son's name was?"

"Worden. William Owen Worden. WOW. His friends call him Wow. Because his name is William Owen Worden—"

Babbling, that final forestalling. Keep talking and people will be polite, Lola thought. They won't talk over you, won't tell you what you can't bear to hear. A thing isn't true until it's said.

Charlie talked over her anyway. "Ma'am. You're going to have to come on down to the office with me."

The woman shook her head. "No."

"You can ride with me. I'll send someone to get your car."

The woman's hands covered her ears.

A thing isn't true until it's said.

Until you hear it.

"No," she said again, and Lola caught her as she started to go down, limbs jackknifing, lips parting to draw breath for the mighty rising scream; and Lola wished, as she wrapped the woman tight in her arms, someone had been there to catch her when she'd found Mary Alice.

CHAPTER FIFTEEN

The ground outside Mary Alice's cabin was white.

"It'll be gone by morning," said Old Man Frazier, to whom Lola had been handed off. He turned out to be only slightly more approachable than his dog. The beast had refused to release its grip on Frank's lifeless leg, and ended up being dragged into the ambulance along with the body. A call to Charlie, who was simultaneously dealing with Billy Worden's mother while trying to locate Joshua, elicited the terse suggestion to shoot the goddamned thing. Instead, the EMTs conferred on the telephone with a vet about a knock-out injection, and then dumped the drooling, staggering creature into the back seat of Old Man Frazier's car, where it emitted a rattling wheeze just often enough to convince Lola it was still alive.

"Snow in June," Old Man Frazier said as he stopped in front of Mary Alice's cabin. He sat behind the wheel, a stumpy gentleman with alarmingly tufted ears, making no move to open her door. Flakes glittered in the headlights. "Bodies dropping like flies. How do you like Montana so far?"

Lola got out without answering. She stood outside the cabin, snow sifting onto her hair and sliding icy fingers beneath her collar, until his taillights disappeared. Bub greeted her at the door, nosing her up and down, narrow-eyed. He ran out to relieve himself, then scratched on the door to come back in. Lola peered toward the corral. The horse lowered himself into the snow and rolled back and forth, grunting in obvious pleasure. She envied his enjoyment. The air in the cabin was glassy with cold. Lola eyeballed a woodstove at one end of the living room. She made a circuit of the walls, looking for a thermostat. She came back to the woodstove. She blew on her fingers and tucked them beneath her armpits and stamped her feet. She jogged to the front door, pulled it open, and contemplated the staves of wood that rose nearly to the roofline. She stood on tiptoe and selected a few pieces from the top, then hurried back indoors and dumped them on the floor by the stove, Bub at her heels.

Her appreciation for his solicitude vanished when he snatched away the only packet of matches she could find, apparently intending a merry chase around the cabin. His eyes went wide and he spat out the matchbook when the piece of kindling Lola lobbed his way smacked the floor mere millimeters from his paws. Thirty minutes later—after a few false starts that involved several days' worth of shredded newspapers, and a cloud of greasy black smoke that preceded her discovery of the flue and necessitated throwing open the windows and letting in still more cold air—a fire hissed within the stove. Bub abandoned further attempts at thievery and lay stretched on the floor, eyelids fluttering, legs twitching in a doggish version of REM sleep. Lola drowsed beside him, languorous with belated warmth and exhaustion. She closed her eyes and let her breathing slow as the day's images began to flicker past. She'd learned it was best not to fight them, lest they rise up in far more fearsome fashion in her dreams.

She saw again Frank's collapsed features, his mutilated body. The fat boy, his livid skin so at odds with his utter stillness. Judith and her labored grip on life. The sheriff's voice, desperate and condemning: "The murder rate in this county has tripled since you got to town." As sleep descended, Lola's thoughts wandered. What was it Jolee had said about Mary Alice that first night? Something about working day and night. And the sheriff: "She's been writing a lot about Johnny

Running Wolf." Johnny's voice ringing through the church. "That name was on top of a lot of stories in the newspaper about me." Nodding, smiling toward everyone else, but ignoring her efforts to catch his eye. Ignoring, likewise, a wave from the toothless guy. Frank. Who'd turned up dead in a ditch.

Lola sat up.

The room tilted.

The sides of the stove glowed faintly. She pushed herself to her feet and tottered to the door and stumbled out onto the porch, sucking in clear, cleansing air. Her thoughts swirled and settled. The first few tumblers clicked into place. Nothing swung open, revealing answers, but questions began to form, the start of a search. Not twenty-four hours earlier she'd righted Mary Alice's desk, restored the pens and paper clips and other things in what seemed to be their proper containers and cubbyholes, and put the printer back on the desk and wiped it clean. Now she reached beneath the desk and pulled hard at a heavy box of paper there, sliding it out into the room. She lifted the top and removed a ream of paper, tore open the wrapping and loaded the printer. She retrieved her laptop and attached the printer and the router. One of Mary Alice's few complaints about Montana lamented the dearth of wireless. Lola grinned as she entered her own name into the access code window. She and Mary Alice had used one another's names for years as a basis for passwords. She followed Jan's instructions for accessing the *Express* archives. She typed in Mary Alice's byline, and sat back and watched as the list of stories scrolling down the screen grew and grew and grew.

Five years' worth. Everything from stories about Magpie town council meetings and casino finances on the reservation, to stories about something called "captive shipping," which sounded intriguing but appeared to be about railroads. Stories about weather. Stories about wheat. Stories, inevitably, about animals. Lola waited until the list was complete and then clicked on the first story and hit Print. The printer whirred into action. She slid the cursor to the next story. Open. *Click*. Print. *Click*. She looked over her shoulder toward the kitchen, where the bottle of Jameson's waited, and ran her tongue across her lips. She went into the bathroom and unhooked the shower radio, hoping for music to help her stay awake, before she remembered that the day's events had thwarted her plan to buy new batteries in town.

The clock's hands inched toward midnight. Open. *Click*. Print. *Click*. There were hundreds of stories and she was going to print out every single one of them, and then read them and sort them according to their potential for trouble. If she were lucky, very lucky—and read very, very quickly—she might accomplish the initial task in a single all-nighter. The Jameson's would have to wait. Open. *Click*. Print. *Click*. Lola pulled the first story from the growing pile in the printer tray. She reached for a yellow highlighter in a container on the desk and pulled off the cap and gnawed on the end as she read. At the end of each page, she looked back at the screen and tapped at the keyboard. Open. *Click*. Print. *Click*.

The first story was about the weather, about a wind so strong that it shoved a locomotive off the tracks. Lola read two sentences, scrawled "No" across it with the highlighter, and started to put it aside. Then she thought: "A locomotive?" She read it through to the end and sat a moment, listening to the printer's buzzing hum, the fire's sibilance in the stove. The dog rolled over and sighed. Beneath it all, slithering over and around the cabin, the low moan of wind. She put the story down.

Open. *Click*. Print. *Click*.

She reached for the next story.

⟡

Sunlight assaulted Lola, cascading through the living room window. She'd closed the bedroom door against the sight of the shattered window and slept on the sofa with the bear spray in hand, the phone at her side. It was six o'clock. She'd last looked at the clock at three, clutching a printout of a story whose revelations were so perplexing it seemed appropriate to note the hour. Now, her stomach clamored. An ache in her hip asserted itself. She rubbed at it, and felt a lump in her pocket. She reached inside and discovered the Zuni fetish she'd taken from Verle's. It was a grizzly bear of fiery coral, about two inches long, with startling turquoise eyes. A strip of buff-colored leather bound a miniature obsidian arrowhead to its back. She lifted the bear into a shaft of sun, admiring the way its turquoise eyes caught the light and glowed.

"Why do you do that? Take things?" Mary Alice had asked her more than once.

Her reply always a wordless shrug. How to explain, even to her best friend, that all of those people had taken little bits of her, security and trust, hope and certainty, pieces she wasn't sure she'd ever get back? It seemed a fair exchange. She cupped the fetish in her hand and moved stiff-legged into the kitchen. Behind her, Bub slid from the sofa with a thump. They yawned in unison, stretching in the luxury of slow waking. She sat the bear on the counter. Its head was raised, mouth open, carved teeth respectfully detailed. Lola thought back to the stuffed bear in the airport, incisors like scythes. These bears didn't simply bite, she guessed. They slashed and shredded, lay waste to whatever got in their way. She liked that. "Grrrr," she said to the bear. She raised her hand to it, fingers bent, in her own approximation of a long-clawed salute. Bub slunk toward the door, radiating canine disgust. Lola remembered what Verle had said about superstitions. She went through the kitchen cabinets until she found the cornmeal. She shook a little into her hand, rubbing its grittiness between her fingertips, and sifted it onto the counter in front of the bear.

"Eat up," she told it. "We're all going to need our strength."

She let Bub out and stood at the edge of the porch, waiting for him to finish his business. For years she'd arisen within one guarded compound or another, yanked from sleep by the muezzin's insistent call to prayer rising above the final defiant blasts of nighttime gunfire. In her house in Kabul, her roommates would already be at work, twisting their lips around indignant French phrases directed at the *stupide* demands from their editors in Paris, the time difference in France making for earlier deadlines than she faced. The cook would be crashing around with all the pans in his arsenal, the end result being only a few green-tinged hard-boiled eggs to go with the previous day's leathery naan. And the guards would almost certainly be asleep on their rope charpoys beside the compound gate, folded into fetal positions within their wide brown woolen shawls, cradling their Kalashnikovs.

Now she stood in unaccustomed solitude, postponing the moment when she'd have to deal with the previous night's discovery. The sun did battle with the blackness of the mountains, its victory preordained. The air smelled of damp pines. The snow was already melting, droplets plinking from the eaves like piano keys. Even the wind had settled into a lazy, tuneful version of its customary shriek. A brown bird, its yellow breast chevroned with black, coasted to a straight-legged landing onto the corral fence. The horse turned toward it and nickered.

The horse. She'd forgotten all about it.

She kicked high fans of snow on her way to the shed, the flakes spangling the air. The horse stood at the fence, waiting. Lola went into the shed and found the coffee can sitting on a shelf in the shed and filled it with grain from the bin Charlie had shown her. She dumped it into one of two rubber buckets hanging inside the fence. The horse plunged its nose into the grain. Lola put a tentative hand against its neck. Its hair was short and smooth. She patted it, lightly at first, then more surely, getting used to the feel of the long muscles beneath the skin. She stroked his bony face, careful not to touch the quivering unprotected hollow above his eye, marveling at the surprising velvet of his nose. She moved a hand behind a tender ear and scratched. The horse swiveled its ears in her direction and leaned into her touch, still chewing. Lola looked around for someone to see her achievement. Bub sat a few feet away. He thumped his tail.

"He likes it!"

Thump.

Bub pranced ahead of her on the way back to the cabin. She scooped some snow and formed a loose snowball. He yelped and turned an aggrieved eye upon her when it disintegrated against his rear. Charlie had said the dog needed a job. Maybe he could catch. She went back into the house and retrieved the softball and Mary Alice's glove, stiff with disuse, from the closet and called to Bub. He was already at the door, waiting.

⟡

ONE HUNDRED pitches into the side of the shed, boards popping like shots upon impact. Inside drops and fastballs. Down on one knee for a while. Arm whips. Wrist snaps. Distance throws and then close. Speed drills. After a half-hour, she was nailing the zone and had worked up a pleasant burn in her arm, but was no closer to making sense of what she'd read the night before. Bub flopped at her feet. His tongue lolled from his open mouth. He'd retrieved each and every pitch, giving, Lola thought as she rubbed the ball against her pants, a whole new meaning to the term spitball. By the time they stopped, the snow was already shrinking from their footprints, grass showing through.

The porch caught the sunlight and held it. A couple of Adirondack chairs beckoned. For all its wide, uncurtained windows, the cabin's interior suddenly seemed dark and confined. Lola went indoors reluctantly and found a heavy sweater in Mary Alice's closet and squirmed into it, throat tightening against the familiar citrus scent of her friend's perfume. She dragged an end table from the living room onto the porch and arranged her various stacks of paper and her laptop upon it. Then she found the highlighter and a pen and some paper. She poured herself a Thermos full of coffee and settled into one of the chairs, its fanned planks already warm to the touch, and gave a last wistful look at the mountains' mocking splendor before trying to decipher what she saw closer at hand.

✧✧✧

"HE CAME *out of nowhere—that is, if you consider one of America's largest cities nowhere. But here on the reservation, that's exactly how they look at Chicago. Nowhere—at least not in any way that is relevant to their reality."*

The highlighter slid with an outraged squeal across the information that had so startled Lola the night before. Most of Mary Alice's stories on Johnny Running Wolf were the usual political fare. The announcement of his candidacy and then the reaction to the announcement. A companion piece, a retrospective of Indian candidates around the country. It was short. In fact, beyond the surprise of his entry into the race, Johnny merited little more than a line or two in Mary Alice's stories until the much bigger surprise of his primary victory. At which point, Mary Alice delivered the standard lengthy profile that yielded the fact that Johnny left the reservation before starting school and grew up just outside Chicago as John Wolf. He'd made his way back to the Blackfeet Nation as an adult, sporting his reclaimed birth name and an avowed desire to help his people. Before that, he'd worked at an oil company after graduating from law school. In Calgary. "We're never surprised when our students go on to prominence," a professor told Mary Alice. A professor named Gallagher. The same name on the voicemail when she'd called the number Mary Alice had scrawled on the back of the campaign card.

Lola shuffled through the stories, looking for something she didn't see. She looked again. She clenched the highlighter between her teeth and turned to the laptop, thinking that maybe in her exhaustion the previous night, she'd failed to print out a story or two that would expand upon the information in the profile. But there was nothing in the *Express* archives, beyond a brief story about the fundraising trip to Denver, about how Johnny was paying for his campaign. Lola bit down on the highlighter. It wasn't like Mary Alice to gloss over such a basic issue, especially for an inexperienced candidate who appeared to be doing so well. There was the matter of gas money for a campaign in a state the size of Montana, funds for the plane travel, the billboards, the suits. Those boots. She opened a new search window for a quick check of Johnny's campaign donors, only to bump up against the unpleasant discovery that Montana apparently had yet to switch to an electronic campaign finance reporting system. She explained to Bub that it was a very bad thing indeed. He yawned and rolled over and flung all four legs wide, ensuring maximum belly exposure to the sun. Lola fought a quick unbidden desire to join him, to spend an entire day moving from one patch of warmth to another. Maybe read a book. A novel. Forget about everything going wrong, all the things she didn't understand, just for a day. "Is that too much to ask?"

The phone rang. Lola dashed inside and snatched the receiver from the cradle. The dog followed and lay down at her feet. "Yes?"

"I'm returning a call from Mary Alice's number," drawled a voice she'd heard only once before. "But this isn't Mary Alice."

"Hello, Gallagher." The dog rose and shook its legs one after the other and padded to the door and whined. Lola shook her head at him. "I'm a friend of Mary Alice's. I'm staying at her place. Mary Alice is dead. Somebody shot her. I'd like to talk to you about your interview with her."

The line went dead before she'd finished. Lola hit redial. "Gallagher. Leave a message."

She retrieved a map she'd found among Mary Alice's things and calculated mileage. Then she let the dog out. "Better stretch your legs now," she told him. "You're in for a quiet couple of days." She watching as he lifted his leg against the porch, against Mary Alice's truck, against one of the fence-posts on the corral. The horse lowered its head and the dog squeezed under the lowest rail. The two touched noses. Lola called Jan at the *Express*.

"It's Thursday, right? I'm losing track of time out here. Any chance we can take a little drive up to Calgary after you get off work tomorrow?"

CHAPTER SIXTEEN

Lola urged Jan to cut her workday short on Friday so they could leave early for Calgary.

"I don't know what it's like at big papers like yours," came the testy reply. "But we lost a third of our reporting staff when Mary Alice died. You should just be glad I'm not working through the weekend."

Lola hung up. The sugar spoon, safely encased in a baggie, lay next to the phone. She went to her laptop and clicked on a file she hadn't used in years. She returned to the phone and dialed a Baltimore number. Ed Sanchez was a Charm City cop whose quest to rise above sergeant was no more successful than his hopeless pursuit of Mary Alice, something he doggedly continued even after she moved to Montana, according to the plaintive emails Mary Alice sometimes forwarded to Lola. Sanchez had been one of Mary Alice's best sources back when she covered the crime beat, work that involved, as she and Lola often joked, "all the 's' stories—shoot, stab, slay, sexual assault." Now Mary Alice herself was one of those stories.

Lola wedged the phone between neck and shoulder, and held the softball beneath the kitchen faucet and scrubbed at it as she spoke. "Hey, Sanchez. It's Lola Wicks. Mary Alice's friend. Right. The tall one." Lola spent several minutes offering fulsome condolences. "You're right. She never should have come out here. But she realized that too late. You know, the last time I talked to her, she said, 'I wish I'd listened to

Sanchez.'" Lola crossed her fingers behind her back. "Yes, really."

She held the phone away from her ear. Sanchez was a little guy, but he was loud. "Listen, Sanchez," she said finally. "I've got a favor to ask. I'm mailing you a teaspoon. I wonder if you could discreetly run the prints on it. I know it's out of order. But we're talking Mary Alice here." She moved the receiver another six inches away and chose a single question from among the barrage he fired at her. "Do I think this guy is the one? He wasn't here when it happened. But I think he might have been involved. If he's clean, that would help me rule him out. Nobody will be the wiser. Thanks, Sanchez. You're the best. Mary Alice always said so."

She hung up, dried the softball on a dish towel and did a little dance step across the kitchen, waving the towel above her head. She tucked the towel through the refrigerator handle. Climbing up on a chair, she stashed the softball in a high cabinet, already crowded with other things Bub had shown a propensity to steal. He leapt against the chair and barked in frustration. "You've had your turn," she told him. "Now I have to deal with the horse."

⟡⟡⟡

LOLA WATCHED Spot from a corner of her eye as she circled the corral with a pitchfork, tossing manure into a wheelbarrow as the sheriff had taught her. The pitchfork was heavier than she'd expected and it twisted awkwardly in her hands, spilling its pungent load, which broke apart and scattered. Bub chased the pieces and then Lola chased Bub, reminding herself not to let him lick her face. She spent entirely too long trying to spear the bits of manure with the pitchfork tines, then headed toward the shed for the wide scoop shovel she'd seen there. As soon as she opened the gate, the horse loomed behind her, trying to shoulder his way through. Lola shouted and threw an instinctive elbow. He half-reared, his hooves flashing large and sharp before her face, and spun away. Lola slammed the gate shut and fumbled with the latch, breathing hard. The horse trotted to the far end of the corral, sulking there when Lola returned with the shovel.

She thought of that first night, how she'd looked at the corral on her way to the cabin, remembering that Mary Alice had mentioned a horse but unable to recall when or why she'd acquired it. While Lola had stood there looking stupidly at the horse, Mary Alice was stiffening on the hillside. Lola posed the question to herself yet again. What if she'd come sooner? The shovel fell from her hand. She sat down in the dirt and put her head to her knees. A heavy footfall sounded behind her. Soft questing breaths whooshed above her head. The horse nosed about her, lipping at her hair. On impulse Lola breathed into the flared nostrils. His ears swiveled forward. His eyes were the color of polished bronze with dark rectangular pupils. Lola pushed herself to her feet and moved to retrieve the shovel. The horse took a step behind her. She took a second, experimental step, a third. It followed doglike. For whatever reason, the creature had been important to Mary Alice. And except for the twice daily, arm's-length feedings, Lola had essentially neglected it.

Even before she'd arrived in Montana, she'd been condescending about Mary Alice's choice to go to work for a newspaper not a tenth the size of the one in Baltimore. And disinterested in the particulars of her new life in Montana beyond poking fun at the log cabin, the pickup, the horse. "Hey, Cowgirl," Lola had addressed her emails. Which were few, and brief. No wonder Mary Alice had mentioned the horse once, and never again. Bub, lavish and apparently indiscriminate with his affections, had forced her to pay attention. The horse—Spot—had been easier to ignore. She noticed now that his tail was a cascade of snarls, his coat so matted and caked that his spots blended into the grime. He watched her uneasily, unused to such prolonged focus.

"Let's get you cleaned up," Lola said to him. "And then I'll figure out some exercise for you, too."

❖❖❖

An hour later, much of the dirt from Spot's coat had settled on Lola as she clumsily wielded a stiff-bristled brush. Spot heaved an occasional sigh and shook himself. Lola learned to shut her eyes against the volcanic cloud of fine grit that rose around her and floated back down, settling onto her scalp and beneath the neck of her pullover. As she swept the brush over and across the horse, the variations in his coat revealed themselves. His head and neck and chest were tinged the color of charcoal. The rest of his body was pale with lavish dark splotches on his rump, a careless grind of a pepper mill onto a snowy linen tablecloth. When she placed a hand lightly on his flank, the skin there twitched specifically, then stilled as she applied more pressure. Lola kept her touch firm as she ran her hand along the cleared paths left by the brush, learning the bulging musculature of his chest, the flat planes of his shoulder blades, the sculpted curves of his haunches. She sat the brush atop a fencepost and tugged at his halter, urging him into a walk, then a slow ponderous trot as she floundered gracelessly beside him. When the sheriff had recommended exercise, he'd meant riding. She knew that, but had decided against it. Hence, the idiotic jog around and around the corral, the horse seemingly puzzled but game beside her. Bub cavorted around them as they made their circuits. Lola let go of the halter and leaned against the fence, breathing mouthfuls of dust. She rubbed a hand against her side where a stitch burned deep, and then pushed the gate open and let it swing shut behind her. She twisted the spigot on the side of the shed and flung bright sparkling handfuls of water onto her face and neck. It ran into her eyes and cut uneven trails through the dust on her cheeks and neck. She straightened and looked around. She was alone but for

Spot and Bub, who stood side by side, rapt. "You two want something to look at?" she said.

She stripped off her shirt and bra and knelt below the spigot, shivering in the icy stream. She turned off the faucet and stood, untangling her hair with her fingers, her skin drying and tautening in the sunshine. She'd spent most of the last few years covered up, head always wrapped in a scarf, her hands and face the only parts of her body that ever felt the sun. She looked down at her breasts, small and pale in the unsparing light. Nipples like tender pink rose petals. She raised her arms above her head and pumped her fists and laughed at herself. Spot flung up his head. Bub barked. "Perverts," Lola said. She hurried back into her wrinkled pullover and jogged toward the house for a real shower. She was almost through the kitchen when she stopped.

Something awry.

The coral bear sat on the counter, regarding her with turquoise eyes.

The cornmeal gone.

A fact that barely had time to register before she lifted her gaze to the window and saw the corral's gate swinging a lazy rebuke. The horse was gone, too.

⟡⟡⟡

"Shit. Goddammit. Hell."

Bub appeared from someplace and flopped at her feet. "Get up," she said. "Find Spot." He swished his tail agreeably against the tiles. "You get more useless by the day. I don't know why Mary Alice kept you around."

She tried to keep her voice light in denial of her rising panic. Charlie said Spot's last escape had taken him to town. Entirely too easy to imagine Spot galloping onto the main road in a heady rush toward freedom. An oncoming hay truck. Shriek of brakes, too late, too late. Maybe, she thought in a sort of prayer, he'd remember that he'd gotten caught in town the last time he went wandering, and had decided to roam elsewhere. She wondered if horses had memories worth speaking of. The porch afforded a decent view down the two-track and she looked hard, hoping to see a spotted rump jogging along it. Nothing. The air hung heavy, smoke from the distant fire smudging the edges of her view. She turned and looked uphill toward the forest. She'd avoided venturing into the trees, unable to shake the image of Mary Alice's body lying beneath them, but on this troubling morning, in the sun's pulsing intensity, they extended a cool and green invitation.

"If I were a horse," she said to Bub, "that's where I'd go."

Before she took a single step, he'd disappeared ahead of her into the forest.

✦✦✦

THE PINES, she quickly discovered as she followed the faint trail that ushered her into them, were hardly the refuge she'd envisioned. They blocked the sun, but also any breezes, and the air beneath them was as close and smothering as a grandmother's parlor. The sun slanted through the branches in opportunistic shafts, the trail in constant transition from light to dark to light again. Lola's steps thudded hollowly against hard-packed ground. Even Bub slowed his usual frenetic dash and kept warily to her side. Lola looked into the shadowy depths surrounding her and imagined bears, cougars, even wolves. Things that could eat her. She'd gathered a few items on her way out the door—a granola bar for her, a lead rope for the horse, and the bear spray. She patted the canister banging at her hip, a new one to replace the one she'd used up on the sheriff. A magpie scolded from above.

"Shut up," Lola told it. How was she supposed to hear the horse over that racket? It shrilled louder, drawing voluble companions. Lola tried to focus on the trail, hoping to see hoofprints. "There," she said to Bub. "Look." A shrub held a few strands of long, silky hair, identical to the ones that had floated around her as she'd dragged a metal comb through the tangles in Spot's tail just an hour earlier. She put her face to them and they brushed like spider webs against her skin. She eased the hairs from the branch and wound them around her fingers. Tried not to think of Mary Alice's hair, so long and beautiful and blood-soaked. Losing the horse was just another way she'd let Mary Alice down.

The trail switchbacked up and up. Lola's legs and lungs blazed pain. She looked ahead and saw a band of light, and then the trees peeled away and the trail led out along a rocky ledge, a cliff wall rising high on one side, falling away on the other. Lola did not like heights. She stopped with the forest at her back. The trail meandered along the ledge for some fifty yards, and then went back into the woods, the inverse of a tunnel, a streak of light bookended by darkness. It was about six feet across, a comfortable width for a rambling country path, but entirely too precarious, given the three hundred foot drop. Dust motes tumbled through the air. Lola stooped and put her hand on one of the rocks underfoot. It burned. The horse wouldn't have gone there. He'd probably just wandered off the trail and deeper into the woods long before she'd ever reached this spot, Lola thought.

Unless.

She put her hands flat against the rock wall behind her and leaned forward by inches. But for a series of ledges, the side of the trail dropped straight away. The ledges were empty. She searched the landscape far, far below for the remains of a horse that had taken an unfortunate stumble. A quicksilver line of water ran along the canyon floor. Two Medicine River, she thought. Lola flattened herself against the wall, its heat suddenly comforting, and kicked a stone over the edge. It bounced off the ledges. Eventually, she heard a small final sound like a rifle crack. She looked up into a scorched sky. The horse might just as well have vanished into the vastness above as the abyss below. She turned to leave. A branch snapped nearby, much louder than the report of rock on rock just moments earlier. She heard a low, heavy breath. *Bear*, she thought. The underbrush shivered and she raised the bear spray and put her thumb on the tab and saw Bub prancing toward her, plumed tail raised high, Spot shambling behind.

She lowered the spray. "You pair of miscreants. You scared me."

The animals stopped just out of reach. Lola held out her hand and Bub ran to her and licked it. She scratched behind his ears, rubbed his stomach. "Good boy. You found him." But when she turned to Spot, he flattened his ears and took a step back. Lola eased the granola bar from her pocket and held it out. Spot made her wait. But when she raised the bar to her own mouth, he rumbled up to her in a flurry of dust and scattered pine needles. She broke the granola bar in half and balanced a piece on her palm and snapped the lead rope onto his halter as he tongued it up. She gave him the rest and tugged at the rope. Spot, apparently having made his single concession, planted his feet wide and stood unmoving. She pulled harder on the rope and he pinned his ears back again and stamped a front hoof. Lola cursed herself for having given him the whole granola bar. She cursed herself for having spent half the day chasing a stupid horse. She cursed herself for ever having come to Montana. Then she cursed herself just on general principles for a while. She let the rope go slack and came close to Spot, standing obstinate and spraddle-legged, and put her face against his neck and thought of how her newspaper was letting the news in Afghanistan go unreported and how the sheriff was letting Mary Alice's murder go unsolved, and somehow it all seemed the same.

"I know just how you feel," she said to Spot, and she thought that it was just as well the path ahead was so discouraging. Otherwise, she'd have been tempted to take horse and dog and keep moving up the mountain, deeper into the woods, where the only things that might hurt someone would do so for reasons that made sense—they were hungry, say, or protecting their cubs, or defending their territory. Spot was large and warm and reassuring and she thought that maybe she'd just stand there awhile longer, leaning on him and trying not to think about all of the things that lay ahead that she didn't understand. But Spot took one step, and another, and at some point Lola realized he was leading her back down the trail, with nothing for her to do but hang onto the rope and follow along.

⟡⟡⟡

Downhill was harder.

Lola slipped and slid on the pine needles underfoot, sometimes reaching for a tree to balance herself. The rough bark tore at her hands. Bub ran ahead and back, ahead and back, seemingly puzzled by her slow progress. Lola had long since ceased to care about bears. A fallen tree lay beside the trail, severed roots twisting high into the air. Lola looked at her watch. It was midafternoon. "Hold up," she said.

She sat on the trunk and held her pullover away from her damp skin, shaking the fabric, trying to coax cooler air beneath the hem. She vowed to abandon her long-sleeved wardrobe, at least for the remainder of her time in Montana, as soon as she got back to the cabin and raided Mary Alice's dresser for some T-shirts. Spot drowsed companionably beside her, hind leg bent, neck down, eyes half-shut. She looked at him, then at Bub, who sprawled panting across the trail. Both appeared supremely bored. Lola considered the horse again and narrowed her eyes. She wound the lead rope once around her hand and clambered up onto the tree trunk. She put her other hand onto Spot's broad back. He opened his eyes and craned his neck and looked back at her. She leaned over and raised a leg and eased herself onto his back, falling forward and wrapping her arms around his neck. Bub stood up on the trail. Lola pushed herself upright. The horse was wide and solid.

"Um," she said. "Walk?"

He nibbled at her booted foot.

Lola jiggled the lead rope.

"Giddyup?"

He lowered his head and yawned.

Lola nudged at his ribs with her heel and he rocked forward in a single step. Lola started to slide. She clutched at his mane and he paused. She balanced herself and again tapped her heel to his side. Another step, another slide, the lunge and lurch of learning to drive a stick shift. Some minutes later, Spot proceeded sedately down the trail, Lola sitting wide-eyed and erect, her hands wound in his mane. The surface of the trail felt very far away. She was at eye level with the lowest tree branches. At first she ducked beneath, stretching herself along Spot's neck, but as she became more accustomed to his swaying gait she unwound her fingers from his mane and reached up and pushed the smaller branches aside. When the trail was particularly steep, she leaned back so as to ease his progress, sitting up again and finding her balance and resting her hands on her thighs when the trail leveled off. She realized that she was enjoying herself. The cabin came into view. Spot picked up the pace. But Bub darted off the trail, nosing hard at the ground to one side. Lola twisted atop Spot to see what he was looking at. She grabbed the lead rope and pulled back on it, succeeding only in turning his head to one side and stopping his forward progress not at all.

"Stop! Whoa!" She dragged harder on the rope, jerking Spot's head nearly around to her foot. He spun a circle, once, then again, and finally stopped. Lola slid from his back, almost falling, but also making sure not to let go of the rope. She had no intention of repeating the day's ordeal. Spot hauled at the rope, trying to move downhill. Lola dug her heels into the ground and braced herself against his weight. She wasn't going to move until she'd had a chance to inspect the spot where she'd found Mary Alice.

⟡

Bᴜʙ ʟᴀʏ beside a flat rock the size of a briefcase, his head resting atop it. He neither looked at Lola as she approached, nor wagged his tail. She stood beside him. Trees in three directions, the cabin barely visible through them in the fourth. Had Mary Alice been setting out on a hike and simply run into a psychopath coming down the trail? Lola would have liked to dismiss such a scenario as needlessly dramatic, but she'd done too many stories about just such horror-movie fare. Or, maybe Mary Alice encountered her killer on her way back, hurrying down the hill so as to give herself enough time to meet Lola's plane? There was the inexplicable note. The lingering matter of her heavy jacket. Lola had gone online to check what the weather had been like in Magpie on the days leading up to her visit. The nights had been chilly, but there'd been a stretch of days in the eighties. She stood rooted awhile longer, seeking insight from the very landscape. None occurred. Spot stamped his foot and tugged again at the rope.

"I give up," Lola said. "Come on, Bub."

He whimpered and refused to move. Lola sat next to him and stroked him. She wondered if dogs felt grief. He lifted his head and keened. She figured that answered the question. "I know, buddy. I miss her, too." She lay down beside him, running her hand over his head. He rested his chin on the rock again. Lola lay her own head next to his and whispered into his ear. "Really, Bub. We have to go home." She rolled onto her stomach and looked toward the cabin. Her eyes narrowed. She sat up. Then again stretched prone.

Standing, the view of the cabin was largely screened by thick pine boughs. But the branches started several feet up the tree trunks, leaving the lower portions bare. Lying on the ground, Lola had a clear sight line to the porch. She thought and thought. She jumped up.

"She was waiting here!" she shouted. "That's why she needed the coat. She called me the night before I got here, and then she went up on this hill to wait! It was cold at night, so she wore her coat."

Her enthusiasm roused Bub from his lassitude. He and the horse turned their puzzled looks upon her, which seemed to be the expression they used most often when she was around. "No, I don't know why she was waiting. Or who she was waiting for," she told them, deciding not to think too much about the fact that she was talking to a couple of animals. "But I'll bet this trip to Calgary will help me figure it out."

CHAPTER SEVENTEEN

Lola walked out of the cafe clutching two paper sacks, and nearly collided with a man on his way in.

"Excuse me," she said, squeezing her arm to her sides so as not to drop the twin cans of Coke she'd tucked beneath an elbow. "*Oh.*"

"Miss Wicks. What a pleasant surprise." Verle lifted his hat, the sun's momentary cruelty throwing the grooves in his face into high relief. He replaced the hat, angling it forward, a wedge of shadow concealing all but his mouth. He made no move to go inside. "I thought you'd left town. I stopped by the Sleep Inn, but they said you'd checked out. Charlie must have found his man."

"No. At least, not that I know of," she said, trying to tamp down a flicker of pleasure at the news that he'd been looking for her. She fumbled for words. "Jan and I are just picking up dinner." She held up the sacks, gone shiny from the fries, without explaining why she was no longer at the motel. "She's waiting for me."

Jan sat across the parking lot at the wheel of a Subaru wagon that might once have been green before dirt and rust went to war on its surface. Joshua stood beside it, gazing off toward the mountains as Jan spoke to him. A hay truck drove past, bits of chaff swirling in its wake. The driver slowed to take the turn out of town, grinding down through the gears, making it impossible for Lola to hear what Jan and Joshua were saying. On the plus side, she thought, they couldn't hear her conversation with Verle, either.

"I'm sorry to hear that."

"That Charlie hasn't arrested anyone or that I'm having dinner with Jan?" The door opened and three men left the cafe. One dug an elbow into Verle's side as they passed. Lola watched closely for an answering grin of conquest, a chuckle of acknowledgment, but saw neither.

"That Charlie hasn't homed in on anybody yet. Not that I'm surprised. But as for dinner, it's a fact that you'd eat better if you were eating with me." A grin plowed new furrows in his face. "Sleep better, too." Jan and Joshua stopped talking. Verle didn't.

"I'm heading down to Denver with the horses for a show there. Depending on how they do, I could get some pretty good offers. Deals like that, I prefer to do in person. I might be gone a couple of days. Didn't want you to think I'd just up and disappeared on you the way you did on me."

Lola looked down the street, hoping to see another hay truck or any vehicle at all that would rend the fabric of the golden evening silence that seemed suddenly to have draped the cafe's small lot. Joshua dropped his cigarette. Small scraping noises reached Lola as he put his toe atop it and moved his foot back and forth. He walked slowly toward the cafe, gravel crunching beneath his boots.

"About that," she said hurriedly to Verle. "I didn't want to disturb you."

Verle lay a finger across her lips. "Shhh. No need to explain." He tipped his hat again, raising his voice. "Goodbye, Miss Wicks. Always nice to see you. And you, too, Miss Carpenter."

The door closed behind Joshua before she realized that Verle had never acknowledged his presence.

◇◈◇

"REMIND ME again," Lola said around a mouthful of cheeseburger, "why we couldn't sit down and eat like civilized people. It's only three hundred miles. We'll be able to get a decent night's sleep before we go find Gallagher. It's not like we'll be driving in the dark." It was six o'clock but she'd quickly learned that this far north, the sun would stay high for hours yet before dipping reluctantly below the horizon around eleven, nudging its way back into dominance before five in the morning. Jan held her burger in one hand and a can of Coke in the other, steering with her wrist as the car whipped around the hay truck they'd seen passing the cafe. Lola glanced at the speedometer and wished she hadn't.

"The sooner we get to Calgary, the better. It'll be a madhouse with the Stampede." Jan had tried to talk Lola into waiting a week to go to Calgary. "We'll never be able to get rooms. People book a year in advance because of the rodeo."

"I'm paying cash," Lola had informed her. "You'd be amazed at how a room materializes when somebody sees green. I'll spring for the gas, too, if you drive."

Jan reminded her of that now. "Here's what's left of the money you gave me. Are you still okay for cash? I gave Joshua more than he asked for. He's going to drive all the way out to Mary Alice's twice a day to look after the animals. And he knows to tell Charlie or anyone else who asks that I'm taking you camping for the weekend, trying to get your mind off things. I figured that was worth some extra money. He's trying to get his sister into a private rehab program. The job in the cafe won't cover that."

Lola squeezed the contents of a foil envelope of ketchup onto the fries in the bottom of one of the bags and held it out to Jan. "That's fine," she said. Jan had no way of knowing just how much cash she was carrying, and she had no intention of telling her. A sign announcing the turnoff to the reservation blurred past.

Jan took a single French fry and bit it in half and pointed the other half at Lola. "About this Gallagher guy we're going to see. Mary Alice must have hundreds of people's phone numbers. Why is it so important to track this one down?"

"Because of the way I found it. And because he hung up on me when I told him Mary Alice was dead."

The car slowed, though not enough for Lola's comfort, as the road wound upward through groves of low, twisted aspens. The prairie fell away behind them. Lola opened the window and let the wind take away the scent of grease. Jan turned to her, eyes round and hard as marbles. "That's it? We're driving into Calgary on the busiest weekend of the year because somebody hung up on you?"

Lola lowered the visor and studied her face in the smeared mirror there. She pulled out a lipstick she'd found in Mary Alice's medicine cabinet and stroked it across her lips, watching her mouth become a bold red stranger. "That's right," she said, wrapping those new lips carefully around the words.

Jan held out her hand for another French fry. "Do you know where he lives?"

"No."

Jan's expression softened, smugness trumping exasperation. "I don't suppose you considered the fact that it's summer, not to mention a weekend. His office will be closed."

"One would assume that," Lola murmured. She reached into her book bag and shook out a black square of silk splashed with chartreuse flowers. She folded it into a triangle and arranged it on her head and tied it to one side beneath her chin. "Unless," she said, as though talking to herself, "one had called the university pretending to be a student with an urgent need to talk to Professor Gallagher. Something about an outstanding assignment from the spring semester, the one assignment that was holding up the award of her diploma, an assignment needing only Professor Gallagher's review. And that student was so grateful to learn that she could call Professor Gallagher at his office this weekend because he always works on weekends to take advantage of the quiet." Lola dove into the book bag again and came out with a pair of black snakeskin cowboy boots inset with a thunderbird pattern of turquoise leather. They were a size seven to her own nine. "The border," she said. "How much farther?"

"About five miles."

"Slow down." Lola curled her toes and shoved a foot into one of the boots. She yanked on the sides until she felt her heel wedge improbably into place, and then went to work on the other one.

"What are you doing? Those are Mary Alice's good boots. And that's her scarf, too."

"I know. I sent it to her from Rome, the last time I had a layover there." Her face was warm with exertion. She put her hands to her cheeks, careful to keep them away from her mouth so as not to smear her lipstick. Ahead, the road peeled off in a Y, a small wooden building on the Canadian side, dwarfed by a post–9/11 concrete fortress across the way. A sign announced the border.

Jan touched her toe to the brake. Lola took out her passport. Its cover was dark red, the lettering stamped in gold: Unione Europea, Repubblica Italiana. "When we get there," Lola said, "I'm your old friend from college. I was an Italian exchange student. Where'd you go to school, anyway?"

A man leaned from the smaller building's window, waving them on.

Jan's eyes went agate again. "What the hell are you talking about?"

"No time for that now. Your school. Quick."

"University of Montana. In-state tuition and all that. Go Griz." She took her foot off the brake. "I don't understand."

The car rolled forward.

"No need. If he asks, tell him everything I just told you. Oh, and my name. It's not Lola. It's Maria. Maria diBianco."

✧✧✧

THE CANADIAN border agent had the broken-veined complexion of a man who enjoyed his liquor, and the distracted air of someone close enough to the end of his shift to anticipate that enjoyment. Good, thought Lola.

He held out his hand for their passports. "Where are we headed tonight?"

Jan's voice was a ragged wisp. "Calgary."

"Mind speaking up? All those big trucks coming through, it affects your hearing after a while." He snapped Jan's passport shut and turned to Lola's. "Remove your scarf, please." She slid it down. "Where are you going?"

"To Calgary," she sang out. "To the Stampede." She twisted in the seat, holding up a booted foot. Her toes burned.

"All the way from"—he looked at her passport again—"Italy to Calgary by way of Montana? Just for the Stampede? Why not fly straight to Calgary?"

Lola lowered her foot, kicking Jan. "*Scusi.*"

Jan's voice was barely louder than before. "We were in college together. She was an exchange student here. She's back for a visit." Her jawline was rigid. Her eyes were ghastly.

Lola leaned across Jan's trembling body. She pumped her fist. "Go Griz."

The man stooped so that his head was level with the car window and scrutinized Lola.

He put a hand to the small of his back and straightened and walked to the booth, indictment in each heavy step. Jan reached for the gearshift. Lola clamped a hand around her wrist. She wondered if they'd send her back to Charlie's jail or if she'd end up in some Canadian form of rendition. She wondered what would happen to Jan. The man came back. He looked at Lola but spoke to Jan.

"That thing on her head has got to go. They'll laugh her out of the Stampede. Make sure she gets a hat to go with those boots," he said. He handed back their passports. "Welcome to Canada."

⟡⟡⟡

"I could kill you. Should kill you."

Jan had held her breath, her face reddening dangerously, as the road unspooled downhill, the border crossing growing smaller and smaller in the rearview mirror. By the time they hit the prairie, the road running through wheat fields dotted with bobbing oil derricks, she'd let it out and sucked enough oxygen back in to fuel quite a rant. "Maybe I'll put you out right here. Let one of those meth-head roughnecks find you by the side of the road. Those guys work two-week shifts without seeing a woman. I'm sure there's an ax murderer among them who might want to turn you into kindling. But only if I don't do it first."

Lola curled toward her burning feet, trying to get a good grip on the boots. "I get the picture. You want me dead. *There.* Oh, that's better." The boots loosened with a series of jerks. Lola rubbed at the top of her feet and flexed her toes. "Ten more minutes in those boots and I'd have confessed to anything."

The car slid onto the shoulder in a hailstorm of gravel, and stopped. Lola's head snapped back against the headrest. Jan turned off the engine. Clouds of dust boiled around them and sifted to earth. The landscape reemerged. The oil rigs were larger than they looked. Lola puzzled over the way the circular motion of their gears produced the drill's monotonous bobbing. She started to ask Jan how they worked, but Jan cut her off.

"Lola. Seriously." Her voice shook. "What was that about? Do you have any idea how much trouble we could've gotten into?"

"But we didn't. Charlie won't let me leave the county, let alone the entire country. It was the only way I could think of to get to Calgary. Besides, this was nothing."

"Nothing? We could have ended up in jail."

Lola thought of border crossings that involved intricate doublespeak about bribes in currencies whose values she grasped only faintly, never sure whether she was paying tens of dollars or hundreds, abandoning mathematical calculations when the muzzle of a gun rose before her face. "Better jail than dead," she murmured.

"What was that?"

"Never mind."

Jan's head fell back. She sent a scream across the prairie. Lola leaned over and turned on the ignition. "Did you even think," Jan gasped when she was done, "about asking me?"

"Of course not. You'd have said no." Lola tapped the clock on the dashboard. "Do you mind driving while you yell at me? Because we're never going to get there at this rate." The car began to move, slowly at first, and then faster until it was hurtling along at what seemed to be Jan's default speed.

"Lesson Number One," Lola said. "Don't ask for anything. Ever. The only way to get what you need is to go after it. Just like we're doing now."

CHAPTER EIGHTEEN

Lola and Jan cut across the campus toward the law building, switching scalding lattes from hand to hand.

The sounds of the waking city eddied around them, leaking through the trees that screened the university from the streets beyond. The sun was already high, glazing Calgary's glass towers, turning the city's broad avenues into sparkling thoroughfares. Lola, who'd grown up beneath clotted skies that absorbed the exhalations of automobiles and industry and returned them as grimy, pelting raindrops, lingered at the edge of campus.

"Come on," Jan urged. "You're the one who wanted to get here early."

"You're the one who insisted on stopping for lattes. It's just that I've never seen a city this clean."

"And you'll never see a latte in Magpie. Have you already forgotten that dishwater at the cafe? Drink up while you can."

Lola tucked the fat morning newspaper she'd bought at the hotel under her arm and hurried to keep up with Jan. After days of scanning the relentless coverage of weather and livestock in the *Express*, she had without protest accepted the extraordinary penalty that involved paying for the paper with U.S. rather than Canadian currency.

"Are you sure?" the hotel clerk had asked. "You know, we have a saying up here for you people when it comes to the exchange."

Lola flipped through the paper's sections. There were many. The food section alone was bigger than the entire *Express*. "What's the saying?"

"BOHIC."

"Excuse me?"

"Bend Over. Here It Comes. That'll be five dollars."

Jan jogged ahead of her to the law school's door. Her hair, still wet from the shower, slapped at her shoulders, leaving a dark stain on her shirt. She grasped the handle and rattled it. "I knew it. It's locked. We drove all the way up here for nothing. Now what do we do?"

Lola dropped the newspaper to the sidewalk. It made a satisfying thump. "We wait. It's early yet." She folded herself onto the concrete beside the newspaper, pulled out a section, and opened it. She took a sip of her latte and licked a bit of foam from her upper lip. Jan shook the door again, then came back and stood over her. Her shadow slid across the newspaper. Lola moved it back into the sunshine and turned the pages, searching for news about Afghanistan.

"Is this the sort of thing Mary Alice would have done? Stake out a place and just wait for somebody? What was she like when she was just starting out? How long did you know her?"

Lola placed her finger on a rectangle of print that re-counted, too briefly, another suicide bombing in Kanda-har with no mention of which factions were involved. She squinted at Jan and tried not to think of a puppy, all quiver-ing eagerness mixed with the confusion of recent loss.

"Longer than you did. Try not to be so gushy when we talk to Gallagher. In fact, don't talk at all. He sounds like a hard case. He'll play you." She turned back to the newspaper so as not to see Jan's face crumple, her shoulders fold in, her arms wrap her torso. "You want to know what Mary Alice was like when she was just starting out? Tough. You need to be, too."

"She *was* tough. But she wasn't a complete and utter bitch." Jan drained her latte and flung the cup into a nearby trash can and tapped at her phone.

"Who are you calling?"

"No one."

Lola turned the page. Another story, a bit longer, about Karzai's slow slide from favor. Except that the newspaper spelled it "favour." "Then what are you doing?"

Jan ran her fingers through her drying hair. "Same thing you are. Reading the newspaper. Same one, in fact. But I didn't have to pay any five dollars for it." She held up her phone to show a miniature version of the story Lola had just read.

"Who's the bitch now?" Lola said. She scooped up the newspaper and stood.

"Indeed," someone drawled. "I'd like the answer to that one myself."

Lola looked around. She didn't see anyone. Then she looked down.

"Are you squabbling young women waiting for someone in particular? Or did our humble law school seem like a particularly good spot for a catfight?"

✧✧✧

DURING THEIR brief telephone conversation, she'd taken in the nasal, dismissive intonations, the corrosive layer of frustration that chafed at the lingering vowels, and pictured an aging product of boarding school, rangy in khakis and a pale summer sweater, someone who'd come up through Canada's version of the Ivy League and had only recently begun to accept the fact that he'd never make his way back there. Even though there'd been no photo of Gallagher on the school's website, there was no mistaking the voice. But nothing else was as she'd imagined.

Gallagher rolled closer, propelling his chair silently across the walk with arms and shoulders like hams beneath a polo shirt that draped to his knees. His legs were those of a boy, dangling uselessly in what Lola could only assume were specially tailored twill pants. Lola had been self-conscious about her height for so long that she took her own discomfort for granted. Now it wormed through her anew as she simply reached over Gallagher's head and wrestled away the door he had just unlocked. "We spoke on the phone," she said. She stuck her foot into the door. Gallagher propelled himself backward into the hallway. "I'm Mary Alice's friend."

Jan squeezed past her and bounded up to Gallagher and held out her hand. "I'm her friend, too. My name's Jan Carpenter. We haven't met. Not even on the phone."

The chair gleamed in the hushed, dark hallway. It looked new. Gallagher looked from Lola to Jan and back to Lola. "You want to talk about Johnny Running Wolf, don't you? Just like Mary Alice did."

❖❖❖

GALLAGHER HAD an electric teapot in his office, and a small refrigerator, too, and he fussed with them as Lola and Jan settled themselves into the chairs before his desk. He shook pungent leaves from a flowered metal tin into a teapot. The hot pot bubbled and sighed. He pulled a carton of milk from the refrigerator and poured some into a pitcher he took from a cupboard behind his desk, along with three cups and saucers. He doused the tea leaves with the boiling water and sat staring at the teapot as though he could see through the translucent china as dark tendrils of flavor curled through the water. His desk was polished and bare, his chair a high-backed leather affair with brass studs. He poured the tea, and then hoisted himself from one chair into the other with those meaty arms and arranged his legs straight out in front of him. "There's lemon if you prefer. And of course sugar. I myself don't use it, but you Americans seem to prefer it."

"Milk is fine," Lola said.

"I like sug . . ." Lola shook her head at Jan, who finished after a pause, "milk, too."

The teacups balanced on three curled feet atop the saucers. Lola wondered if Gallagher and Mary Alice had established a working relationship based on discussions of antique china. Gallagher slurped when he drank.

Lola waited until he swallowed. "Do you know Johnny Running Wolf well?"

"Of course. Our program for aboriginal students is quite fine. They go on to noteworthy careers. Which makes Mr. Running Wolf's outcome doubly unfortunate."

"Unfortunate? You told Mary Alice you weren't surprised that"—Lola fished the story's phrase from her memory—"he'd gone on to prominence."

"I spoke of our students in general. I did not specify Mr. Running Wolf. Mary Alice quoted me accurately. Your memory, it appears, is less than accurate."

Lola sat her cup down so hard that some tea sloshed into the saucer and tried again. "What do you mean, unfortunate? He won the gubernatorial primary. That sounds pretty fortunate to me."

Gallagher wrapped his hands around the chair's arms and flexed first one bicep then the other, swinging the chair from side to side. "Miss Wicks," he chided. "You want me to give you a story without giving anything in return. That's not how we play this game. Mary Alice learned that when she spoke to me."

"I didn't tell you I was writing a story," she retorted.

"What kind of lawyer would I be if I didn't do my research? You left your name on my voicemail. I looked you up. Of course you're doing a story. It's your nature to find out things. You're like the scorpion that stings the frog carrying it across the river. You can't help yourself. Even if it means"—he pulled a linen handkerchief from his pocket and coughed wetly into it—"you die."

Lola thought that Gallagher sounded like the one who was about to die. "What can I possibly give you?" What could Mary Alice have given him? One of her grandmother's teacups for his collection?

Gallagher lowered the handkerchief from his mouth and dropped it in his lap, drawing her unwilling gaze to his shrunken legs. "Travel is difficult for me. As you can see. But you've spent years in one of the world's most storied locations. Barbarism! Tyranny! Blood running in the streets! Give me something of that. Tell me a story in exchange for the one you want from me. Play Scheherazade to my poor King Shahryar." He lifted the teapot and held it above her cup. His knuckles were swollen, the back of his hand puffy, distended. "Yes?"

Lola calculated the tea she'd already drunk, along with the latte that preceded it, and wondered if she'd be able to get through even a short story without having to excuse herself to use the restroom.

"Tell him," Jan urged.

Lola crossed her legs. "When I went to Afghanistan the first time," she began, "you couldn't fly in. The Americans were still bombing Kabul. The border with Pakistan was closed. The only way in was through Tajikistan, overland across the border into territory still held by the Northern Alliance and then on through contested territory to get as close to Kabul as we could. We crossed the Oxus"—

"The Oxus," Gallagher sighed. "In the very footsteps of Alexander the Great."

"We floated across on a raft. There were men on the raft with grenade launchers and on the far shore, on the other side of a hill, you could hear mortars. They made a big thump when they blew. Closer by, there was a popping noise—like someone stepping on bubble wrap—and they told me it was rifle fire. It sounded innocuous, but there it was, and I wanted to ask the man to turn the raft around so I could get to shore and fire up the satellite phone and call my editor and tell him I was coming home."

"But you didn't."

"No." Lola cleared her throat. "It was sunset. It looked as though the entire horizon was on fire. But overhead, the stars were coming out. Thousands, millions of them. You could see the Milky Way. I couldn't remember the last time I'd seen so many stars. I stared at them and tried to lose myself in their light in the hopes that if I caught a bullet, the last thing I saw would be something beautiful."

Gallagher shook out his handkerchief again, examined it, and folded it back into a palm-sized square. "It's a good story. Yes. I'll tell you mine about Johnny Running Wolf."

Lola's fingers itched for a pen. She saw Jan succumb to the same impulse, reaching for her recorder, and mouthed *no*.

"His mother was aboriginal and his father, too, but when he wasn't much older than a toddler, his mother left his father and married a white man and went to live outside Chicago. Johnny got one of your good suburban educations. He went by John Wolf then. As I understand it, he went back to his real name once he left his stepfather's home. His nose is a fright—I think he said something about boxing in high school—but other than that, he was a good-looking fellow. His grades weren't perfect, but good enough for us to accept him."

"Why here?" Lola asked, breaking her own rule about interrupting a source once he started talking. "Why not Chicago? There are plenty of good law schools there."

Gallagher paused so long that she wished she'd just kept her mouth shut. "His mother was a Blood," he said finally, as if that explained everything.

Lola didn't understand, but didn't want to stop him again. She dug her fingers into her palms, as if she could capture her own words there, keep them from escaping.

Jan supplied her answer. "That's how the Blackfeet are known in Canada. Same tribe, different whitepeople name for them. The border doesn't matter to them, but I imagine it does when it comes to law schools looking to admit students, right, Dr. Gallagher?"

"That's right," Gallagher said and Lola uncurled her fingers as he went on. "We recruit widely for promising students. And he performed well once he got here. At least, at first."

"Then what?" Jan again. Lola glared at her.

Gallagher made a series of small motions, shifting in his chair. "He drank. It can be an issue with people from our First Nations. He pulled himself together for a while, enough to graduate, and to get a job in the legal department of one of our local corporations. But the last I heard, he'd started drinking again and got fired. We'd see him on the streets once in a while, cadging change. Tragic. End of story." He steepled quivering fingers beneath his chin. Lola wondered if he were ill.

"But he must have pulled himself together." She couldn't lose anything by speaking up now. "Well enough to run for governor. It's odd that Mary Alice didn't write any of that."

"Clearly he recovered, and quite well, too. Why dredge it up? It does no one any good. I'm sorry to be of no use to you." He lowered himself back into his wheelchair, forestalling further questions.

Lola and Jan followed him back into the hallway, lighted now, students drifting past, toting volumes beneath their arms, dark circles beneath their eyes. The border might have mattered in terms of who got accepted where, Lola thought, but law school's toll on its students was universal.

"My condolences on the loss of your friend," Gallagher said. He closed the office door behind him. A lock clicked.

Jan swayed backward down the hallway, bending at the waist, drawing her hand veil-like across her face and then waving her arms in an approximation of a dance, her harsh words at odds with her exotic movements.

"Tell me a story, Scheherazade. In fact, tell me this. Exactly which one of us got played here today?"

CHAPTER NINETEEN

Jan and Lola walked back across campus in a brittle silence that lasted until they stood before the coffee shop where they'd begun their morning.

Traffic streamed past in a rise and fall of purposeful sound. Jan spoke into one of the pauses. "We should leave now. Cut our losses on a wasted day."

Lola pushed open the coffee shop door. "We're not going anywhere. Two lattes," she told the clerk. "Triple shots. We're going to be up late." She put a twenty on the counter.

"Don't you have Canadian?" the barista asked. He wore a cowboy-style snap-front shirt over Hawaiian shorts, and hiking boots with no socks. Lola couldn't tell if he meant to be ironic or had just dressed in a hurry.

"I know. BOHIC. Where's your restroom?"

When she returned, Jan had taken her own latte to a corner table and left Lola's on the counter. She jingled her car keys in a warning as Lola approached. "You seem to forget I'm the one driving. You can stay here if you want. I'm going home. I'd like to salvage what's left of my weekend. Good luck getting that fake Italian chick back across the border."

Lola hooked her ankle around a chair leg and pulled it away from the table, turned it around and straddled it. "If you really meant to leave me here, you'd have gone while I was still in the bathroom. Don't bluff. You're bad at it. And we don't have time for it. We've got too much to do."

"Such as?"

"One of us—me, actually—is going to go back to the law building to spend some time in the library looking through the yearbooks for all the years Johnny Running Wolf was a student here, and the alumni bulletins for every year since he graduated. And you're going to go to the university bookstore and buy anything Gallagher's written. If he's like every other professor on the planet, he'll assign his own books to his students. Then go through them. Just look for anything that grabs your attention. Trust your instincts. If something makes you stop and look twice, it's significant. Look for his publications on the Web, too. I meant to before we left, but I didn't have time." She thumbed some bills from the rubber-banded bundle in her pocket, thought a minute, and added more. "That should take care of the BOHIC. Why don't we meet back here in, say, four hours?"

Jan set her jaw. "This is insane. The guy can't help us. He sure didn't help Mary Alice. He didn't even tell her that the guy drank."

"We don't know that Gallagher didn't tell her. She just didn't write it. Why, I don't know. I think she was saving it for a bigger story. Gallagher told us about it because he wanted us to know. He just doesn't want anything coming back on him. Which is fine with me. I'd rather have it all to myself anyway." She stood up and carried her cup to the counter.

Jan hurried behind, calling, "To ourselves, you mean. It's our story. We're working on it together. So you meant to say ourselves, right?"

"Yeah," Lola said. "Right."

❖❖❖

AN HOUR into her search, Lola had unearthed only two photos and a single paragraph in an alumni bulletin. The yearbook lay open to Johnny's formal portrait, his features behind the ruined nose sharper then, thin lips clamped defiantly against the smile—either triumphant or merely relieved—sported by so many of his fellow graduates. The other photo was the sort of candid shot used to brighten columns of dreary type about the students' accomplishments. In it, two shirtless young men leaned against one another, arms held high, fists encased in puffy boxing gloves. The pose accentuated Johnny's youthful leanness, shoulder blades like scythes, ribs defining a hairless torso. His companion looked as though he outweighed Johnny by a good fifty pounds, a pad of flesh bulging over the shiny stuff of his shorts. Beneath a beetling mustache, his upper lip was split and swollen and an unerring strike had charcoaled a half-moon beneath his left eye. The caption writer played it law-school cute: "Vince Fantonelli guilty of underestimating the strategy of Johnny Running Wolf." Six years later, the alumni bulletin reported: "Together again—Faculty of Law chums ('95) Vince Fantonelli and Johnny Running Wolf reunite at Fantonelli Transport, where Running Wolf will work in the legal division."

Lola tapped a text to Jan: "See if there's anything about a Fantonelli Transport in Gallagher's stuff." She opened her laptop to search for herself. She found the company on the first click. It had started decades earlier in Chicago as a trash hauler, moving to corner the market on carrying nuclear waste to Nevada—hence, a branch in Las Vegas—but as that field waned, the company had found a far more lucrative focus in the booming agricultural and oil markets just north of the border. Lola clicked through screen after screen of flatbeds and tankers and slatted cattle trailers that dwarfed the hard-hatted company executives standing next to them on the occasion of opening yet another new office, this one in Calgary. Lola went to the list of directors. Vince Fantonelli looked to be a man in his sixties, his face a series of layers melting into one another, brow to cheeks to chin, jowls indistinguishable from neck. There was no bio. Just a single word—founder. Lola flipped back through the yearbook to the boxers, knowing already that Johnny's sparring partner was far too young to be the man on the computer screen. They had to be father and son.

She paged back through the yearbook until she came to Vince Junior's portrait. Unlike Johnny, he beamed at the camera. Glossy dark hair waved thickly away from an assertive forehead that sat brick-like atop broad features. But when she went back to Fantonelli Transport's website, she found no mention of a Vince Junior. She typed "Vincent Fantonelli" into Google and wasn't surprised that the first entry was an obituary. Heart attack, she thought, given the excessive avoirdupois of the company's founder. Or a stroke. She wondered if Vince Junior had inherited the company. Maybe Fantonelli Transport's website just hadn't been updated with that information, she thought. She clicked on the obituary. She stared at the screen, then at the yearbook lying open in her lap. This time, the photos matched. The obituary was for Vincent Fantonelli Junior and apparently it had taken quite a bit more than a heart attack to kill him. He'd been murdered.

⟡⟡⟡

LOLA'S PHONE buzzed and buzzed in her pocket. She'd set it on vibrate the first time it rang and had ignored it ever since as she jotted notes about Vince Fantonelli—Senior and Junior both. Or, as she was learning to think of them, Big Fanny and Little Fanny. She'd groaned in belated recognition when she read about Fantonelli Transport's mob connections. Of course, she thought. Trucking. That old cover. The nicknames, hated equally by father and son, apparently had been bestowed by resentful undercover federal agents who'd spent too many hours lurking outside restaurants as they tailed Big Fanny. Now Big Fanny was sitting in a Canadian prison, no doubt growing even larger on an inmate's starchy diet while his lawyers fended off one attempt after another from the U.S.

Attorney's Office in Chicago to extradite him on extortion, racketeering, and all the other usual charges that screamed "mob." The Canadians had filed but a single charge against him—murder. In the death of his son.

Newspapers had a field day. "Mob Boss Suspected in Son's Slaying," read the *Chicago Tribune*. "Heir's Death, Founder's Arrest, Threaten Stability of Major Trucking Firm," fussed the *Calgary Herald*. Lola went to the tabloids, chuckling over headlines that inevitably spanked Big Fanny or sent him off to the Big House. Which was nothing compared to the frenzy they'd gone into over his son's death.

It started with a body in a Calgary alley, its sharp suit all the more notable because the parts that would usually have protruded from its fine-weave worsted—namely hands and feet—were gone entirely, lopped off at the hemlines. Its head mercifully remained, albeit as a shapeless mass, crushed by repeated blows from a brick, the whole gelatinous mass embedded with bits of reddish, crumbly stuff, like sand in a jellyfish. One tabloid ran a full-page photo of the nattily clad torso with an arch headline. "Do You Know This Suit?" The sartorial remnants had survived more intact than the body within. And indeed, somebody did know it, a Chinatown tailor whose wizened features and mangled English were the stuff of central casting—or at least, were made to seem that way—as he described the day Little Fanny came into his shop and special-ordered the fabric from London, demanding a dandyish nipped-in waist and snug-fitting pants. The tailor had held an impromptu news conference. Videos abounded on YouTube.

"Mr. Fanny, he dress left," the man said with a sly smile, his hands sketching a substantial bulge. Lola imagined too well the delight of the assembled reporters and cameramen, to whom the only possible thing better than a handless, footless, faceless corpse was a handless, footless, faceless, well-hung corpse.

Authorities made short work of arresting Big Fanny once the body had been identified. His difficulties with his son, who'd caused the family no end of trouble by an inexplicable push into routes commandeered by Mexican cartels, had been an open secret for years. Little Fanny was banished to Calgary at the turn of the millennium to run the company's branch there, with the added insult that he was to confine his activities to the legitimate end of things. His gruesome end indicated he hadn't. Different newspapers quoted various unnamed law enforcement sources saying that shortly before his death, Little Fanny had tipped off a go-between that his father had put out a hit on him, and that he was ready to talk. But Big Fanny had proved quicker than the Mounties. The Canadians kept the whole fiasco quiet until after Little Fanny's funeral, waiting politely until the cortege of limos delivered Big Fanny to the Calgary airport for his return flight to Chicago before whisking him—as much as someone Big Fanny's size could be whisked—away from the boarding area in handcuffs.

Lola went back once again to the company's website. She tried using the search field, and then viewed pages individually, unsuccessfully seeking mention of Johnny Running Wolf. She wondered when, and how, he'd eased out of the job with Fantonelli Transport after the hit on Little Fanny. If maybe he'd been the one who turned on his friend, passed damning information to Big Fanny about his son's wayward loyalties. She paged through her notes, looking for more particular connections and saw none. She threw down the pen. It took a hop and caromed off the wall, leaving a mark. Lola flexed her fingers. The woman at the front desk glared her way. The library's door burst open.

"I've been calling and calling." Jan's voice rang aggrieved across the room. Students, earbud cords snaking across their work, stayed focused.

"Wait until you see what I've got," Lola began.

"No. You wait and see what *I've* got." Jan stood just inside the door, refusing to move in Lola's direction.

"Wait until you see what happens if this continues one minute more," the librarian snapped. "Both of you. Out."

◇◇◇

JAN GRABBED Lola's hand with steel fingers. "Let's hope he's still there," she said, tugging her down the hall. Lola tried to shake her off, then broke into a lurching run behind her.

"Who?"

"Gallagher. You're right. He wasn't telling us everything. And with good reason." Jan let go when they reached the stairs, taking them two at a time, her steps echoing off the walls. Lola caught up with her at Gallagher's office door, bending to catch her breath as Jan pounded the heel of her hand against it.

"He's gone," Lola said. "What was so important?"

Jan blew on her reddened palm, then held it out to Lola. "His hand. Did you see his hand?"

Lola had, in fact, paid particular attention to Gallagher's hands, guiltily so, knowing it to be a way of avoiding looking at his legs. "He'd hurt it," she said immediately. "It was all swollen and scraped. I thought maybe he'd fallen."

"He had," Jan crowed. She held out her phone so that Lola could see the story there from the *Calgary Herald* about the attack on the esteemed Professor Gallagher. The call to police had come shortly after midnight. When they arrived, Gallagher lay in his bathrobe just inside his smashed front door beside the broken remains of his wheelchair, blood curling from the corners of his mouth. But for the defensive wounds to his hands, his injuries were all internal, ribs broken, kidneys bruised. One man, he'd told police. Masked. Silent, but for the grunt that accompanied each blow. No, he had no idea why someone would do that to him. None. He was adamant.

"Look at the date," Jan commanded.

"June fifteenth." Lola counted back. "About ten days ago. Mary Alice was still alive then."

"That's right. She wrote this a day earlier." Another story flashed on the screen. Mary Alice's profile of Johnny Running Wolf. "I think that's why he got beaten up. And maybe why Mary Alice got killed. I'll bet whoever killed her knew they'd talked. Gallagher wasn't playing us. He's just scared to death. No way he could risk telling us directly whatever he told Mary Alice."

Lola put her hand to the locked office door. "No wonder he hung up on me."

◇◇◇

"AT LEAST we're going the right way," Jan said as she drove southbound through Calgary. The northbound lanes were clogged with traffic. She stopped at a light. "Everybody's heading into town for the rodeo. Except for those guys." She jerked her thumb at a pair of cowboys emerging from a bar. "They must have been cut early."

The men headed down the sidewalk, swaggery in their boots. Lola's eyes went to the W stitched atop their back pockets, to the whitened circle worn into each right pocket by the container of chew within. "Pull over," she told Jan.

"What for?"

But Lola was already out of the car, calling to the men, holding up her phone. "Mind if I take a picture?"

"You're embarrassing us," Jan hissed from the car. "These guys aren't some sort of tourist attraction. Those aren't costumes. Rodeo is how they pay the bills."

The men stopped, uncertain. Lola snapped a couple of pictures and handed the phone to Jan. "Can you take one of all of us?" She turned to the men. "We don't have cowboys where I'm from." She wrapped her arms around waists that felt like steel bands beneath shirts smelling of starch and sweat. The men grinned obligingly.

"Cheese!" said Lola.

⟡⟡⟡

LOLA DOZED as the car sped back toward the border, awaiting with resignation the images behind her eyelids, Mary Alice on the ground and awake, her mouth moving in a soundless question, the motion tugging at the hole in her cheek. It winked redly at Lola. She turned her face away but Mary Alice's hand flew up and wrapped the soft flesh of her upper arm, fingernails digging through the fabric of her pullover, calling to her. "Lola. Lola."

"Oh, Mary Alice. I'm so sorry," she murmured, and then her head cracked against the window and she opened her eyes.

Jan let go of her arm. Her voice was small and scared. "We're at the border. What do we do now? Tell me, Lola. I mean, Maria. What do we do?"

"Shhh," Lola murmured. "I'm trying to sleep." She slumped back against the headrest. The guard approached with heavy, purposeful footsteps. "Passports." He raised his voice. "Yours, too. Miss. Your passport."

Lola yawned and stretched her arms above her head, opening her eyes by degrees. She handed her passport to Jan, who gave it to the guard without looking at her. As he thumbed through it, Lola leaned across Jan and held her phone to the window. "Smile!"

"What do you think you're doing?" The guard grabbed the phone from her hand. Her passport slapped against the ground. "Photographs are absolutely not allowed. How do you delete . . . okay, I've got it." His big hands worked at the phone. "There. Oh. *Oh.*" He chuckled and his expression, when he turned back to the car, had changed entirely. "Enjoyed ourselves at the Stampede, did we?" He held up the

~ 197 ~

phone, flicking through the photos of Lola and the cowboys. "I'd say we have ourselves the makings of a buckle bunny."

Jan shrugged and smiled and flipped her hair around. "You'll have to excuse my friend. It was her first rodeo."

He snapped the phone shut and retrieved Lola's passport from the ground and handed both back to Jan. "I can see that. You drive carefully. It's getting late and you've still got a ways to go. Welcome home."

✧✧✧

"WAIT," LOLA commanded. She slitted her eyes and watched the customs station recede in the side mirror.

"Wait," she said. The car rounded a curve. She sat up.

Jan turned to her. "Now?"

"Wait." Another bend in the road. The bobbing oil derricks were behind them. They were back in cattle country. A mile rolled by. Another.

"Okay. Now."

Jan steered to the side of the road. Stopped. She and Lola looked at each other. They flung open the doors. Ran circles around the car. Whooped. High-fived as they passed one another. Slapped at the hood, the doors, the rear window. Cattle wheeled and scattered, tails kinked high. Meadowlarks exploded like shrapnel from the high grasses.

"We did it," Jan gasped. "We made it."

"You." Lola jabbed an index finger at her. "You did it. You were right there with me."

"God," said Jan. She was upright, standing tiptoe in triumph, and then she was down, cross-legged in the dirt beside the car, head in her hands, shaking. "Tell me this isn't par for the course. I thought for sure you'd blown it when you took his picture."

"Diversionary tactic. The picture became the issue, not my passport. Same thing with the scarf on the way over. It distracted him."

Jan raised her head. "I don't think I'm cut out for this."

Lola stood above her. "For what it's worth, I've never done anything quite like that. Maria's my emergency backup. I've never had to use her before. Mary Alice getting killed, though. That seemed like an emergency." The cattle wandered back, curious. "And it worked. It got us across the border, got us to Gallagher. And to Fantonelli. I don't know what it means yet, but I'll figure it out."

"You?"

"We. I meant we."

Before Lola could react, Jan was back in the car, engine running, windows rolled up, and doors pointedly locked. She lowered her own window an inch. "You didn't mean any such thing. You just used me to get across the border. You didn't even need to do the whole Maria thing. You could have sent me up to Calgary alone to talk to Gallagher and do the research in the library. You just didn't trust me. Either that, or you want it all to yourself. I don't know which is worse."

Lola considered the fact that during the long minutes the car had been stopped beside the road, not a single vehicle, not even one of those ubiquitous hay trucks, had passed. She looked to the darkening east, turned to the west, where the sun wobbled atop the mountains. The cattle were dwarfed by their own immense shadows. The wind coolly explored the back of her neck, still a caress at this point. Soon it would feel more like a slap.

When Lola had first met Jan, she'd taken her for one of those perfectly nice young women who drifted into journalism, frequently from an English major, and who lingered there awhile, maintaining their girlish softness on a diet of sugary feature stories, until they married a fellow reporter whose surface cockiness masked an insecurity that preferred a woman not quite as talented as he. The women, wives now, would disappear into the world of babies and freelancing and the wistful line that accompanied introductions at parties: "I used to be a reporter."

But something smoldered beneath Jan's deceptive earnestness. It lit up her features when she'd discovered the news about Gallagher, propelled her confident flirtation with the border guard, and flared in her eyes now as she issued her ultimatum to Lola. Lola knew she should just say something agreeable, defuse the situation so they could be on their way. The wind shouldered past. "I don't trust people in general," she said. "That's how you make mistakes."

She thought that would probably piss Jan off. Instead, Jan nodded thoughtfully. "You may have a point. For instance, you trusted me to get you into Canada and back. Which I did. But maybe you shouldn't have trusted me to get you all the way back home. That may have been a mistake."

The wind took another whack at Lola. She was tired. She was cold. She wanted to go home. Which, it jolted her to realize, meant the cabin. She thought of the woodstove's steady glow, the dog curled at her side on the commodious sofa, sprawled on his back, his feet pawing the air in doggy dreams, a spectacle so ridiculous and tender it always made Lola laugh—but quietly, quietly, so as not to wake him.

"Fine," she said. "A real partnership."

The window hummed lower. Jan held her hand out. "Wanna spit and shake?" And spent the next five miles protesting to Lola that she'd been joking, she really had.

CHAPTER TWENTY

Joshua had left the cabin unlocked.

Of course, thought Lola, shaking her head. She turned the handle. The door scraped across the floor, shoving things aside. Lola froze. Something flew through the opening, whomped her in the gut. She fell backward onto the porch, hands automatically cradling her head. Bub's cold nose shoved them aside. His tongue bathed her face. He barked in her ear. Lola lay still until her heart resumed something resembling a normal, if galloping, rhythm. Then she pushed herself up to see what had happened inside.

It wasn't as bad as the night she'd found Mary Alice. But it was close, so close that she'd reached for the phone, ready to call 9-1-1, when she realized the dog had vanished. Fright turned to suspicion as she scanned the disarray. A Tupperware container lay on its side, empty but for the crusted remnants of her attempt at a spaghetti-and-meatballs meal. She turned toward the refrigerator. The door stood open, Bub nearly disappearing into the interior, balancing on his back paws, front legs scrabbling for what remained of its pathetic contents. The refrigerator door swung wide, the newly tattered dishtowel fluttering from its handle. Lola's eyes narrowed. She reached for the door and closed it, Bub standing his ground until the last possible moment, growling as the door's rubber gasket pinched him against the frame. He shimmied away and cast a resentful glance at Lola. Then he braced his legs and sank his teeth in the dishtowel and tugged until the door gave way, diving once again into the chilly interior before Lola hoisted him bodily and tossed him behind her. She shut the refrigerator, this time removing what was left of the towel.

"Do you have any idea what a pain in the ass you are?" She righted the chairs. "I'll bet you were cute as a puppy." She picked up the salt and pepper shakers and replaced them on the table, wadded up the lone placemat and napkin and tossed them in the general direction of the washing machine. "That's probably why Mary Alice got you. She took one look at that blue eye and fell for you." She lifted the Tupperware container, noted the teeth marks, and threw it in the trash. She looked awhile for the lid and gave up. "She didn't know you'd grow up to be a devil dog." She worked the floor over with a broom, then a mop, Bub watching intently from the living room doorway. As soon as she was done, the floor gleaming damp and clean, he danced across it, trailing paw prints. Lola hoisted herself onto the counter and swung her legs above the wet floor. She picked up the grizzly bear fetish and tossed it from hand to hand while she spoke, feeling the stone warm against her palms. "I could bean you with this thing right now. I had a seventy mile-per-hour fastpitch in college. If I bounced this off your head, you'd be done for."

The dog leapt from the floor onto one of the chairs. He turned his head, fixing her with that blue eye and, before she'd divined his attempt, flew through the space between them, landing on the square foot of bare counter beside her. He climbed into her lap and curled himself against her and closed his eyes and sighed, deep and contented. Lola's hand dropped to his neck, slid to his back. She stroked him mindlessly, trying to sort out the puzzle posed by Johnny Running Wolf's association with Vince Fantonelli.

✧✧✧

THE NEXT morning, she reminded Bub that he wasn't the only one needing attention. She thought of the instructions she'd

Googled a few days earlier. People rode horses all the time. For fun, or so she'd been given to understand. She went into the shed and located the bridle, hanging on its hook. Its wide leather straps and nickel hardware felt heavy, substantial. She held it up and studied it awhile, matching parts with her memory of the drawings on the Internet. She looped the reins over her arm and let herself into the corral, making sure to latch the gate securely. Her feet sank into the soft dirt. Spot raised his head. She held the bridle's hinged bit in her hand to warm it, then nudged it against his teeth, surprised when he actually opened his mouth and let it slip in. She arranged the headstall behind his ears and fastened the throatlatch, sliding two fingers between it and the soft loose skin behind his jaw to make sure of a comfortable fit, and then undid the halter completely and slipped it out from under the bridle. She hung the halter on a fencepost and tied the bridle's reins around the top rail and went back for the saddle and a fleece blanket. She hefted them together. The saddle horn dug between her breasts. She approached the horse from the left, the way the Internet instructed—but why? She'd wasted a good ten minutes trying to ascertain the answer, to no avail—and hoisted the saddle high. The far stirrup swung and caught the horse in the ribs, and he shied away and the saddle came down onto thin air, dragging Lola with it. It hit the dirt and her face hit the seat and she realized she'd done a wholly inadequate job of dusting it. She sneezed and slid the blanket from beneath the saddle, and walked to the far side of the corral and shook it out so as not to further spook Spot; then came back and arranged the blanket on his back, smoothing it away from the bump where his neck met his back. "Withers," she'd learned the spot was called.

She lifted the saddle again, this time hooking the stirrups and the cinch to the horn, and got it onto his back and unhooked everything without giving offense. The cinch, soft and ropy, dangled almost to the dirt. She eyed Spot's hooves, but his feet stayed planted while she caught at the swaying cinch and then tried three times before catching and buckling it. She stepped to Spot's head, stroked his nose and waited. Bub crept close. Lola waited. Bub whined. Spot let out his breath with a long, resigned sigh and Lola yanked at the cinch and buckled it tighter, taking up the slack. He'd filled his belly with air when she plopped the saddle down, and had she ignored the instructions to tighten the cinch after a few minutes, the saddle would have slid sideways and she'd have gone into the dirt. Or so Google had told her.

Lola congratulated herself.

Too soon. A moment later, she lifted her foot toward the wooden stirrup, its instep rubbed shiny by Mary Alice's boot. Just as she was about to slide her toe into it, Spot sidled a half-step away. Lola came down hard, falling against him. She lifted her foot again, with the same result. She edged him against the fence, but when her foot left the ground, he took a step forward, all the while maintaining an alert, interested look as though watching something happening over which he had no control.

Lola thought back, but could not remember the instructions covering this particular development. Spot yawned. Lola moved fast, but he moved faster, just a last-minute half-step, one that, due to her momentum, sent her sprawling onto hands and knees, staring at his cinched belly. She remembered how she'd fallen across him up on the mountain, somehow managing to stay on even as he moved forward. She grasped the horn with both hands, bent her knees and crouched so low that her head brushed the bottom of the stirrup. Then she tensed her calves and pogoed upward, using the horn to leverage herself high, ignoring the stirrup entirely, falling once again across his back, grateful for the saddle and all of its strange protrusions, loosing one hand from the horn and grabbing at the leather strings—"latigos! latigos!" she grunted—somehow getting a leg over, even as Spot stepped and turned and moved about on the short tether of the reins, agreeable look long gone, ears laid tight against his head.

Lola fitted her wide hiking boots, barely, into the stirrups. She reached and stroked Spot's neck, babbling soothing nonsense until he stilled and his ears, those barometers of intent, stood upright again. She gathered up the reins and wound them around one hand, keeping a death grip on the saddle horn with the other. She took a breath and flexed her calves. Nothing. She flexed again and squeezed her knees against his sides and he stepped out, sedate as a granny out for an after-church stroll, as though there were nothing more he wanted to do than walk slow, crooked circles around the corral.

⟡

WHICH WAS all she did that first hour, trying to get the hang of steering—"No," she reminded herself. "Reining"—laying the leather against his neck with varying degrees of firmness, astounded every time at the immediacy of his response, from a long looping turn when she touched the reins low on his neck, to a spin that unseated her when she put them high and hard just inches behind his ears. It was the first of a half-dozen falls that day, and the only thing she could say about those was that she greatly improved her skill at getting back onto him, so that he finally abandoned his antics and stood resignedly as Lola—with increasing stiffness—hauled herself back aboard in preparation for her next fall. The more comfortable she got with the horse, working her way up to a jolting trot, the more he tested her. But gently, gently, and with great equanimity, though always just a little beyond the limits of her ability, forcing her to push herself. Next thing, she thought, as she lifted the reins and touched her heel to his flank, he'd probably try to buck her off.

And so he did, giving an obliging crow-hop, arching his back and then kicking out both back hooves, adding some velocity as she left the saddle, a little outside herself so that she could almost see the perfect backflip described by her body, jackknifing in the memory of some childhood dive, her timing all wrong because she slammed shoulders-first onto the ground, its surface suddenly rock-hard. Then she was back inside herself, gasping, turning her head away as the horse's nose swam close, outsize and distorted. She shut her eyes and tried to catch her breath, knowing that with oxygen would come pain.

She tried her voice—"Always get right back on"—but didn't like the sound of that. Not one bit. She looked up at the stirrup. It seemed very far away, the horse's back farther still. She wanted to lie back down in the dirt. She wanted to drag herself into the cabin and go to bed. She wanted to hobble to Mary Alice's truck and start it up and drive to the airport. She wanted to take enough sleeping pills to get her through the subsequent flights to Kabul, and then she wanted to find a fixer who would take her back to the border highlands where the people she met would be straightforward in their hatred and open about their reasons for shooting people and leaving their corpses staring open-eyed on rocky hillsides. She wanted to understand things again. She didn't understand anything in this new place and at that very moment, the main thing she didn't understand was why she had to get back on that goddamned horse.

"Come here," she said to him, and when he stepped closer, she grabbed a fistful of his mane and used it to pull herself to her feet, and then she hitched along his side until she came to the stirrup and raised her foot and jammed it in, the horse standing frozen as she worked her way crablike onto his back. She wished, achingly, for Mary Alice; wanted to see her lean against the corral fence, shake all of that blond hair out of her face and say, "Well, I'll be damned, Bub-ette. You did it. Surprised yourself, didn't you? Now what?"

Now what, indeed. Lola took the reins and latched onto the horn in preparation for a repeat performance, but the horse apparently had had enough because he moved serenely forward. They made a final circuit of the corral, Lola nudging him into a brief trot and even—breathlessly, both hands wrapped around the horn—a few steps of a slow, rocking canter. Spot slowed of his own accord. Lola sighed, wishing, almost, that she'd fall again, knock herself completely senseless, anything to get her past the fact that despite all the progress it felt as though she'd made, she wasn't one bit closer to figuring out what had happened to Mary Alice.

✧✧✧

SHE LAY that night in a tub full of water as hot as she could bear it, every so often lifting a blister-pink limb free of the cloud of steam that hung above the water, inspecting the bruises blooming yellow and purple along her skin. The color reminded her of the dead boy she'd seen in the trailer. She wondered briefly about Joshua's sister and then sank into the water again and groaned, so exhausted and sore that when the phone rang it took her three rings to answer it.

She looked at the clock. It was eleven. She wrapped a towel tight around herself and put her ear to the phone and braced for some sort of threat. The voice on the other end was anything but furtive, spilling from the receiver and filling the room. Bub growled.

"Wicks! Bet you'd forgotten all about me. Hope I didn't wake you."

"Sanchez. It's"—she calculated—"one in the morning there. What are you doing up?"

"I'm back on nights. This spoon you sent me. Pretty good prints, actually. Nice job."

Lola put her hand to Bub's muzzle and lowered herself onto the sofa. "Shut up."

"What?"

"Nothing. Sanchez, please. Was there a match? What did he do? Kill somebody? Any record of him buying a rifle? An M-16, maybe? Or an AR-15? That's the civilian version, right?"

"Hold up, hold up. Who are we talking about here?"

"Johnny Running Wolf. He was tight with Little Fanny Fantonelli—Vince Junior. I think maybe he took out Mary Alice. Arranged it so it would happen while he was in Denver."

The night's stillness closed in, a dark wave of silence flowing toward her, breaking against the yellow island of light cast by the lamp. Lola fell onto the sofa and reached out her hand as though to push it away, afraid that somehow the phone had gone dead, that Sanchez had vanished into it, along with the answers she so badly needed.

"That may well be," he said. Her heart thudded. "But here's another scenario."

The towel fell away as Lola bounded to her feet, breathing hard, head spinning, reaching for something, anything in what Sanchez was saying that she could catch and hang onto, to help her make sense of the impossibility he had just described.

They spoke a few moments more. She hung up the phone and stared into space. Then she dialed again. "Charlie?" Once again, she held the phone away from her ear. "Yes, I know what time you start work in the morning. I'm sorry. I wouldn't be calling if it weren't really important. I need you to meet me at the cafe tomorrow. Bring your cuffs."

Bub lifted his ears at the renewed blast from the phone. Lola waited until the sheriff finished. "I've figured some things out," she said, and treated him to a sample. "There's more. Please trust me on this one." Her smile lingered even after Charlie hung up on her.

"That's the problem," he'd said before he'd clicked his phone off. "God help me, I do trust you."

CHAPTER TWENTY-ONE

Lola's fingertips tattooed the Formica tabletop.

The salt and pepper shakers rattled against the ketchup bottle. Except for the blur of fingers, she was motionless, eyes fixed on a space beyond the cafe window. Smoke over the mountains boiled up black. Helicopters buzzed the perimeter, giant canvas buckets swaying like dancers beneath them. Joshua and his coffeepot walked into her field of vision.

"How's your sister?"

"In rehab," he said in his characteristic whisper. "Finally. She doesn't know about Frank yet. It's going to kill her when she finds out what those so-called friends of hers did to him."

Lola tried to look as though she were paying attention. She pressed her hand against her shirt cuff, her fingers tracing the reassuring outline of Jan's digital tape recorder inside her sleeve. She'd stopped on her way to the cafe to borrow it, saying she wanted to dictate some notes for the story, and then practiced with it in the car, draping her arm casually over the wheel and reading aloud from the newspaper. Even when she'd lowered her voice, the recorder picked up the words, muffled but still intelligible. She wanted everything documented, for the story's sake, and for Charlie's, too, although she had a feeling he might not approve. She lifted her cup for a refill and looked at the clock.

11:53.

She'd asked Johnny to meet her at noon. Charlie would join them at 12:30. "He'll spook if he sees us together when he walks in," she'd insisted, and the sheriff had finally agreed. The room's sounds came separately. The racket of cutlery on porcelain. Ice cubes crashing against one another in tall water glasses. Lola was back on the battlefield, as on edge in this cafe as in a highlands gully awaiting the opening rattle of rifle fire, focused, ready. As prepared as she ever could be for the moment when all hell broke loose and preparation counted for shit.

11:56.

The door opened. Lola's hand jerked and a wave of coffee broke over the lip of her cup and shuddered into a puddle. Joshua's rag flicked. A rancher walked past, earth flaking from his boots in a trail across the floor. "You bunch of do-nothings. What are you doing sitting on your behinds in the middle of the day while I'm out making an honest living?" Chairs scraped to accommodate the newcomer. Lola held out her mug again.

11:58.

When the door opened again, she didn't look up, not until he slid into the chair across from her. She'd forgotten how big he was, the way he filled the space between her and the rest of the room. She launched the smile she'd practiced. "Johnny," she said. The first time she'd called him by name.

His hair shone blue-black in the dust-filtered light. "At your service, ma'am. One of those big cinnamon buns," he told Joshua. "Warm it a little if that's not too much trouble. I suddenly find myself with a powerful appetite."

Lola had spent a fair amount of time in front of the mirror working on her smile, and it held. "It's good to see you."

"To what do I owe the pleasure?" he asked. "Or is this business?" His standard opening, but probing, too, just the way he'd done on the phone when she'd called early that morning to set up the meeting. "I'm in the middle of a campaign here," he reminded her now. "I'm supposed to be over in East Bumfuck talking to the Elks. I had to cancel. Riley chewed my ass."

Joshua arrived, bearing the cinnamon bun as though offering something precious. It glowed warm and golden, crystalled with frosting, nearly filling a plate.

"Do you actually intend to eat all of that?" Lola asked, her astonishment unrehearsed.

"Two forks," Johnny said to Joshua.

Lola shook her head. "I'll have the fruit cup." She said nothing else until it arrived.

Usually she enjoyed this part, watching them fidget through the silence. On her best days, they broke it first, sometimes blurting what she wanted to hear before she even had a chance to ask. Not Johnny. He stayed where he was, rocking a little on the back-tilted legs of the chair, leveling a steady half-smile at her. She was, she reminded herself, dealing with a pro.

She wondered if Mary Alice had likewise confronted Johnny, confident that she'd gotten the goods, bracing herself for anger made more dangerous by fear of exposure. Mary Alice would have been smart enough to have had that confrontation in public, too, knowing that people—no matter how angry or afraid or embarrassed—generally don't want those emotions on display for the world. It was an old safety measure and a good one, given that once they cooled down, the subjects of such interviews usually didn't summon someone with a high-powered rifle and dead aim.

Lola chased her fruit around in its syrup, peach slices swimming like goldfish among the pale, peeled grapes, the scarlet surprise of the occasional maraschino cherry. She lifted the paper napkin to her lips and put it back down, brushing her thumb against her wrist to activate the recorder. She looked at the clock—12:10—and raised her eyes to his; noted for the first time the contacts sliding dark across the irises. "I just couldn't get over Calgary."

Johnny attacked the cinnamon bun. "What about it?" he said around a mouthful that filled his cheeks.

Lola speared one of the sickly grapes. "Your having gone to school there. With Vince Fantonelli."

"Damn. I haven't thought about Vince in years. Shame about what happened to him. But school—those were the days. We had ourselves some good times." He threw his head back and laughed, showing that pale throat beneath the cured-hide tan of his face.

12:18.

The cinnamon bun was half-gone.

Johnny moved the plate toward her. "You've got to have some of this. Nell's are the best. But you've been hanging around here long enough to know that. Isn't it about time for you to go?"

Lola pushed the plate away. "And then, going to work with Vince. Getting all tangled up in the mob."

"My job for Fantonelli Transport was hardly, as you put it, all tangled up in the mob. I was just another lawyer with a good-paying employer. Last I heard, everybody has a right to legal representation," he said. He dragged his fork across the plate, icing piling up against it like drifts on a snowplow blade.

"Nice that your father put you on the payroll. How much did you get under the table?" She picked up her bowl and put it to her mouth, tipped it and drained the fruit syrup in a long swallow.

12:28.

"My father?"

A final piece of cinnamon bun sat lonely on the big plate.

"Last chance," Johnny said.

"All yours."

He ate it, taking his time, swallowing before speaking. "My father. I never knew him. Do you mean my stepdad? He was a pharmacist. I never worked for him, though."

Lola leaned in, savoring the physical sensation of the moment, the withheld knowledge humming within her like a strikeout pitch, gathering force with the windup: "I mean your father. Vince Senior. Big Fanny."

"What the hell are you talking about?"

Sweet, sure release, the ball hanging high and lovely before dropping into the inevitable curve below the slicing bat.

It was 12:30.

"Oh, come on, Little Fanny. How long did you think you'd get away with playing Indian?"

✧✧✧

THE BACKGROUND noises rushed back in, loud enough to drown out the sound of the opening front door. If it had opened. Which it apparently had not, no collective turning of heads to see who could be enticed to sit down, share a cup of coffee, jaw about the wildfires and wheat prices and the inexplicable bumper crop of bodies.

"I have to admit," Lola continued, talking fast now, needing to keep Johnny there until the sheriff showed up, "it's impressive. The hair—dyed *and* conked. The spray tan. I found all the boxes in the bathroom trash can at your—Johnny's—grandmother's place. That's a lot of work. Time-consuming." She looked at the top of his head, the white slash of the part, the hair drawn tight into the braids on either side. "How often do you have to touch up those roots?"

He reached across the table, picked up her coffee cup. Put his nose to it. "Funny," he said. "I don't smell anything. What'd you spike this with, vodka?"

Lola squeezed her next question past the anger fighting to escape. "What I can't figure out is the nose. How'd you do it?"

He hung onto her cup, took another ostentatious whiff. "With your permission," he said, and drank from it. He shook his head. "Well, I'll be damned. It's clean. Did you start your morning with a snort? Because what you're saying, that's crazy talk."

Lola let herself look toward the door. No one there. The only thing to do at this point was keep firing questions, one fastball after another, watching as he deflected them into foul territory, knowing sooner rather than later would come the big swing and the miss. "Did you get somebody to hit you? Or did you do it yourself?" She shivered, pantomiming agony. "Must have hurt like hell."

"Funny," he said. "You talking about the Fantonellis. It was Little Fanny who hit me, back in law school. He'd boxed some, but wanted to get better, so we got into it one day, just fooling around, and he landed one right on my nose." He shook his head, his face going soft and fond.

"What about Frank's pony?"

"What about it?"

She'd hoped to do this part with Charlie sitting beside her, but she was too deep into the game. He'd just have to bat cleanup. "Johnny broke his nose riding Frank's pony. Back when they were little kids. Guess he never told you that, did he, Little Fanny?"

"Quit calling me that."

"You quit. It's over. I ran your prints."

The skin around his eyes tightened. A muscle jumped in his jaw. "You're bluffing," he said, and she knew for sure.

"It's all there," she said. "The prints. Your record. How long after you'd arrived on the rez before you started running drugs again? Couldn't help yourself, could you? It's what you know. The campaign, though. I've got to give you credit for using it to launder your money. The tribe was suspicious, you know. Or at least some people were. Showing up the way you did, saying you'd forgotten all their traditions because you'd lived so long with white people." She was beyond bluff now, spreading it out for him, thinking as she spoke how she'd finally found her way to him, the hints from Mary Alice's stories and the sheriff and Wilson and Gallagher scattered like crumbs along a Hansel and Gretel trail. And she'd been the one to scoop them up. "Know what else gave you away?"

"Do tell." Voice like sandpaper.

"Going into tipis. Lodges, I guess they're called. See, I didn't know that before I came out here. You didn't either. And I'd probably turn right, too, if I ever went into one."

He shrugged. "So?"

"Wilson told me people always turn left."

"I'd been away a long time."

"Even little kids know that. Everybody does it, so it's more like instinct. I figured you can change everything else— you can undo that hard-squeeze whiteman handshake, you can stop looking people right in the eye in a way that would be rude, you can lower the decibel level when you talk— but that thing about turning left, that's so little and insignificant no white person would ever notice it, so there's no need to change it. Except that you never changed it because you'd never learned it in the first place. Mary Alice figured it out. She was just about to bust you. Wasn't she, Little Fanny? That's why you had her killed. Who'd you get to do it? Frank? Or did he just happen to come upon her after the fact?"

Sometimes the fight just went out of them. Maybe it didn't even matter that Charlie wasn't there to snap the cuffs onto his wrists and haul his sorry ass off to jail. Lola could probably offer Johnny a ride over to the sheriff's office and he'd come along, glad it was finally over. He had to be weary of this witness protection program of his own design.

"I don't know what Mary Alice was going to do," he said, and his tone was all wrong, no defeat in it. "But I know this. It's nothing but one big load of horseshit. There's no story. Wasn't then and isn't now."

"Oh, there will be," she said. "I can promise you that. But that's the least of your worries. If your father finds out you're here—and he will when the story runs—then it won't matter what color contacts you're wearing. Federal prison won't stop Big Fanny from putting out that hit again, and this time, he'll make sure it's done right."

He shifted in his seat and Lola knew she didn't have much time.

"Did you kill him yourself? Johnny, I mean. Track him down at a homeless shelter, give him some good clothes, lure him into an alley, something like that? Must've hurt, to waste one of your pretty suits that way."

She knew she was talking too loud, and still her voice rose.

"How'd Mary Alice find out? And why'd you have to kill her? Why didn't you just take off again, like you did from Calgary? You'd be gone and she'd still be alive."

Joshua had come over to their table and stood rooted with his coffeepot.

"You've got it all wrong," Johnny said. "She was a nosy bitch, but I didn't kill her. I wasn't there. Remember?" He came upright in his chair, legs knocking hard against the floor. His hand shot out and clamped her arm. Lola twisted in his grip. He thumbed her cuff away from her wrist and deftly extracted the tape recorder. It went into her coffee cup with a splash.

"Oops," he said.

Lola grabbed for the cup. He held it away from her and sloshed the coffee around. The recorder clacked against the sides of the cup. "The light just went off. That can't be good. You seem to know so much about the mob. Funny how it didn't occur to you that spotting a wire is part of Mob 101." He extracted a sheaf of green from a billfold and fanned a few bucks onto the table.

Lola didn't even bother looking toward the door. He wasn't coming.

"You have fun writing that story of yours. Here." He pulled a fifty from the wallet, slapped it on the table. "This says it never runs."

She ran to the cafe door just in time to watch the Suburban pull away, heading north, the windows down, Johnny waving a grand goodbye.

CHAPTER TWENTY-TWO

"Where the hell were you?"

Lola swept her arm across Charlie's desk. The cribbage board skated to the floor, pegs and cards patterning around it. Before the sheriff could navigate to the desk's far side, manuals followed. Pages fluttered, seeking their place.

"Are you going to tear up my entire office? Because if you are, we're going to have to find another place for you to tell me whatever it was that you found so urgent." His hands banded her wrists. Lola aimed a kick at his shins but he sidestepped it, not letting go. She tried again; again, he moved easily with her, his ponderous body suddenly light, Lola the clumsy one in their dance of anger and avoidance. "I was right here," he said. A slight hesitation between his words the only betrayal of the effort required to hold her in place. "Look, I'm sorry. But I had to take a call. I was just on my way over when you came busting in." Shadows swept past the frosted glass window of his door and returned, lingering. "Could you lower your voice, Lola? Half the county employees are in the hallway, taking in the show."

The effort made Lola's chest hurt. "Get back on that phone. Do that all-points-bulletin thing you did with me. Because he's getting away."

The shadows swam closer to the window, a school of fish coalescing into a single focused mass. "Everybody back to work," Charlie called. The mass broke apart and the room grew lighter. "You," he said to Lola. "Sit down."

She shook her head.

His arms were straight as steel. He lowered them and Lola found herself in a chair. "I could arrest you. Seriously. You have got to knock this shit off. Now"—he made the mistake of loosening his grip—"what's going on?"

Lola threw his hands off and shot up from the chair. "Johnny Running Wolf killed Mary Alice—at least, he set it up. And now, thanks to you and your asinine phone call, he's gone. Go after him."

He slid his hand along his nylon duty belt, touching the black anodized pistol, the orange-handled Taser, the cylinder of pepper spray. The brick-sized radio, the deceptively weighty flashlight, the hard circle of cuffs. He made a movement toward the door. Checked it.

"How do you know this?" Suspicion warred with weariness in his voice. "All you told me when you called last night is that you think Johnny Running Wolf is running with the mob and isn't even an Indian. At least, I think that's what you said. I was only half-awake."

"I don't think. I know. His real name is Vince Fantonelli Junior. A.K.A. Little Fanny, to distinguish him from his father, Big Fanny." Lola paced as she spoke, seeking words that would persuade him. "Little Fanny got crosswise with his father during a drug war up in Calgary a few years back, and Big Fanny put out a hit on him. So he offed his old friend Johnny Running Wolf and showed up on the reservation pretending to be him. It might have worked, but a guy like Little Fanny was never going to be content sitting in an old lady's house out on the prairie. He went back to his old line of work. He probably made some connections in Helena when the tribe sent him there to lobby. And you were onto it. You and Frank. But Frank wasn't running booze for him. He was running drugs." She stopped for air.

Charlie leaned against the desk and crossed his arms. "I don't know that he was running them for Johnny. But I do know he was running drugs."

Lola paused in mid-stride. "You do?"

"That was the phone call I took. They finally got the tox screens back from Frank and Judith and Billy Worden, too. You called it. Those kids OD'd on heroin."

Lola indulged in a flash of triumph. Knew he could see it in her face. "What about Frank?"

"They found traces of it in his backpack. The kids probably thought they'd hit the jackpot when they jumped him. They were tweaking when they did it—that's something else the tox screens showed—and that's probably why things got so out of hand. And then they found the heroin and decided to give it a try. Heroin on top of meth. It's a wonder more of them didn't end up dead. So, yes, you were right about that. But how do you figure Johnny is really this Italian guy?"

Pride puffed through her urgency. "I found all of his stuff. He had dye, hair straightener, that fake suntan goop in his bathroom. I've got photos on my cell phone if you want to see them."

Charlie retrieved the things she'd knocked from his desk. He squared the deck of cards and replaced the cribbage pegs in the holes. He crouched and felt around on the floor and straightened. "Huh," he said. "One must have rolled under the desk. About the Indian thing."

"What about it?"

"You know, a lot of us are conflicted when we don't look Indian enough. There's all kinds of mixed-blood combinations, starting with French like me and getting more complicated from there. It doesn't even have to be white blood to make things confusing. I've got cousins that are damn near pure Indian but not enough of any one tribe to enroll for membership. Given that he's running for governor as the first Indian candidate, maybe he thought he needed to look a little more authentic. Doesn't mean he's a mobster. Besides, when you're talking heroin, you're talking real money. You've got to launder that stuff somehow. Johnny has a lot of spendy stuff, but not nearly enough to account for the kind of money heroin brings. Where would he stash it all?"

"His campaign," Lola said. "It was a front." She reached for his phone.

"If we were in California, I'd say maybe. But campaigns in Montana are still cheap. You're throwing around a lot of accusations. I like you, Lola. I like you a lot. But we're getting into some pretty strange territory here."

She gaped at him. "Like? As in . . ."

He pulled the phone away from her. "First you mess up my crime scenes, now you trash my office. I don't even want to get into how you've messed with my head. Leave my phone alone."

"Relax," she said. "I'm going to dial a number. The cop who picks up is going to tell you about the fingerprints. The ones that prove Johnny Running Wolf is really Little Fanny Fantonelli." She felt for the phone again. "So, when you say *like* . . ."

Charlie moved the phone farther out of reach. "Never mind about that now. There are prints? Why didn't you say so? Give me that number. I'll dial it myself. On my cell. I can talk to your guy on our way to the reservation."

⬦⬦⬦

LOLA SAT in silence after Charlie's brief conversation with Sanchez. She wasn't going to ask a third time about that *like* business. The cruiser plunged through the smoking landscape. A venerable plane, seemingly too cumbersome for the propellers that powered it, passed overhead on its way toward a flaming hillside. Orange plumes billowed from the plane's belly as it heaved itself over the ridge. The chemical cloud rolled down the hill into the smoke.

Charlie nodded toward a line of men in yellow near low flames undulating across the hillside. "They're setting backfires. That's good. They need to get this thing under control before it gets down into grazing land."

Lola felt his gaze upon her. She stared stubbornly ahead. He switched on the cruiser's lights and chased them through the smoke. Wilson was waiting outside the tribal offices when they pulled up.

"I sent tribal police up to his gran'mother's place," Wilson said. "His outfit went tearing by here a little while ago, headed that way. Half the town saw it and the greater part of those people were happy to let me know about it."

"Why don't you tell Wilson what you told me?" Charlie suggested as they drove out of town, Wilson sitting in the back seat behind Lola.

"Johnny's not an Indian. He's a white guy. Italian, for what it's worth."

Wilson passed a hand over his face. "You know, we get people all the time at powwows, women, mostly, a few men, all decked out in turquoise and headbands and fringe and whatnot. Blond hair in braids. A Cherokee princess in their background. For some reason, it's almost always Cherokee— although Lakota, they're real popular, too, thanks to *Dances with Wolves*. And for damn sure it's always a princess. Everybody wants to be us, but nobody wants to live like us. But this is more than some powwow wannabe. The guy's running for governor, making a big deal about how he's Blackfeet. If nothing else, it seems like a pretty risky thing to do if he's not who he says he is."

"That's why it works," Lola said. "Hiding in plain sight, the more public, the better. Oldest trick in the book, mainly because it works. I think he killed Mary Alice. Or at least set it up."

Hazy sunlight refracted off Wilson's glasses.

"I know you do," he said. And then nobody said anything else until they pulled up in front of Johnny's grandmother's house.

⟡⟡⟡

THE SUBURBAN, if it ever had been there, was gone. Tribal police cars surrounded the house. Two officers flanked the doorway. "Nobody here," one of them said.

Charlie looked to Wilson for permission.

"Go ahead."

Charlie disappeared inside. A moment later, he was back, motioning them in. The three of them filled the little kitchen.

"I know," said Lola. "Don't touch anything."

The sheriff snapped rubber gloves over his hands and opened and closed cabinet doors. They were empty—as were the closets and the medicine cabinet, the trash cans and the dresser drawers and the refrigerator. The dishes were gone, along with the cutlery, even the ice cube trays. "Man works fast," Charlie said. He inspected the stainless-steel faucet, the refrigerator door handle. They shone brightly. "Looks like he wiped everything down."

"Where'd he go?" said Lola. "If he's been here and gone, he'd have passed us on the way back. There's only the one road, right?" She followed Wilson and Charlie outside. The two men walked a few yards from the house, then crouched in unison and examined something. Lola hurried to them and saw only prairie. She said as much.

"What do you smell?" Charlie asked her. He made it a command. "Smell."

Lola lifted her face. The air was acrid. "I smell the fires." She took another breath, tasted something sharp and sweet undercutting the air's charcoal tinge. Charlie tore a grey-green leaf from one of the woody shrubs and rolled it between his fingers. He held it beneath her nose, the scent coming strong now, welcome against the smoke.

"It's sage. Look there." He pointed toward the prairie.

Lola looked.

"No," he said. "*There*," and lowered his arm a little, and then she saw it, the faint twin tracks of bruised plants leading away from the house. Wilson took off his hat and rubbed his hand on his forehead as if to erase the creases there, then shaded his eyes, looking north.

"What are you looking at?" Lola asked.

Wilson turned with a tight smile.

"Canada."

⟡⟡⟡

WILSON CALLED his counterparts on the Blood Reserve in Canada while Charlie talked to Border Patrol. "Not that it'll do much good," he told Lola.

"Why not?"

Wilson jumped in. "No way he went to the formal crossing. And the Blood Reserve is only twelve miles north of the border. We go back and forth all the time. He'll probably try to move from one reserve to the next."

Charlie held the car door for Lola. Wilson got in behind her. She took a long last look at the northern horizon, and put her head on her knees. Charlie closed her door and came around to his own side and slid in.

"We'll run the prints again, officially, at my request. I'll get that started the minute I get back. I'll put the word out at airports, too, in case he tries to get on a plane. The technical term at this point is 'person of interest.' Doesn't mean he's a suspect, but for sure we think he could help us in the investigation. By the time they pick him up—and they *will* pick him up, Lola, don't you worry—I plan to have enough to justify holding him."

"As soon as I get back," Wilson said, "I'll email the Blood some photos. If anybody up there has seen him, they'll remember him. That nose might have been his best friend for a long time, but now it's his worst enemy. He can't un-break it, at least not overnight."

Charlie spoke again. "Oh, and you're free to go back home, or wherever it is you want to go. I know you're not happy with the way we've handled this, but I had to rule you out, not just as a suspect, but as somebody who might have useful information. Which you might not have had then, but you sure as hell found some." He steered with his left hand out and extended his right in a handshake. Lola had gotten used to the way Indian people shook hands, quickly touching fingertips and then pulling away, but Charlie folded her hand in his and held it until a series of snaking curves demanded his full attention. He rounded them and reached for the radio.

"Tiffany? Whatever else you're doing, drop it. We're going to be busy, really busy, for the rest of the day."

CHAPTER TWENTY-THREE

At Charlie's insistence, Lola met him at the cafe for a final breakfast before leaving Magpie.

"I'll buy," he said. "It's the least I can do after keeping you here all this time."

Lola had already picked up a rental car after dropping off Mary Alice's truck at the dealership in town, where it would be sold and the proceeds sent to Mary Alice's parents. Charlie was keeping her waiting. Lola put her menu down and studied the dirty yellow stratum of smoke above the mountains, the result of the fire's latest run. Joshua topped off her coffee.

"Everybody's talking about Johnny Running Wolf. Half the people on the rez say they knew he was a whiteman the minute they saw him. The other half are saying the guy really *was* Johnny. That this is just one more way to make the tribe look bad."

Lola knew better than to protest that one man's actions couldn't possibly reflect on an entire people. She ran her hand across the tabletop. It came away grimy with soot.

"You think he killed her," Joshua said.

"Sure. Set it up, anyway."

Joshua pulled a damp rag from his back pocket and rubbed at the table, leaving circular dark smears. "Maybe he did," he said. "Maybe not. Just when you think something's one way, it turns out to be another. That's something Mary Alice learned."

Lola wondered if anybody in Magpie ever said a thing directly. Joshua snapped his wrist and popped the rag and put it back in his pocket. His eyes met hers. Lola remembered Mary Alice telling her that among Indian people, a direct stare was considered rude. "It gets them in trouble, Bub-ette," she'd said in one of their rare phone calls. "People think because they don't look you in the eye, they're all shifty and evasive, when all they're really trying to do is show some respect." Lola had been dissed, and she didn't know why. Joshua left without taking her order. Nell came out of the kitchen and Lola waved her over. "I'll have the cinnamon bun."

Nell stopped. "Come again?"

"I'm going to spend the next two or three days on airplanes, with nothing to eat but pretzels and peanuts. I might as well put as much food in my stomach as I can in one fell swoop." When the cinnamon bun arrived, though, she had second thoughts. Her fork hovered. She pondered the best way to launch her assault. Carve away at the sides, or dive right into the middle, where the icing pooled in a viscous lake? The ranchers rose, a herd on the move, and ventured bets.

"A buck says she won't eat it all."

"A buck says if she doesn't, you'll be the first one going for the leftovers."

"Har. Neither one of you has got a buck. It's a wonder Nell lets you eat here."

The door banged behind Charlie. He looked at the commotion around Lola's table. "What am I missing?"

"Lola ordered the cinnamon bun," Nell said.

Charlie brought out his wallet.

"Put your money away," one of the ranchers said. "You're late to that party."

Lola took a quick bite, and then another. "Oh, my. This is fine. Somebody's going to lose some money. I'm eating all of this." The ranchers departed singly and in pairs, turning square, good-humored faces upon her and commenting on the efficient dispatch of the cinnamon bun, on the money she would cost them in lost bets, on a waistline that they insisted had expanded visibly since she'd walked in the door that morning. Lola tried to remember another place where a remark that a woman appeared to have gained weight was offered as a compliment. She'd taken their initial silence as hostility. It occurred to her now that it might simply have been shyness, or even an excess of good manners, not wanting to impose themselves on someone without an initial greeting, an offhand comment about the weather that invited response. She'd never so much as said hello.

Charlie pointed to the bun. "Bet they don't have those where you're going."

Lola waved her fork at him. "Found him yet?"

"Not yet. But I'm not worried. For a place that barely has Internet, word travels pretty fast in Indian Country. Somebody will spot him. A lot of First Peoples live in Calgary. Wilson's making sure the word gets to them, too. Hey, Nell. Where's Joshua?"

"Don't know. He just took off in some sort of snit. But don't worry. I've already got it started. Eggs over easy. Toast no butter, bacon and hash browns burnt unto crispy."

Lola turned her plate and carved away at the bun from another angle. "Something's been worrying me. What if they catch him in Canada?"

He hooked his fork in the remainder of the bun. "What if they do?"

"Canada doesn't have the death penalty. They don't like extraditing people in murder cases. How are you going to get him here to try him for killing Mary Alice?"

He slid the plate to one side to make room for the breakfast Nell sat before him. "For one thing, we don't have a murder case yet. We either need to catch Johnny and get him to fess up, or get hold of one of his partners and sweat it out of him. He had to have help. But I'm not worried about getting him back to Magpie."

"How's that?"

"The heroin. One thing I've found out, talking to the other sheriffs, is that it's been popping up all over Montana, mainly along the I-90 corridor—Missoula, Bozeman, Billings—and then down onto I-25 through Wyoming to Denver. Same old routes meth took. But you can make a lot more money off heroin than meth. Canada would be happy to send him back here on a drug charge and let us pay the costs of prosecuting him. Once we get him here, we can start working on the Mary Alice piece of things. It could take some time before we track down both him and his partners and get this whole thing nailed down. You need to prepare yourself for that."

A hay truck filled the cafe window, churning up dust that rose and blended with the smoke. The lettering on the cab— Two Medicine Ranch—reminded Lola of something else. She pushed his hand away from his plate.

"Pay attention. I know where to look. Two Medicine."

"The river?"

"The campaign. Not the campaign itself, but the interest group. TMResources. I always figured the TM stood for Two Medicine. Remember Mary Alice's note? *Camping on the Two Medicine.* There was no reason for her to be that specific. If you can find out who's behind the group, I'll bet that'll lead you to his partners. I've already checked it, but those groups don't have to list their donors. When you think about it, they're great vehicles for laundering a lot of cash. You're an officer of the law, though. You can probably get the names. Start there."

"Good idea." He looked at his watch. "When are you out of here?"

"I'm on the five-thirty flight."

"What are you going to do with the rest of your day?"

"I've got a couple of things left to do at the cabin. Speaking of tying up loose ends—" She handed him a document. "It's a bill of sale. For the horse. Mary Alice's parents gave me power of attorney. So if you give me a dollar and sign here, that horse is yours." She'd fill in some zeroes behind the $1 on the copy she'd send to Mary Alice's parents, withdrawing a thousand dollars from her fast-dwindling savings account, and mail the money along with the document. To Charlie, she said, "I figure now we're even, after that knock on the head I gave you."

He borrowed a pen from Nell and scrawled his name. "It's going to take me months to get that horse back to the condition Mary Alice had him in. That is, if you haven't ruined him completely." Grinning down at the tabletop like a ten-year-old boy.

The dog was going to live with Jolee. "What with all the goings-on around here lately, looks like a watchdog would be in order," she'd scowled when Lola offered. "Aw, honey," she said a moment later. "He's just a dog."

Lola had already delivered Mary Alice's kitchen table to Jan.

"Shouldn't you have this?" Jan had asked.

"I travel light. It won't fit in the overhead bin." Lola found herself talking to the top of Jan's head as the younger woman surprised her with a quick hug. Even as Lola's arms rose to return it, Jan ducked away.

"I still think you're a bitch."

Lola grinned. "Look who's talking."

When Lola had finally sold her paper on the story, Jan had insisted on an agreement that it would run the same day in the *Express*. "With my name on top of that one."

"Fair enough," Lola agreed. She'd even turned down the paltry freelance fee offered by the *Express* in exchange for free real estate ads for Mary Alice's place, one less thing for Mary Alice's parents to worry about. She folded back the newspaper to the classifieds and showed it to Charlie, a handsome display with a large photo of the cabin, Bub striking an uncharacteristically well-behaved pose on the porch.

"I'll bet her parents would rent it to you," Charlie suggested. "The *Express* has been down a writer ever since it lost Mary Alice. You could stay. I say this knowing it's to my detriment. If you stuck around I'd probably have to hire a deputy just to handle all the extra crime you seem to attract." He paid close attention to his plate as he spoke, polishing its already spotless surface with the final piece of toast.

Lola thought of how she'd inadvertently insulted his Indian-ness during that first interview. The wine bottle smashed against his head. The damage to his office. Not to mention the stolen cribbage peg. She decided not to call Charlie's attention to the utter faux pas of suggesting that someone with her experience would consider even for a second the possibility of working in a suburban newspaper bureau in Baltimore, let alone in a backwater like Magpie. She simply said nothing at all, and they finished their first and only meal together in a silence that left her feeling small and ashamed.

CHAPTER TWENTY-FOUR

Spot was at the corral gate, working at the latch with his teeth, when Lola drove into the clearing.

At the sight of the car, he trotted to the far side of the corral and affected not to notice her. He whinnied, as though just realizing she'd arrived, when the car's automatic lock sounded its beep. "Just you wait," Lola called to him. "Your life of leisure is about to come to an end. And I know for a fact Charlie's stopping by the hardware store to get a new latch for his corral."

She reminded herself how much easier things would be when she no longer had to worry about feeding, cleaning, exercising and otherwise spending surprising amounts of time on two creatures whose sole purpose appeared to be to undermine her sanity. Bub chose that moment to lean against her. She worked her fingers along his spine. He arched his back and groaned. "It'll be so much better with Jolee," she told him. She wondered if he believed it any more than she did.

⟡⟡⟡

LOLA SAVED the coffeepot and the telephone for last. She wrapped the glass pot in layers of old *Express*es and sat it in the bottom of a cardboard box. She squeezed the phone jack and pulled it from its wall connector. Then thought about how Verle had chided her for slipping from his bed without saying goodbye. He was from a generation that set store by formalities. He'd been kind to her, and then some. A call seemed the least she could do. She plugged the phone back in and dialed. One of Verle's workers—Carlos? Eduardo? She couldn't keep them all straight—sounded rushed, impatient. "You wait," he said. She heard heavy sliding sounds, as though things were being dragged across a floor. Verle picked up. "Verle here."

"It's Lola. What'd you buy this time? Another sofa?" she teased.

"Hold on." He must have covered the receiver with his hand because his next words were muffled, indistinct. *"Silencio! Hey, hey. Cuidado con eso."* The noises ceased. "Lola. I wasn't expecting your call. Looked for you last night. Thought maybe you'd stop by. I wanted your opinion on a new desk. It's supposed to have sat in Wyatt Earp's office, maybe even while he was there, although I doubt that. Either way, it's a beautiful thing. Maybe you'll come see it tonight?"

Lola squeezed the phone against her neck and fitted the rest of the coffeemaker into the box as she spoke. She glossed quickly over the fact that she wouldn't be stopping by—"I've got to be out of the cabin in a couple of hours to make my plane. Maybe sooner, depending on how bad the smoke is"—and got quickly to the why. "Charlie's pretty sure they'll pick him up within the next few days. He's going to keep me updated. I'm hoping he's in custody by the time I get to Kabul."

"Well, now. Charlie got his man after all. That is a surprising thing. Sounds like he couldn't have done it without you. Congratulations."

"It's a bit of a problem, actually," Lola admitted. "If there's a trial, I'll have to come back and testify. I'm his main witness. But that shouldn't be for months and months. He says that'll give him time to hit up the state for plane fare to get me back here."

Verle's voice brightened considerably. "But you'll be back. Lola, you just made my day. You travel safely now. Until next time."

Lola unplugged the phone with a bit of a flourish, twirling the cord lasso-like before winding it around the phone and putting all of it into the box with the coffeemaker. She crumpled some more newspapers around everything and folded down the flaps on the box and drew a tape gun across them with a ragged tearing sound and then dropped the gun to the floor. Bub promptly retrieved it. "Thanks," said Lola, "but I'm done with that." She picked up a marker and printed Mary Alice's parents' name and address on a label in large block letters, then peeled the protective paper from the adhesive and smoothed the label onto the box. She lifted the box, gauging its weight, and wished she'd accepted Mary Alice's parents' offer to reimburse her for shipping costs.

The wind sideswiped her as she stepped off the porch and sent her staggering. She caught her balance and looked up the hill into a swirling wall of smoke. The fire was within two miles of the cabin, according to Charlie. "Any closer and I'd be issuing an evacuation order," he'd said. Lola sat the box on the porch with the others that Charlie had promised to pick up when he came for Spot, and went back into the bedroom. Her remaining cash lay in neat stacks atop the bare mattress, along with the note from Mary Alice. Charlie had made her a copy.

Camping on the Two Medicine.

She ran her fingers over the words. "You did it, Mary Alice," she whispered. "You led us to him. He's not going to get away with it."

She went back to the kitchen and opened the cupboard before remembering that she'd packed all the glasses. She drank directly from the faucet. The grizzly bear fetish she'd pinched from Verle's house stood on the counter. Twice, she'd tossed the bear into the trash, along with the paperweight and the cribbage peg, thinking it was time to end a pointless habit. But twice, she'd beheld the bear's turquoise stare from the depths of the can and retrieved it. Now, she picked it up and put it in her pocket. Its weight dragged at the fabric.

She walked through the cabin for a final check, trailing her hands along the peeled logs, so much warmer and more welcoming than the rough whitewashed surfaces of the Kabul house that had never, as long as she'd lived there, seemed like adequate protection against the turmoil just beyond the high, double-barred courtyard gate. In just a short time, the cabin had come to feel more like home than the Kabul house ever had. "Go figure," she said to Bub, who'd returned to her side. She wondered yet again how long it would take her to stop looking around for him once she was back in Kabul. "You're just a dog," she reminded him.

She went into the bathroom and opened the medicine cabinet to ensure that it was, indeed, empty. She closed it and examined her reflection in the mirror, willing away the twin vertical lines beginning to segment her face between mouth and chin, their horizontal counterparts running in triplicate across her forehead. She tugged at her hair. Maybe it was time to let it grow out, brush disguising curls across her brow in what Mary Alice used to call the poor woman's facelift. She turned to go, and saw the radio hanging from the shower head. She never had gotten around to buying batteries for it, and she'd forgotten to box it with the rest of Mary Alice's things.

"Too late," she told Bub. She picked it up and lobbed it underhand through the door toward the trash can. He leapt for it as she threw, messing with her aim. The radio bounced off the lip of the can and slammed against the floor, the impact popping apart its hard plastic shell.

"Hell," said Lola.

She crossed the living room to pick it up. In the next moment, she was on the floor, the radio still in pieces around her, staring at the objects in her palm. They must have been in the radio the whole time, wedged into the battery compartment—Mary Alice's flash drives.

⟡⟡⟡

LIGHT FROM the laptop pulsed across Lola's face as the files from the flash drives transferred into her computer's memory. The file names were a jumble of nonsensical-seeming numbers, in a code known only to Mary Alice. She'd developed it after she lost a laptop in one of Baltimore's routine smash-and-grabs, watching from inside a Starbucks just a few steps away as a leather-gloved guy shattered the window of her illegally parked car with a short, practiced punch. He'd had the audacity to turn and wave in mid-dash as she ran down the sidewalk after him, screaming curses and sending her perfectly frothed latte in a high, helpless arc in his direction.

"He was just a punk," she'd said to Lola. "But what if he hadn't been? What if he'd cracked the password and saw a file labeled 'Cops on the Take?' Worse yet, what if the cops had recovered it and held onto it for evidence?" Lola agreed that would have been a very bad thing indeed. So Mary Alice invented an elaborate system to protect her important files, transferring them nightly to the flash drives, giving them innocuous names as a backup. The list of files in front of Lola marched down the screen and disappeared somewhere below its bottom margin. She picked one at random and clicked and almost laughed. The first screen—as well as the second, third, fourth and fifth—was occupied by an interminable, years-old story on abuses within the Baltimore Parking Authority. Another ruse. Lola knew Mary Alice's habit of putting boring stuff atop short takes of important information. Lola held her finger on the down arrow and eventually was rewarded with a list of names and numbers:

Hassan Fouad, $9,799
Juanita Alfonso, $8,095
Jonah Yazzie, $9,006
Akram Shadden, $8,705
And so on.

"TMResources," she breathed. She'd found their donor list.

✧✧✧

LOLA SAT at her laptop, fingertips tingling. She went first to the Federal Bureau of Prisons website, typing in one name after another to see if any had drug trafficking convictions. None did. "That would have been too easy," she told Bub. She went next to the federal court system site and through the slightly more cumbersome process of determining whether anyone on the list had at least been indicted. Again, she drew blanks. She opened another of Mary Alice's files. More names, more amounts. And more unproductive searches. She clicked faster and faster. Nothing. Nothing. Nothing. She went back to Google and tried pairing the names with Fantonelli. Nothing. Then with Montana. Nothing. She tried a couple of the names individually, a search so broad she usually avoided it as meaningless. The results reminded her why.

Yazzie turned out to be the surname of about half the Navajo Nation. There were dozens of Juanita Alfonsos, among them a teacher, an artist, and an accounting student who posted all sorts of inappropriate photos of herself on Facebook. All of the Juanitas, however, apparently abided by the law. The various Akram Shaddens included a horse, of all things. But no heroin dealers. Or even a wealthy oilman who might have served as a clean front man for a dirty issues organization.

Lola looked at the clock. It was nearly noon. She went to the sink and took another awkward gulp from the faucet. She picked up the flash drives and rattled them like dice in her hand. She'd imagined a blessed moment of clarity, bright lights, the whole package tied up in a big bow of certainty. She sat back down at the laptop and blew ash from the screen. She wiped her hands on her pants and set her fingers back on the keyboard, hitting all the wrong keys. The screen blinked crazily, flashing back to an earlier search. Juanita Alfonso, artist-not-political-donor. Lola struck at the keyboard, trying to get back to Google, and opened the page instead. A photo display of pots filled the screen, then disappeared as Lola's finger found the backspace key.

"Wait," she breathed. "Come back."

But she'd already gone back to the main search screen. This time she typed slowly, carefully, spelling the name aloud as she typed. Juanita Alfonso.

Got the link to the website. Clicked it open.

Went to "Works." Clicked again.

The screen full of pots. Pots glazed black, patterned with unglazed geometrics.

Verle's voice in Lola's head. "Noticed you went for that one first. You've got a good eye for quality."

Lola clicked back to Mary Alice's list, chose another name. There were several Jonah Yazzies, but one turned out to be a weaver whose pieces sold for tens of thousands of dollars. Lola thought of the rugs on Verle's walls and floors. She went back to one of the Arabic names and pasted it into Google, ready this time for what she'd see. Akram Shadden was a promising Arabian stud. Verle must have been smart enough to buy the horse before his price soared beyond ten thousand dollars. Bub rose from his position across Lola's feet and put his head on her thigh, divining as always any change in mood. "Ten thousand," Lola told him. "The magic number. The tragic number."

Pay less than ten thousand dollars and the IRS—mostly— didn't give a rat's ass. More than that, though, and the agency got interested. Very interested. Folks who wanted their cash clean and clear bought things that cost less than ten thousand dollars. Lola thought of Verle's house, its pottery and rugs and paintings. All the renovations outside, probably done in small, nine-thousand-nine-hundred-and-ninety-nine-dollar increments. The horses. The Charlie Russells. Entire cellars full of wine. Cash to the sellers, twice the asking price, with the understanding that half the cash would go toward a political donation. Johnny would have needed somebody local to work with, the sheriff had said. And he'd reminded her that a campaign, even one for governor, wouldn't have begun to soak up all the money flowing from heroin. But rebuilding a ranch inside and out, even in ten-thousand-dollar increments—that, thought Lola, might have done the trick.

Lola thought of Verle.

Whose hay trucks and horse trailers had been rolling in or out of his place whenever she'd been there. The horses on their way to shows in Denver and Boise and Billings, all the places the sheriff said heroin had shown up. Verle's people had been driving more than prize horseflesh to all those shows. Had hauled more than hay on those flatbeds.

Verle, with his handcrafted, probably-just-under-ten-thousand-dollar rifle leaning by his front door. "I can drop a bear at a hundred yards," he'd said. Which was double the distance from Mary Alice's cabin to where her body had been found. She remembered the rifle's big bore. That gun hadn't killed Mary Alice, but Verle probably had another that had. Of all the bullshit Johnny had slung Lola's way, one comment had been genuine. "I didn't kill her," he said. "I wasn't there. Remember?"

But Verle was.

Verle.

Who knew Lola was alone in the cabin.

Lola's fingers froze on the keyboard.

She looked at Bub.

"Run," she said. "Run."

CHAPTER TWENTY-FIVE

They were halfway to the car, Bub flinging himself ahead of her, when a high sound ripped the air.

Spot stood at the corral gate, neck extended, sounding another prolonged and agitated neigh. A deeper call answered him. Lola hissed to Bub and ducked into the underbrush, grabbing at low branches to still any telltale movement. She heard the heavy hoof beats before she saw him. Verle entered the clearing atop the big bay, the rifle tucked into a scabbard. His head swiveled toward her rental car and he kicked at the bay and urged him toward it. He circled the car, the bay bending around it as though it were a balky steer. Verle reined the horse closer and leaned from the saddle and put a hand on the hood. Lola knew it would feel cool.

Verle straightened in the saddle and spurred the horse toward the cabin. He dropped the reins to the ground and pulled the rifle from the scabbard. He swung a leg over the horse, slid to the ground and climbed the steps. He stopped in front of the door and turned, surveying the clearing. Lola closed her eyes and held her breath. When she opened her eyes, the porch was empty. She rose from her knees and crept hunched toward the car, careful not to move the bushes above, Bub slinking beside her. She reached the edge of the underbrush. The car sat twenty feet away, the cabin another thirty feet beyond it. Verle almost certainly would have realized she wasn't in the house. But maybe his attention had been distracted by the laptop. Lola calculated the time it would take her to spring that twenty feet, turn on the ignition, and outdrive the bullet that would zing her way within seconds of his hearing the engine turn over. She fumbled in her pocket for the hard plastic key holder.

The key holder with the lock button she'd automatically pushed when she'd left the car.

The mocking beep echoed in her brain. The beep that, if she hit the unlock button, would signal her presence to Verle, give him that extra split second's warning, enough for a long stride onto the porch, the rifle moving from crook of elbow to its fixed position against his shoulder as she turned the key in the ignition. More than enough time for one shot. The only shot he'd need.

Even as she fingered the keychain, the cabin door opened.

He cradled the rifle in one arm, his hand on the trigger guard. Lola watched again the sweeping scrutiny that would take in the silent car, the empty stretch of road beyond. A turn of his head would bring the corral into view above the cabin, Spot still attentive along the fence.

The door banged shut. He'd gone back inside.

Lola dashed through the brush until she was behind the cabin, drawing herself up tall and narrow behind a thick-trunked ponderosa pine, Bub pressed against her ankle. She stared at the bedroom window until Verle's silhouette appeared. He'd be checking under the bed this time, opening the closet doors, stepping into the bathroom and pulling aside the shower curtain. The silhouette was gone, then back again. She counted—one, two, three, four, five—enough time for him to leave the bedroom and go back into the living room. She crossed the clearing at a sprint. The bay raised its head and stepped back. A noise began deep in its chest. Lola grabbed a lead rope and went for Spot, no time for a saddle or even a bridle, just snapped the rope to his halter and made a desperate scramble onto his bare back. Leaned and stretched to unlatch the gate and squeezed her knees to urge Spot into a swift walk, the soft dry earth absorbing the sound of his hoof beats.

Behind her, Lola heard the bay's outraged whinny and the answering sound of the cabin door as she slammed her heels into Spot's sides and urged him into full gallop up the trail.

✧✧✧

SPOT PLUNGED through the trees, Lola clinging monkeylike, hands wrapped in his mane, knees high on his shoulders, wondering how long she could possibly stay aboard.

She'd forgotten about the path's steep switchbacks. The horse sank onto its hindquarters and wheeled at the turns, nearly unseating her at each one. Bub was a black-and-white blur, crossing the path ahead of them. Lola wanted to turn and look for Verle, but was afraid even such a small motion would send her dangerously off balance. Spot tilted through another corner. Lola flung her arms around his neck. Ahead, just yards off the trail, flames licked the ground beneath the trees. Spot backpedaled to a halt. Lola pushed herself upright and stroked him, afraid to waste even a second, more afraid that he might, in his panic, turn and gallop straight back toward Verle. "Easy," she said. "Easy." Bub waited, flanks heaving. Lola nudged at Spot's ribs. "Let's go," she said. He sidestepped and stopped again.

"Lola!"

Verle's voice rang through the trees.

"Christ," Lola gasped. She lashed the end of the lead rope back and forth across Spot's withers. "Move!"

The horse leapt ahead into a choking swirl of smoke that muffled the voice behind them, even as it failed to disguise the fact that it was getting closer.

And still Verle kept calling.

"Lola! Lola!"

✧✧✧

Lola's lungs burned. She couldn't see the fire anymore, but she heard it, the stiff swish of taffeta rubbing against itself. Smoke drifted in shreds, obscuring and then revealing the trail. Lola clutched tighter at the horse's mane and finally chanced a backward glance, caught a glimpse of the bay's head, lather dripping from its mouth, its eyes rolling white with exertion. Spot lunged up another switchback. The blistering wind scorched their faces, briefly lifting the smoke. Again, Spot stopped. This time, Lola let him. She'd forgotten how the trail came out onto the canyon edge, the way it threaded along the cliff wall until it met the forest beyond. Far below, the cool waters of Two Medicine River taunted her, and then the rifle cracked. Spot spun away from the sound and Lola flew through empty air, soaring so inevitably toward the river that the smash of rock against shoulder and hip came as a shock. She reached out a tentative arm and felt nothing at all. She'd landed at the canyon's rim.

She rolled toward safety, clawing at the hard earth. The horse's spotted rump, the color of soot and smoke, newly punctuated with red, disappeared into the trees. Verle's horse approached, saucer-sized hooves paddling through the loose shale. Verle sat him easily, reins loose in one hand, rifle at the ready in the other.

The big horse stopped a few feet away and Lola looked up, into the rifle's bore. She rolled onto her stomach and put her hands on the rocks beneath her and pushed herself to her knees. But when she tried to stand her left leg bowed at mid-calf and she twisted to escape the pain, fighting to fall away from the canyon edge. She lay still, ignoring Verle, ignoring the gun, ignoring everything but the scarlet intensity of the pain pulsing between the long bones in her calf and radiating through her body, so that the sudden throb in her head, the numbness in her hands, all seemed somehow connected. She flexed her fingers and then slid her hand down her leg, wondering at the way that simple motion drew the pain with it, a line of concentration so fierce she wondered that it remained invisible. She pressed her hand against her ankle.

"Oohhhh." She pressed harder, getting used to it. She'd need to walk on it. Somehow.

"Got your wings clipped, didn't you?"

Lola kept her hand on her ankle and rolled her head to look at Verle. Soot shadowed the lines and hollows of his face, throwing the expansive forehead, the beaked nose into high relief, giving it the pitiless appearance of a medieval woodcut. She raised herself onto her elbows and hitched toward a skinny tree that leaned over the trail's edge, grasping at the rough bark. She hauled herself to her knees.

Verle sat and watched, patting the restive bay to still him.

Lola put one hand over the other and then repeated the motion, hoisting herself by degrees to her feet.

"This should be interesting," said Verle.

Lola put a little weight onto her left foot and forced a rising moan back into her throat. She planted her right foot more firmly and let go of the tree and dragged a hand across her face, letting it come to rest against her throat. Her pulse jerked, fast and uneven. "I'm fine." She took a wobbling step and grabbed at the tree. "I'm fine," she said again.

Verle waved the gun. Lola flinched. "You have an unusual definition of fine."

Lola watched the gun. She'd had a longstanding bargain with God, and God was letting her down. The more time she'd spent in Afghanistan, the more she figured she'd increased the odds of the inevitable. Fair enough. But she looked at how some journalists had died—beaten, tortured, raped, throats slit with rusty knives or beheaded altogether with several awkward chops—and made her deal: a bullet in the back. "I just don't want to see it coming," she'd say during the punchy late-night conversations at the Kabul house when the talk veered in that direction, as it always did. "Quick, clean. One minute I'm there worrying about making deadline, the next minute deadline's not an issue anymore. I'd leave an editor hanging. Is there any worthier way to go?" A line that brought a raucous laugh and a new round of drinks.

She'd always wondered whether the unlucky ones ever really let themselves admit they were about to die. If they thought the steady gun, the twitchy trigger finger, was just one more bluff. If, in those final few seconds, they regretted the decisions that had led them there. If a job in a suburban bureau would really have been so bad after all. She looked at Verle and looked at the gun and figured she wasn't ever going to get the chance to find out. She wasn't even going to get shot in the back. She thought of Mary Alice, saw again the wound on her face, wondered if at the last second Mary Alice had closed her eyes.

Verle lifted the gun.

There was the motion and Bub barking and a shot. Lola fell, twisting her leg yet again. She screamed.

The pain came and came, waves of it, and Lola thought it was a lousy deal that things went on hurting after you were dead. Bub barked again and Verle shouted and Lola saw him juggling the gun that he'd almost dropped when Bub launched himself, sending the shot wild. Lola did a sort of leap and hobble across the trail, dragging herself to the cliff face and then along it, grabbing at the rocks, her back to the drop-off, moving away from Verle as fast as she could, her own searing breaths nearly drowning out the struggle behind her. Another shot cracked and Bub's snarls changed to a prolonged wail and she looked, once, and saw the dog on the ground and then Bub was quiet; and it was just her own breathing and the sound of the pebbles dislodged beneath her feet, tumbling over the cliff edge and pinging off the rock below.

She stopped.

The gun came up again.

Lola let go of the cliff and stood in the middle of the trail, a foot from the drop-off. She stared hard at Verle, the sight line like a steadying rope.

"Go ahead and shoot," she said. "And when you're done with me, go find the horse and kill him, too."

"I just might." He brought the gun up again.

Lola ducked.

"Go ahead and shoot," Verle parroted. "Big talk."

Lola took a step back. He took one forward.

"It's not going to work," she said. "Johnny can do his disappearing act over the border, but you can't. They'll get you. You might as well give up now."

Telling him to quit because she wasn't ready to, not yet, bargaining as though she were back at a border crossing, habit kicking in, trying to give herself time to think. She put her hand to the knobbed cliff face as though for support, feeling for a loose stone. But the rock was solid. "Just tell me why," she said. She had to get him talking. "Before . . ."

"Before you get what's coming to you," he said agreeably. "You've been to my ranch," he added.

Lola nodded. Keep talking, she thought. Come on.

"Then you know why."

Lola wondered if she'd figure it out before he shot her. He advanced another step. He was probably forty feet away, entirely too close for comfort.

"I don't get it."

"Teaming up with Johnny. Whatever his name was. I didn't care. He knew how to move drugs. I knew how to hook him up out here. It's what you might call a win-win. There was more than enough money for both of us. He got to fling his take around, making like he was a serious candidate for governor and I got to bail out the ranch, keep the tribe from getting their hooks into it. They were set to buy it until I outfoxed them. I fixed it up, gave it the care it deserves. Until that friend of yours started poking around. Her bad luck. Now yours, too."

Lola tried again. "It's all on Mary Alice's files. I emailed them to Charlie. And to Jan at the *Express*."

He laughed. "No, you didn't. Your email was up on your computer. I looked through the file. You didn't send anything."

Lola slumped against the rock, trying to look nonchalant. Like she was settling in for a nice long chat with the man who was going to put a bullet or three into her. She slipped her hands into her pockets, hoping she'd shoved the flash drives in there on her way out the door. Thinking that maybe, if he killed her, it wouldn't occur to him to go through the pockets. That somebody else might; that they'd find the drives, open the files, think to look below the stupid stories Mary Alice had stacked atop the real information. She imagined sitting with Mary Alice on some sort of afterlife barstools. "Poor bastard. Joke's on him, huh, Bub-ette?"

She slithered her fingers within her pockets in slow, small movements and talked fast. "It's not going to work. One woman shot dead, maybe you could get away with that. But two? They're going to look at anybody who had contact with us. That's a pretty small circle. They'll look at Johnny, sure, but you'll be right at the top of the list with him."

"I'm not going to shoot you," Verle said, and the hope rose hard in her even as he spoke again.

"You're going to jump."

He pulled the trigger.

Lola fell awkwardly, hands still in her pockets. The bullet powdered the rocks in front of her feet. Shards ricocheted around her. Verle stooped and picked up the shell casing, then waited as she freed her hands and went through the manipulations required to bring her more or less vertical again.

"Looking for these?" he said. He held out his hand. The flash drives lay like flattened bullets in his palm. "They were next to your computer." He flicked his wrist and sent them into the vast gulf below.

Lola let go of the wall and balanced on her good leg. She glanced over the edge.

"Just get it over with," Verle said. "I can stand here and shoot around you all day, but you'd save us both some time and trouble if you'd just jump. Suicide, fall, it won't matter. People will believe either one. Anything's possible."

"Anything's possible," Lola murmured.

She tested a little weight on her bad leg. It was bearable. Just. A sprain, maybe, or a hairline fracture. It would do.

"Go on," Verle said. He gestured to the edge with the gun. "You go on now. I haven't got all day."

Lola lifted her arm. Pulled it back. Quick windup, theatrics not advisable at this point. A split second's full weight on her leg. Heard a snap as she shot her hand forward, opened her fingers, and let fly.

The bear fetish rocketed straight and true, connecting with the pulsing dimple above the bay's right eye. The horse shrieked and reared. Verle swayed forward with the motion, as comfortable as a grandmother in a rocking chair, not even grabbing the horn for balance. Of course, thought Lola. He was a horseman. Yet again the gun rose.

Lola collapsed onto the trail, shouting her frustration to the sky.

The horse, already unnerved, blood streaming into its eye, shied from the sound, a sideways leap across the trail. It planted its outside legs firmly upon air. Lola watched its one good eye roll back, its body lurching off balance, the recognition crossing Verle's face, the desperate scramble from the saddle, too late, too late, the tilt over the edge and beyond, turning clumsy arabesques into the smoke-filled canyon.

CHAPTER TWENTY-SIX

"Lola! Lola!"

Lola raised her head by degrees. "No," she moaned. How had he survived? He must have landed on one of the rocky outcroppings on the way down. With movement came sensation. The leg, a good sharp stab. Her palms, raw patches burning. She put them gingerly on the ground and began a three-point crawl, pain sending her off balance with each lurch forward. Stop. Breathe. Move. Smoke scouring her throat with every gasp. All the while, staring at the drop-off, expecting to see Verle's rifle-wielding arm rise above it. Or had he somehow found a way back onto the path? She crawled faster. Uneven hoof beats sounded an ominous drumbeat. Her lament turned to protest. "No!" The horse, too? Lola slumped onto her good knee and peered down the trail into the roiling cloud. Something moving in there.

Spot limped out of the smoke, Charlie beside him. "Lola!"

For the first time in her adult memory, Lola Wicks burst into tears.

⟡

"WHAT ARE you doing up here?" Lola sniffled into his chest.

"I got worried when I didn't see you come back through town. I was afraid you'd miss your plane."

She pressed her face harder against his shirt. "How did you know I hadn't come back?"

"I was watching for you. I had something to tell you. And then Jolee said when I went over for coffee that something was up at Verle's, that his people had been tearing up and down the road all morning. And I started thinking—you know, it's always bugged me that Johnny was in Denver when Mary Alice got shot. Somebody had to do the shooting for him. I got a bad feeling and headed up to the cabin. Your car was there, but you weren't, and there were two sets of hoof prints headed off into the woods. It didn't take a genius."

"Thank you," she said. Then she said, "I took your cribbage peg."

"I know." His voice nearly as reassuring as his arms around her. "Wilson can make another one." He stroked her hair.

She pulled back. "What did you want to tell me?"

"Never mind about that now."

"He shot Bub."

"Bastard." He drew her to him again.

"I killed him."

He lifted one of her hands and inspected her bleeding palm. "That's a matter of debate. Did you shoot him?"

Lola started to shake her head. Even that slight motion spurred new waves of pain. "He was the one with the gun. I just . . ."

He put his lips to the broken skin. "Just what?"

"Threw something at his horse. It shied. They went over." She saw again Verle's eyes, staring terribly into hers in the endless second before he plunged from view. Her teeth chattered.

A dull boom sounded. Then another. Charlie stood up. "I don't know what that noise was, but it wasn't anything good. Lola, you didn't kill anybody. Let's get this leg splinted. You look shocky. If I can get you onto that horse, think you can hang on?"

Lola looked at Spot. Blood crusted along a deep furrow in his flank. "He's hurt."

"But he can walk. You can't. I'm going to let go of you now." He unbuttoned his shirt and shrugged out of it and wrapped it around her. He peeled off his undershirt and tore it into long strips. He took a Leatherman tool from the end-less assortment of gadgets on his duty belt and selected a blade and slashed two thin branches from a nearby tree. "I won't lie. This is going to hurt like hell. Ready?"

"No. I am not. But, Charlie?"

"Yes?"

"If I holler, don't stop. Keep going. Just get me out of this place."

◇◇◇

LOLA QUESTIONED Charlie through gritted teeth, wielding words against agony as the horse jolted down the trail. "Why do you think he threw that rock through the window instead of just shooting me?"

"I don't think he did. I think Frank threw it. Maybe he came across Mary Alice's body after she got shot and wanted to warn you, to keep the same thing from happening to you. Who knows?" Charlie's shoulders lifted and lowered. They were shiny with sweat. Thirty yards away, a pine exploded into flames. Spot limped faster. Lola hadn't thought her leg could hurt any worse. She'd been wrong. She hung onto Charlie's words, grateful for any distraction.

"Or maybe you're right—Verle could have been trying to scare you away. He didn't need another shot-to-death woman on his hands. Besides, maybe he didn't want to kill you unless he absolutely had to. Given that you two . . ."

"Slept together?"

Charlie made a choking sound.

"That thing," she said. "It was just . . . nothing. A mistake. One in a long history of mistakes, I'm afraid."

His back was broad, muscles sliding easily beneath his skin as he walked, no sign at all of the pudginess Lola had assumed when she'd first met him. He was not a fat man, just a big one. He looked over his shoulder, his expression utterly devoid of condemnation. "Maybe your luck will turn."

Smoke rolled across the trail like ghostly tumbleweeds. Lola used it as an excuse to cough away still more tears.

"We're almost there," Charlie said. "We'll take my car down. You're doing great."

"Can you do me a favor?"

"Sure."

"It's a big one."

"Shoot."

"Can you go back and find Bub and bury him?" It was the most she could push past the sob lurking in her throat.

"Consider it done." Charlie's own voice was none too steady.

Lola closed her eyes and concentrated fiercely on maintaining her balance for the final few yards. Spot stopped. "Are we there?" she said without opening her eyes. She was very tired. As badly as she wanted to be flat on her back in a bed in the clinic, pumped full of every single painkiller Margie had on hand, she dreaded the maneuvering necessary to get her off the horse and into Charlie's cruiser. "Let's get my stuff out of the cabin and get this over with."

"That's going to be tough."

Lola opened her eyes. Shut them against the sting of smoke.

Maybe, she thought, if she didn't look again. Maybe it wouldn't be true. But even behind her closed eyelids, the image remained, the lick and leap of flame, the hungry snapping sound, the burnt skeletons of the rental car and Charlie's cruiser, the crashing collapse of roof, Mary Alice's cabin whirling away into the hideous sky in a great pillar of ember and ash.

CHAPTER TWENTY-SEVEN

Lola sat at a computer in the Baltimore newsroom and clicked on the *Express* website.

The homepage was nearly all headline. "Friends Eulogize Area Rancher Killed in Fall." Jan's story from Verle's funeral summarized the information she'd included in her piece a few days earlier about his death. "It appears Mr. Duncan's horse lost its footing on the trail above Two Medicine River," said Sheriff Charles Laurendeau. "It's pretty unforgiving up there. No second chances."

Lola chuckled over the eulogies themselves, the verbal contortions that avoided mention of the near-daily revelations that had run in the *Express* since Verle's death: Mary Alice's cell phone, fished out of the irrigation ditch along the road where Lola had first seen Verle. Along with a semiautomatic rifle, a spent shell casing, and a bullet. Ballistics tests would take another week. But Charlie confidently predicted they were the weapon and ammunition that had killed Mary Alice. "Hah," Lola said to the screen.

The story that she and Jan had written together about Johnny Running Wolf, hastily amended to include his ties to TMResources and thus to Verle, would run—with both their bylines—in the Sunday papers in Baltimore and Magpie. The cafe, she'd heard, had tripled its order of Sunday *Expresses* for the breakfast crew. As for the Baltimore paper, Lola had assumed her insistence on including Jan's name at the top of the story would result in an extra year's exile to suburbia. Instead, someone in one of the layers of management that never seemed to be thinned by layoffs had pulled rank on her behalf. The suburban assignment was rescinded altogether in favor of a coveted posting to City Hall, with its reliable stream of corruption stories.

An editor—the same one who had yanked her from Kabul—stopped beside her desk, stepping around the crutches that leaned against it. "Looks like you've gotten signed into our new system." Resentment narrowed his eyes, dragged at his mouth. "Now try to find that same story on your phone." He handed her a flat black oblong.

Lola tossed it from hand to hand. "How do I turn this thing on?"

He gave her a manual with a number inked on the cover. "Here's your security code. I have to say, I never thought I'd see you again. I was sure you'd head back to Afghanistan. We had a pool. I lost some money." He pointed toward a placard mimicking a movie poster hung in the newsroom. "Run, Lola, Run!" was printed in red across the top, above an old photo of Lola kicking at her Jeep in frustration during a particularly prolonged delay at a Khyber Pass checkpoint. She wore a headscarf that had come loose, its ends lofting in the winds that skated down from the Hindu Kush, revealing a face contorted in anger. The poster featured a roughly sketched map of the world titled, "Where's Lola now?" Stickpins affixed with flags littered its surface.

"They sold for a buck a pin. There's a name on each one of those. People put them where they thought you'd end up." A clot of pins nearly obliterated Afghanistan. There were a few in the general region of Montana—"Some of the women thought you might find yourself a cowboy and stay, but I think that was more about their fantasies than yours"—some in Europe, quite a few in Africa and more than one in Antarctica. Not one, Lola saw, was anywhere near Baltimore.

"There's one in the middle of the Atlantic," he pointed out. Sure enough, a flagged pin adorned a crude drawing of a raft. "That might be closer to here than Montana. I think that one belongs to Bob. Looks like he wins fifty bucks. Just think, back in the old days, with everybody playing, it would've been something like two hundred."

Lola's new desk was near his office. She looked through the glass wall. He'd acquired another paperweight. This one rested on a high shelf, out of easy reach. "I was going to," she said. "Go back to Afghanistan, I mean. I had it all planned."

"What happened? A sudden decision to abandon your lonely, noble quest for the real story?"

So she'd wounded him after all, all those weeks ago.

"What changed your mind? You get a good look at somebody who'd been shot and finally figure out a newspaper story wasn't worth it? Because that's what was going to happen if you went back to Afghanistan. Sooner or later, everybody's luck runs out."

Lola thought of her savings swirling away in the ashes of the fire. Her luck ran out before she'd even gotten a chance to get back on the ground in Afghanistan. She considered the Baltimore streetscape through the window, the sluggish river of people and automobiles moving between the grey canyons of tall buildings, and conjured instead mountains and endless sky.

"Stay," Charlie had urged. "This is your home now."

Lola balked. "It was Mary Alice's home. Not mine. Besides, all my money's gone. The paper's paying me four times—well, three times, or at least twice—what I'd make at the *Express*."

"We none of us make any money here to speak of," he'd said, his body so warm and comforting against hers that she'd reversed her opinion of the lumpy beds at the Sleep Inn on the spot. "Somehow we survive. You might be broke, but you'd never be bored. As you well know." He waited until she was back in Baltimore to start the emails. No message in the box, just the subject line. "Come home." Same thing, same time, day after day. Four P.M.

Jan, too, sent notes, but hers came at all hours. "Idiot," she typed into the subject line. "Fool." Lola looked at the clock. It was 3:55. Activity picked up in the newsroom. Deadline neared, editors glaring meaningfully over the tops of their computer screens at reporters who'd spent most of the day screwing around drinking coffee and Googling their own bylines before getting down to the business of writing their stories.

Her computer pinged. Lola looked at her email list. There it was, right on time. "Come home."

She smiled. Then looked again.

This time, there was an attachment, a photo file. She opened the email. He'd written a message, too. "Look who's waiting for you."

Lola rolled her eyes. He was upping the ante, sending a picture of himself. She wondered if he'd be in his sheriff's uniform.

"Get off that computer and get on your phone." The editor again. "You've got to learn to use that thing."

Lola clicked rebelliously on the paper clip signifying the attachment. Then shoved so forcefully away from her desk that her chair sailed into the aisle. She grabbed at the crutches as she rolled past, nearly dropping them. She stopped the chair, struggled to her feet and fitted the crutches under her arms.

The editor narrowed his eyes. "What's going on?"

Lola balanced on one crutch and reached for something on her desk. "Catch!" She launched the phone at his head. He ducked. She laughed.

From her computer screen, a photo of a black-and-white dog, one leg bandaged, another gone entirely, fixed an approving stare upon her with one brown eye, one blue.

"Wicks! Goddammit. These phones are expensive. Where are you going?"

Lola planted the crutches and swung her body. Another hop and swing, catching the rhythm, moving with sudden certainty toward the door.

"Home," she called. "I'm going home."